MY MIDNIGHT SUN

A NOVEL

JOHN SHORS

Author of *Beneath A Marble Sky*

ISBN: 978-0-9991744-8-7

Published by Blackfin Books.

Cover design: Caroline Johnson

Interior formatting: Mark Thomas / Coverness.com

PRAISE FOR THE NOVELS OF JOHN SHORS

"Shors is an immense talent."

—AMY TAN, BESTSELLING AUTHOR OF *THE JOY LUCK CLUB*

"I was deeply moved by this poignant and life-affirming novel."

—WALLY LAMB, BESTSELLING AUTHOR OF *SHE'S COME UNDONE*

"Shors transcends politics and headlines and finds the timeless and deeply human stories that are the essence of enduring fiction. This is strong, important work from a gifted writer."

—ROBERT OLEN BUTLER, PULITZER PRIZE-WINNING AUTHOR OF *A GOOD SCENT FROM A STRANGE MOUNTAIN*

"A maelstrom of riveting action. I loved this book."

—KARL MARLANTES, BESTSELLING AUTHOR OF *MATTERHORN*

"This is a beautiful heart speaking to us of the beautiful world we could and should find, even in the darkness that so often floods the world with fear."

—GREGORY DAVID ROBERTS, BESTSELLING AUTHOR OF *SHANTARAM*

"John Shors is an author of sweeping imaginative force."

—SANDRA GULLAND, BESTSELLING AUTHOR OF
THE JOSEPHINE B. TRILOGY

"An epic, historical page-turner with a beating heart. I loved it."

—JAMIE FORD, BESTSELLING AUTHOR OF
HOTEL ON THE CORNER OF BITTER AND SWEET

"Destined to be this decade's *The English Patient*."

—*BOOKLIST*

"Stunning and profoundly moving."

—*NATIONAL GEOGRAPHIC TRAVELER*

"A work of art, rare in a debut novel."

—*THE DES MOINES REGISTER*

"An epic love story."

—*SOUTHEAST ASIA GLOBE*

"As luminous a jewel as any that adorn the Taj Mahal's walls."

—*FOREWORD MAGAZINE*

"An intense, historical page-turner.... [A] legendary tale."

—*THE SHANGHAI DAILY*

"Shors' narrative reads like a poet's description of the jungles, the temples, and the hearts of each character."

—The Phnom Penh Advisor

"An absorbing novel about the extremes of passion—with much relevance for our own time."

—Denver Rocky Mountain News

"[A] story of redemption ... where the prophets, saints, and deities of the great religions have been silenced, but where human decency, even heroism, survives in small, fertile patches."

—The Japan Times

"An author to anticipate."

—Omaha World-Herald

"A majestic novel that irresistibly draws the reader within its saga of human struggles, failings, alliances and betrayals."

—Midwest Book Review

"Shors seems to draw on a deep well of resolve to give back."

—Jakarta Globe

"A thriller, complete with camera-ready scooter chase scenes…. Shors excels at plotting, and his Saigon street cred is impeccable."

—*Kirkus Reviews*

"Touchingly personal, Shors' vivid descriptions throughout the novel are enough to transport you elsewhere."

—*Sierra Club Magazine*

"Shors is a genius storyteller."

—*Adventure Travel News*

"Those familiar with Ken Follett's *Pillars of the Earth* will find strong correlations between the novels. This is a page-turner."

—*Romantic Times*

"Destined to be a blockbuster. Highly recommended."

—*Historical Novels Review*

AUTHOR'S
NOTE

When I was in my early twenties, I was fortunate to backpack around Asia for many months. One of the highlights of that trip was trekking through the Himalayas on what's called the Annapurna Circuit. This journey took more than two weeks and involved climbing over one of the world's tallest mountain passes. It was a unique, difficult, and extraordinary experience.

After being back in America for a few years, I decided to sit down and write a novel based on my adventures in Nepal. Though *My Midnight Sun* is fictitious, many of the scenes within it are founded on experiences I had. And while the core relationship within the novel is fabricated, for me, rereading this novel is like walking back through time.

Upon finishing *My Midnight Sun,* my literary agent tried to find a suitable publisher. Unfortunately, editor after editor after editor rejected the tale. Undaunted by these rejections, I went on to publish ten other novels—mostly works of historical fiction set in Asia.

In the spring of 2020, as COVID-19 shut down most of the world, I became housebound for a few months without much to do. At this point, I decided to dust off *My Midnight Sun* and simply publish it myself. I changed the very first scene in the novel, as well as the overall timeline. But everything else I left as was.

Were all of those editors right to reject my story? I don't know. I'll let you decide for yourself. But I've enjoyed rereading the pages.

Finally, I'd be remiss not to mention the wonderful people of Thailand and Nepal. Perhaps not the faces, but certainly the deeds of these strangers will always linger in my mind, tangible and permanent, like names etched in oak by a past generation.

For all of my past, present, and future
traveling companions…

CHAPTER 1

THE END OF ME

December 26, 2004
Phuket, Thailand

I heard the tsunami before I saw it—a rumbling, grinding roar that sounded like an old building being brought down by explosives. I heard the screams next—shrieks of terror, pain, and confusion. Turning on my side, I only had time to notice that Sarah was no longer wrapping the sarong about her waist. Instead, she had paused to look at me, her mouth open but still.

A heartbeat later, the sea assaulted our bungalow, spewing up through the wooden floor as if our tiny hut were being forced down into the froth by a giant's hand. Water shot up like miniature geysers between the gaps in the floorboards. It then raged through the windows, rising with each second from our ankles to our knees to our thighs.

Instinctively, I threw myself against the bungalow's door. The sea mirrored my action from the opposite side, though, smashing into the door as if a battering ram—ripping off its hinges, hurtling it inward against me. I tasted salt and blood. Sarah screamed as we were both lifted and then compressed against the roof. Suddenly we were underwater. As the sea stung my eyes I tore at the thatched roof with my hands. I slammed my head against it. I bit it. Ripped it. Kicked it. The hole I opened was no bigger than a toilet seat, but it was big enough. The sea shoved us through it, and suddenly we were on the surface, being driven inland somehow by a mass of water that was infinitely powerful and irresistible.

"Sarah!" I screamed, kicking toward her, pulling her close. She clung to me, wiping blood from a gash above her eye, struggling to stay afloat. She tried to speak but seemed powerless to do so.

The sea spewed forth, collapsing bungalows, tossing cars and motorcycles about as if they were made of plastic. A man clinging to a palm tree screamed as an overturned boat plowed into the tree, severing his arms from his body. He shrieked again and disappeared. In his wake swirled bodies—those of water buffalo, cats, and children. The bodies were torn and incomplete.

Something snagged on my swimming suit, and I was dragged underwater. In the blackness objects battered me, striking my head, my ankles, my groin. I managed to get out of my suit and, following bubbles upward, swam. Sarah shouted when she saw me, and we were together again. Our fingers merged.

The speed with which we moved astounded me—at least as fast as a passenger train. A dead elephant tumbled past. A cement truck rolled into and through a barber shop. Next a hotel collapsed before us, its balcony falling atop a trio of Thai children clinging to a floating door. A woman wailed as she saw them die. She dove after them and was swallowed by the hotel. People on the upper level screamed as the building toppled. They jumped from windows. They stood still. Clinging together, they disappeared as the hotel and the sea consumed them.

A mound of steel and concrete remained slightly higher than the water. A Thai man swam frantically toward this island, only to be impaled upon the rubble. I shouted at Sarah to swim away from it, and we did, wincing as our feet struck debris. The brown, filth-laden water choked us, and we spat and struggled. A fishing net filled with thrashing creatures entangled us, and we went under for a few heartbeats. A sea turtle hammered into my side, and I desperately held my breath. Kicking upward, we emerged from the net, our bodies now bloodied in a dozen places.

Sarah was weakening. The sea had stolen her sarong, and I glimpsed angry welts about her body. Her left arm seemed lifeless, and I feared it was broken. I shouted at her to fight, to clear her mind of anything save survival. But to my dismay, she didn't seem to hear me, not even when I pressed my lips against her ear.

A life-sized wooden Buddha floated by, and I grabbed its torso with one arm and Sarah with the other. We were moving more slowly now. For an instant the water ceased to flow. Then we were being dragged backward, out toward the sea. Something crunched against my knee, and I yelped in pain.

As we were dragged toward the deep, I struggled to keep us alive. I tried to do so many things—to hold Sarah afloat, to kick toward a distant palm tree, to not lessen my grip upon the Buddha. The thought of losing Sarah provoked a fear within me the likes of which I had never experienced. My world seemed to spin, and I panicked, clutching her against me so hard that my fingernails made her bleed.

Again something struck my legs, raking them as if a pair of mailed hands. Ferocious pain penetrated my fog of fear and horror. I screamed. I screamed again and again, and this newfound despair gave me the strength to lift Sarah higher out of the water. She was barely conscious, and a large contusion dominated the side of her forehead. I begged her to stay awake, salt from the sea and my tears clouding my vision. Sarah seemed to recognize my voice, and her lips drew into a fleeting smile.

I prayed as I kicked toward the palm tree, kicked with my pulverized and aching feet. I prayed to God, to the Buddha I grasped, to anyone or anything listening. I cried as I prayed, dozens of lifeless Thais and tourists swirling about me like leaves in a stream.

"Please ... don't leave me," Sarah whispered through bleeding lips.

"I won't. I promise."

I pulled her closer and kicked harder, groaning when we snagged upon the outrigging of a partially sunken fishing boat. My body was caught within ropes and cables, as was Sarah's. The sea continued to withdraw, and the pressure against us was enormous, unbearable in fact. Debris jammed against us, striking us, slashing our faces. Abruptly, the boat moved deep below, pulling us under. I continued to hold Sarah with one hand. With my other, I tore at the ropes that bound her as if they were snakelike demons. I ripped them with talons, not fingers. I severed them with my teeth. When my lungs threatened to burst I let go of Sarah so that I could attack the ropes with both my hands. She struggled now too—yet with no sense of purpose. She tried to swim upward but only further entangled herself.

Suddenly the ropes about my legs parted, and I was free, tumbling through the water. I reached for Sarah, and our hands met but then separated. Frantic, I grabbed her long hair and tried to pull her with me. Some of her hair stayed in my fingers. Most did not, and we were yanked apart. Sarah stopped struggling and turned to watch me drift away. She opened her mouth, and even in the blankness, even with the clash of steel against wood and stone, I heard her scream. It was the scream of someone watching herself die a hideous death, of someone who desperately wanted to live but knew she would not. The sea suffocated my efforts to shout her name as I was swept away.

Sarah disappeared into a cloud of distant debris. I kicked and clawed wildly toward her but might as well have tried to swim up a waterfall. The sea took me where it wanted, finally depositing me against the very tree I'd earlier sought to reach. Only now I didn't care. It didn't matter. I wanted to let go and die with her, to travel with her as I thought I always would.

But I was too much the coward.

CHAPTER 2

REMORSE AND RETURN

February 12, 2005
Moab, Utah

The red sandstone—as curved and smooth as Sarah's hips—was cool against my hands. Sitting with my knees drawn up toward my chest, I gazed down the endless and windswept formation of rock. The trail next to us dropped sharply, following the contours of what looked like a giant skateboarding park. For miles in all directions the sandstone stretched and soared. Aside from a few clumps of juniper bushes, this world was dominated by the red rock and a rich, cloudless sky. Far below, a lone figure on a mountain bike churned along the trail—his or her bike winking at me as it reflected bits of sunlight.

The view should have inspired me, as should have the descent below. The passage was laced with swooping drops and leaps—sections of trail that would test my bike and me. Though I'd visited and enjoyed this spot for years, it meant nothing to me now and, in fact, actually magnified my hurt, for I'd been here last with Sarah. And memories were plentiful.

"It didn't work, did it?"

I turned toward my best friend, Drew, who sat at my side. "What?"

"This trip," he replied, setting down his water bottle. "It didn't do anything for you."

I started to lie for his sake but stopped myself. "No. Not really."

"Maybe I—"

"But thanks for bringing me here. Thanks for trying."

He shook his head slowly. "You know, I loved her too."

"I know."

"Like you said in your wedding toast, she knew how to lift everyone up. Everyone around her. She did that to me. She was really good at that."

I made no reply, remembering the many pronouncements intoned that night, as well as the words exchanged with Sarah when we were finally alone. The hole in me deepened, as it always did when I walked through the past. I pressed the tips of my fingers against the corners of my eyes to stop myself from crying.

"What are you thinking about?" Drew asked quietly.

I sniffed, shaking my head. "I can't … there's no way I can live like this. I can't work. I can't eat or think or sleep. It's just … it's too much. Way too much. If I stay like this … I'll never leave this hell."

"Then you should go back. Go back to Thailand. Find something good."

"I think I have to. Even though I'm afraid."

"Of what?"

"Of what I might find there. Or of finding nothing." I felt the sandstone with my hands, pressing my palms against it as if to keep myself from being blown away. "But I can't stay in San Francisco. I see her in every restaurant, in every park. She's everywhere we've ever been. And all those places are ruined for me."

"Do you—"

"It's worse than that. I sit for hours outside our old apartment. I look into the windows. It's like I think that I might see her. I … I try to see her. Sometimes I kind of do."

"How often do you sit like that?"

"Don't ask. You really don't want to know."

"Jesus, Owen."

I continued to clutch at the sandstone, barely aware of the tears that raced down my dusty cheeks. "It just hurts so much. I didn't know anything could hurt like this. I really didn't. It's like … remember when I broke three ribs?"

"You were coughing up blood and you still wanted to ski down the damn mountain."

"It hurts like that, but so much worse. It hurts to breathe. To think. To sleep. And it never gets better. And I can never escape it."

Drew scratched at his wispy beard, but his eyes didn't leave mine. "You have to try and somehow let her go."

"She's a part of me. How do you let someone go who is a part of you?"

"She'd want you to try."

"She'd want me to? Do you know she begged me to hold onto her? To not let go?"

"That's different and you know it."

"It doesn't matter. I'm not letting her go. I can't. And I don't want to."

"But I think that you have to somehow. You do." When I didn't respond, Drew took another drink of water. He offered me some, but I made no move to take it. "What do you hope to find in Thailand?" he asked.

"Hope?" I muttered, shaking my head. "I don't know. Something ... something to make me understand."

"Should I go with you? Maybe I could help."

"Maybe. But I have to go alone."

"You don't have to do anything."

In the distance the sun settled upon the horizon. The rock beneath and around us reflected and enhanced the light, glowing like lava. "We should ride," I said, rising, hating the feeling that the world had nothing left to offer me. Hating the fact that I could care less about a beautiful sunset.

"When will you leave?" my friend asked, still sitting on the sandstone.

"Soon. It should be soon."

I climbed atop my bike and within seconds was hurtling down the trail, the straps of my untethered helmet bouncing against my face.

CHAPTER 3

CHANCE ENCOUNTER

April 12, 2005
Bangkok, Thailand

E ven for Bangkok it was hot. The city teemed with the kind of heat that made the air feel leaden, smell like the inside of an oven. Taking a long draw from a Singha beer, I tried to forget about the beads of sweat descending my brow, dropping to the table before me.

The night was alive as it only could be in Bangkok. As always, the streets surged with people. Among the multitudes of flesh and faces, my eyes drifted between a blind man selling dried fish, three monks clad in saffron-colored robes, and a woman sitting in a polished and manicured BMW.

Beyond these figures, the city stretched and soared with great contrasts—ultra-modern skyscrapers mingling with century-old shops and markets.

I wearily studied the scene before me as I awaited my food. Patience must have been invented in Thailand, a realm where waiters moved as unhurried as elephant grass swaying in the wind. To hope for my meal's quick arrival was something I might have done when Sarah and I first landed here. But not now. Not after nearly two months of wandering alone, of searching for answers I never expected to discover.

The beer was soon gone. Swiveling in my chair, I pointed to my bottle. A girl sweeping the floor smiled and set her broom against a table. She vanished through the restaurant's battered door, reappearing in the time it took me to clean my spoon on the frayed tablecloth.

Putting a fresh beer beside me, she asked, "Why you sit outside, mister? Much better inside. We have air-con. It very cold."

"I'm fine here," I replied. "But thanks for asking."

She shrugged and returned to her broom. I tilted the beer back, savoring the way it foamed in my mouth. I noticed the fish vendor hand several dried squid on sticks to a teenage couple. The monks shuffled toward an idle bus, in the throes of a passionate discussion. The BMW was nowhere to be seen.

I wondered where the driver had gone and how she had made her fortune. In a city where poverty loomed under countless streetlights, it was odd to see the sleek steel of a

German automobile. The car was worth more than many Thais would make in a lifetime.

My thoughts diluted as a waiter placed a heaping mound of rice and garlic shrimp on the table. Picking up my oversized spoon, I began to eat, marveling at the size and taste of the crustaceans. They'd been prepared perfectly, full of spices found only in Asia.

I was so engrossed with my meal that I almost didn't hear him. His voice rose softly over the horns and sirens, the breath of the city. "I hungry," he said. "Please give money for food."

The boy must have been no more than twelve. He wore a filthy Chicago Bulls jersey, torn shorts, and sandals. His hands and face were the color of gold. Though I felt badly for him, I knew I shouldn't help. By giving, I'd perpetuate a cycle from which he would never escape. Lacking the valor to speak, I shook my head.

"Please—"

"I'm sorry, my friend. You should go home to your mother and father."

"No mother, no father."

I'd heard the story before and guessed his parents were nearby. His earnings might buy his mother a pair of sandals or his father a drink. "I'm really sorry, but I can't help you," I said.

The boy nodded submissively, as if he heard the line a dozen times each night. "Can I see watch?"

I showed him my wrist. He studied my digital Casio, then announced proudly, "It seven, zero, three!"

I managed to smile at his bravado. "Very nice. Who taught you to tell time so well?"

"My sister. She say after I learn how to read time, she buy me watch. I almost ready."

"Good for you."

"Thank you, mister." He swatted at a fly. "Little money, please?"

"Could I buy you something instead? How about a book?"

"Me no need book. Need money."

"I'm sorry, but I just can't do that."

"Plea—"

Hating to disappoint him, but knowing that it was just another scam, I turned and ate. Only now the meal didn't taste so delicious. The shrimp seemed bland, as dry as dust. But I was hungry and finished them, scraping at the chipped plate until not a single grain of rice remained.

Sipping my beer, I looked for the boy, spying him a few buildings down at another set of tables. Though I wished he were at home, playing with his siblings or studying, I knew that begging was in his immediate future. He'd do it for a couple of years, then probably become some sort of laborer.

My waiter returned, unceremoniously removing my plate. I watched him shuffle to a counter, set the plate beside him, and start to tally up my bill. Knowing it would take him a few minutes, I reached into my fanny pack and withdrew a water-damaged passport. It had been found a mile inland and returned to me by the U.S. Embassy. Its first page bore a photograph of a young woman. Her face was tan. A splattering of freckles corralled her nose. The sun had bleached her hair until it mirrored the color of ancient ivory. Sarah had been only twenty when the photo was taken, four years younger than when we'd met. But she'd remained largely unchanged. Her eyes had always gleamed with passion. Her smile had harbored an uncommon sincerity.

A tear welled and I quickly wiped it away. I vowed not to cry about her tonight, though her passport usually made me weep. So did the few hairs that I had taped to the inside of the little blue book. Aching with the knowledge that I would never hold her again, I gripped her passport tightly. I thought about what could have been as I gazed at her photo—if only I'd saved her instead of watched her die. We'd have merged, grown until we completed each other. But because of me, because of my failure, no such merging would ever take place. We'd been cast apart like gulls in a hurricane, never to meet again.

I winced, shutting her passport. The memories it evoked were more often curses than blessings. Promising myself not to look at it again until tomorrow, I paid my bill. My room was distant and I relished the thought of a walk. It might clear my mind, numb my pain. Maybe tonight I wouldn't dream of her death, wake up whispering her name.

My thoughts roamed. I wondered what I was doing in Bangkok, why I wasn't on one of the beaches to the south, helping someone rebuild, doing something to try and somehow make peace with the past. Bangkok had sucked me into its innards much like the tsunami had. My seven weeks in the city had been full of drifting. I'd felt disconnected on the streets, perhaps even more so in the squalid room I rented. At night I'd take a cold shower in my floor's only bathroom and lie down on my cot without bothering to dry. I'd pity myself until sleep rescued me.

Turning down a potholed street, I circumvented heaps of refuse. Mangy dogs scavenged through the trash, pausing to glance in my direction. Most of the dogs limped. One was missing a leg. All were emaciated, ribs protruding like long fingers.

When I was past the reeking piles, the dogs snarled. A fight ensued. I heard one yelp repeatedly, then whimper. After a few more steps, sirens replaced its cries. Wanting to flee this road, I turned right, striding down a familiar thoroughfare. My room wasn't far. Another ten minutes and I'd be there.

I couldn't help but think of my precious wife and how I'd failed her, failed her just two weeks after exchanging rings. I saw her face as she was yanked from me, remembered her horror as her world went black. The memory made me bitter and my pace increased. Though it had been almost four months since she'd died, I was still haunted with visions, brimming with unfulfilled dreams. When we were together I'd loved her so much that oftentimes I had ached with want. Now I simply ached.

It was Sarah who'd planned our long honeymoon throughout Asia. Her father had once captained an aircraft carrier, and she'd spent much of her childhood visiting him in Guam, Japan, South Korea, and Thailand. We'd plotted our honeymoon over takeout food in our Berkeley apartment. All her memories would be rekindled. Each port revisited. We'd also venture into uncharted lands, trekking through Nepal, exploring the ruined forts of India.

Thinking of our plans, my eyes watered. I'd returned to Thailand hoping to find some trace of her spirit. But today, like each day preceding, reminded me only of our separation, of her muffled scream as I was dragged from her.

As I wiped my tears, a woman stepped from the shadows of a splintered doorway. Clad in a miniskirt and a nearly transparent blouse, she reached out, touching my shoulder. "I give you anything you want, handsome man," she said. "I give it to you for ten dollar."

I shook my head, avoiding her eyes.

"You know who you look like?" When I didn't respond, she grabbed my arm, pulling me close. "You like young Robert Redford."

"You've been … you've seen too many American movies," I stammered, glimpsing the curves of her body.

"Maybe yes, maybe no. But you look same. Your face same, your hair same, your eyes same. Though you have more muscle than he. I think you bigger too."

I wondered if Redford's eyes had ever been bloodshot from tormented nights, if the skin beneath them looked bruised. "He's a lot better looking," I finally replied.

"Anyway, I give you good discount. Only ten dollar."

"Good night," I said, quickening my pace. "Be careful out here."

Her laugh could have been a hyena's cackle, long and abrasive. "Maybe tomorrow?"

"Maybe," I whispered, hoping to be rid of her.

"Don't forget me!"

Only when I heard her stop following did I slow. Though such encounters were a part of life in this slice of Bangkok, tonight I found them grating. They put me on edge, made me want to look up and see trees instead of buildings.

While I pondered why fate favored some people and spit on others, a tuk-tuk came shrieking past. The Thai version of a taxi, tuk-tuks resembled three-wheeled golf carts. The tiny cars reached terrific speeds and were perfect for Bangkok's nightmarish traffic. They were able to penetrate jams, capable of driving down a sidewalk or dodging oncoming cars.

The tuk-tuk receded, trailing loud music. It zigzagged through traffic, moving like a prizefighter. I watched its flashing purple lights fade into the night. Soon all I could see was its abundant exhaust.

As I neared Ko Sahn Road—the area where most backpackers stayed—vendors grew thick, hawking everything from fresh pineapple to tattoos to fake Rolexes. Though midnight neared, the street was inundated with foreigners. I heard English, Japanese, French, Thai, German, Russian, and several other tongues I didn't recognize.

Spying the sign that pointed to my guesthouse, I turned into a nameless alley. My feet fell on dirt and broken glass. I watched darkened doorways. Digging into my fanny pack, I withdrew a bottle of purified water and drank deeply.

Then I saw him. Curled next to a young woman, he slept with his Bulls jersey pulled over his head, shielding himself from fluorescent lights. Their legs intertwined, neither stirred. He used his shoes as a pillow. She slumbered beside a mound of decaying vegetables, which seemed to move as dozens of cockroaches sorted through the reeking rubbish.

Guilt suffocated me. I bent down, cursing myself for not giving him some of my shrimp, for so callously rejecting his tale.

The boy's eyes widened when I touched him. Recognition eclipsed his face. "How are you, mister?"

"Fine. And how about you? Can you sleep here?"

"No problem. I come here every night with sister."

As if prompted, the woman stirred. Only when she sat up did I notice her extraordinary beauty. Her eyes were vast, dark moons. Her skin was so flawless that I wanted to reach out and touch it, see if it was real.

Her full lips quivered. "You lost?"

"No. I've met your brother before."

"He not brother. Just good friend."

The boy giggled. She ruffled his hair playfully as he spoke in Thai.

"What did he say?" I asked.

"He say you not believe him."

"Well, I was—"

"It okay. No need for sorry. It not easy for foreigner to believe such thing."

Uncomfortable with the subject, I replied, "Your English is great. How did you learn it so well?"

Her face transformed, a smile rising. "It not so great. I make many mistakes. And my vocabulary not so much. Big words is big problems."

"No, you speak well."

"Thank you."

"Can I ask your name?" When she hesitated, I said, "I'm Owen. Owen Sterling."

"I Suchin. Like your American name, Sue, and then a chin. My friend is Ratu." She stood, body arching backward as she stretched. Only then did I realize how thin she was. Though loose clothing hid much, her tapered frame seemed to cling to itself. Her legs could have been those of a gazelle. Suchin fought back a sudden series of coughs, straightening her long, black hair. "Why you stop to talk with us?"

"I don't know," I replied, disheartened, believing that she was sick.

Ratu interrupted my thoughts. "Please give money, mister."

His friend muttered something and he quieted. "He no learn how to fight hunger," she said.

"Where are his parents?"

"He not know."

"And yours?"

I didn't think she heard me. But then she glanced to her left, her gaze resting on a plastic picture frame, which was propped up against a bottle. Though I was too distant to see it clearly, the frame held a black and white photo of what might have been a family. "They farmers in countryside," she finally answered, "far, far from here."

Noting how sadness had crept into her words, I thought about my photo of Sarah, about how the image had branded itself upon my mind. Perhaps this woman and I were less different than circumstances indicated. "How long have you been away from them?"

"Why you ask this question?"

"Because I've been away from—" I paused, wishing Sarah was with me. "I'm just curious. That's all."

"You should go to hotel, forget what you see here. It better that way. Easier for you."

"But I'd like—"

"To have this be memory from your trip? Talking to homeless woman?"

"I'm not looking for memories," I replied. My thoughts wavered as a one-eared rat ambled from a nearby gutter. It came directly at us, heading toward the pile of vegetables. Suchin picked up a brick and tossed it at the foot-long rodent. Her aim was true. The rat hissed, retreating back to the gutter. A portion of its tail remained twitching on the pavement.

"I no like this rat," she said disdainfully. "He bite me once.

That night I take his ear. Tonight I take his tail. Soon there be nothing left of him."

I wasn't sure how to respond. "Isn't there somewhere else … you could sleep? What about a park?"

"Police give us problem if we sleep in nice place. Here they leave us alone."

"But the rats?"

"Streets of Bangkok not easy place. We worry about food, clothes, clean water. Not rats." She stifled a yawn. "No American dream here."

"What about a Thai dream?"

"Not for me, not for Ratu."

"Do you mind if … what happened to yours?"

Her laugh was a combination of bitterness and incredulity. "Money buy everything in Bangkok. Even dream."

Though I knew I was pushing this woman, I wanted to understand what had happened to her. If I understood, perhaps I could help, perhaps for a moment I could think of something other than Sarah. "How so?"

"You no want to hear my story. It only make you more sad."

"Why do you think I'm sad?"

"Your eyes, your face, your body look tired. You like old man."

Thinking of her earlier smile, and hoping, no, needing to see it again, I replied, "You're as observant as you are beautiful."

Her face tightened. She took a sudden breath as if to reply angrily but then paused. Looking at the boy, she muttered, "I no care about beauty. It give me nothing but problem."

"I'm sorry," I replied quietly.

Suchin lay down, curling up next to Ratu, who had returned to his dreams. "Good night," she said. "Maybe we meet again. If not in this life, in next for sure."

I wanted to reply, to somehow comfort her, but she'd closed her eyes. Her spell upon me unbroken, I watched her chest rise and fall. At times, her hair stirred in the breeze. For the most part, however, all was still, more like a painting than a moment in time.

Noticing that one of Ratu's shoes protruded from under his head, I leaned forward, reaching into my pocket. Though I didn't have much money, I put all my crumpled bills into his shoe, forcing them toward the toe. After making certain no one else was around, I pulled off my watch and stuck it in the shoe.

"Sleep well," I whispered.

Soon they receded from me, distant but not forgotten.

CHAPTER 4

A WAR OF WATER

I was glad for the new day. In the amber light of dawn I'd dreamt of demons—finned and scaled beasts that tore at Sarah with primeval bloodlust. The grinning creatures had left me alone, opting to pull her apart. Others writhed within the crimson water, racing to hunks of drifting flesh. No matter how hard I'd tried to swim to her, I remained immobile. My limbs, so unappealing to her assailants, had been worthless to me.

"Stop it," I muttered as I strode down the street, trying to vanquish her tortured face from my mind. As I often did when I was upset, I grasped my wedding ring, which hung from a leather cord about my neck, so that it could be closer to my heart. Steadying myself, I moved down the sidewalk, caressing the golden circle. I took several deep breaths, still attempting to collect myself. A familiar sense of dread welled up within me, and my back and neck grew damp with perspiration.

Suddenly desperate to shed her from my thoughts, I looked about. A few blocks ahead, I saw the first hint of celebration. People were gathering on the streets—collecting in doorways and outdoor restaurants. At a nearby intersection, three men next to a fire engine held a thick hose, dousing the crowd before them. Most being drenched fought back, hurling buckets of water in their assailants' direction.

"Songkran," which meant *water festival* in Thai, dated back centuries in Thailand. A holiday that used to mark the coming of the New Year, Songkran had lost some of its meaning over time but was still the biggest celebration in the country. So renowned was it, in fact, that people from all over Asia flocked here to participate.

Understanding Songkran's history, but only knowing it to be some kind of colossal water fight, I'd eaten breakfast and bought the biggest bucket I could find. The blue bucket had some twine attached to its handle.

I'd heard that the most frenzied festivities took place along Bangkok's many canals. Fortunately, some weren't too far from my guesthouse. Hoping that the celebration would provide me with some sort of reprieve from my misery, I scurried forward, holding my sloshing bucket with my right hand. As I neared a crowd, a group of shrieking youths ran forward, dousing me with pails of ice water. Taken a bit by surprise, I was slow in my counterattack and my water struck only the ground. The children cried out triumphantly and hurried across the road to drench a street vendor. Laughing, he grabbed a bucket and emptied it onto them. Watching the children scamper away, I shivered, glad that my bucket still had some water in it.

A pickup truck drove in my direction, veering toward me at the last second. A handful of children stood behind the cab, surrounding a pair of massive barrels—both overflowing with water and ice. As the truck passed, the children used long ladles to fling water at me with incredible precision. I ran for cover while the kids shrieked and shook their fists in the air.

A nearby traffic light turned green, and a legion of pickups approached. Though my bucket was only partially full and I was clearly overmatched, I stepped into the street and assaulted the first to arrive. I timed my throw well and soaked the riders in the truck's rear. They attacked a microsecond later and fared better. Water hit me in the eyes so hard it hurt.

For the next half hour I worked my way north. Refilling my bucket from huge tubs of ice water along the road, I constantly attacked, and retreated from, the hordes of people gathered on the sidewalk. All wanted to soak the foreigner, or "farang," as I was called. I heard the word dozens of times while I fought, often holding my bucket above my head in an effort to collect ammunition.

Soon the communal tubs were empty. Knowing the only way I'd be able to fill my bucket was to reach the canals, I increased my pace. Everyone shared the same thought, and armies flowed to the north.

When I stumbled upon a canal, the sight was staggering, so chaotic I felt as if a revolution were unfolding. Tens of thousands of Thais bordered the waterway, fighting against the occupants of hundreds of pickup trucks passing on a parallel road. Those assaulting from the ground offered no mercy. In addition to attacking the pickups, they inundated motorcycles, taxis, police cars, trucks, buses, and bicyclists. The few drivers daring enough to counterattack must have regretted their bravery, for untold gallons of water cascaded through each open window, drenching everyone and everything inside.

Eager to help fight the heavily armed pickups, I ran to the canal, my mood improving with each step. Throwing my bucket into the murky water, I quickly hauled it up with the twine. By now I'd perfected the art of timing my throws. Dozens riding in the backs of pickups were soaked by my assaults. Beside me, Thais of all shapes and sizes fought shoulder to shoulder against the convoy of vehicles. The Thais sang and shrieked as they fought—many acting decades younger than their wrinkles revealed them to be.

Suddenly, I felt a tap on my arm and turned. My eyes widened as I faced the young woman I'd met the previous night outside my guesthouse. Before I could say anything, Suchin yelled, throwing a bucket of water into my face. The cold liquid struck me directly in the eyes, causing no small amount of pain. Seeing me grimace, my attacker shrieked in victory, then squeezed my nose. She laughed, turning away.

My spirits rising as a strange sort of mania unfolded within me, I dropped my bucket and lifted her up from behind. Unaware of my intentions, Suchin didn't struggle until it was too late. Walking to the edge of the canal, I heaved her into it, and she landed with a terrific splash. Several of her companions, including Ratu, then pushed me, and I toppled into the canal, pulling Ratu after me, holding my breath as I went under. The water, brown and warm, was only about four feet deep. Standing on the muddy bottom, the three of us splashed and dunked each other mercilessly, laughing as we fought.

"I not know monkey like water," Suchin exclaimed, feigning puzzlement.

"This one does."

"Then he not so smart. He should know that big snakes live in river. Can eat him."

Suchin dove beneath the surface. Though I could see her kicking legs coming at me, I didn't move, enjoying the moment. Her hands found my ankles and she pulled them upward with surprising strength. Yelling, I fell backward. My adversaries then pounced on my chest and sent me under. Growing a bit more determined, I sprang up, forcing them aside. Grabbing Ratu under his armpits, I threw him as far as I could. He screamed in glee and vanished in a heap of spray.

Laughing, Suchin came at me again. I knocked her outstretched hands away, wrapping my arms around her. She giggled, thrashing about as if a worm on a hook. Ratu heard her pleas and swam toward me. When he was about to attack, I let her go, holding my arms up in a gesture of peace.

After retrieving our buckets, we dragged ourselves from the canal. My hat was gone and my wallet was a complete mess, bills sticking together as if wet leaves. The two Thais were in equally bad shape. The petals of pink water lilies clung to Suchin's long, matted hair. Ratu's jersey was ripped where I'd grabbed him. Fortunately, our losses didn't dampen our spirits. Standing next to each other, we worked as a unit, sending barrage after barrage into the oncoming motorists, who retaliated gleefully. By now, in the growing heat of the day, their ice water felt refreshing and we were happy to be hit.

For the rest of the afternoon we celebrated together. Fighting with thousands, we filled trucks, streets, tuk-tuks, and gutters with the brown water. As the day matured, we seemed to be winning the fight against our mounted foes, though traitors on our side kept the struggle about even.

Much later, when dusk was gleaming, Suchin suddenly thanked me in Thai and leaned forward to give me a hug. As I held her, she dropped her arms about my waist and spun us to our left. We pirouetted on the slippery ground, unaware of the world around us. It felt liberating to embrace her, and for the first time in months, I remembered what it was like to have a moment of happiness. Not bliss, but the sort of warm contentedness that makes one feel at home. Suchin must have understood my mood, for she playfully kissed me on the cheek as she whispered good-bye.

"Stay," I muttered.

"Good-bye, monkey."

She threw a final bucket of water at me and took Ratu's elbow. When they walked away, I waited for her to turn, to glance once more in my direction. But she didn't. And I started to shiver, wishing that I wasn't once again alone.

*

Later that night, I sat at my guesthouse's outdoor restaurant, my damp clothes reminding me of the day's bombardments. The scarred table before me, hardly benefiting from a recent face-lift of blue paint, carried a lone candle. This burnt slowly, its flame gyrating in the wind. Nearby, a couple from Amsterdam was engrossed in a game of chess. A German was at the only other occupied table. I knew him to be a friendly guy, but he sat quietly, concentrating on the fat joint he was rolling.

Though far from silent, the evening was, without question, more tranquil than usual. The Thais must have been resting after the long day of celebrating. I certainly was ready for sleep, awash with yawns and stretches. To watch the candle flicker was calming, and I studied how the wax pooled on the wood. My eyelids soon felt like heavy curtains.

The spell was broken when a bald waiter brought my meal, placing a chicken taco on the table and thanking me for my patience in broken English. The taco was gargantuan, steam rising off it as if smoke drifting from a wet log. I grabbed a fork, pleased when the taco's taste surpassed my expectations.

I tried to eat it slowly but found myself devouring increasingly large pieces. As I made short work of the meal, I noticed a pair of mangy dogs at my feet. Their eyes locked on mine as they skillfully begged for food.

I ignored the dogs for a long time. But whenever I glanced down they pleaded, never altering their stare. Growing full, as well as sympathetic, I tore a piece of chicken in two and casually tossed each animal a hunk. Before the meat hit the cement floor, a fight exploded—a cataclysmic battle out of some Hollywood blockbuster. Stained teeth sought necks as the carnivores struggled over the morsels. The dogs snarled, yelped, and drew blood. They leapt and tumbled and rolled. My tablecloth became ensnared in claws and was dragged to the ground, plates and drinks cascading upon the dogs. Uttering curses, people hurried away. I jumped from my chair, certain my legs looked like giant drumsticks to the crazed animals.

When the fight finally died down, the German laughed. The couple from Amsterdam didn't think much was funny as they picked up their scattered chess pieces. When I apologized they glared at me, each muttering something in Dutch. Feeling like an ass, I quickly cleaned up the mess beneath my table. After paying my bill and leaving a large tip, I said good night to the German and walked into the tired building.

I climbed the worn stairs to my third-floor room. Unlocking my door's padlock, I stepped inside. A swell of heat engulfed me, as if I were a pizza being thrust into an oven. I flicked on my ceiling fan, pulled off my shirt, and opened the window. A rusty ladder was to my left, running from the top to the bottom of the building, apparently a fire escape.

Wanting to leave my room while it cooled, I climbed out the window, placing my right foot on the rung below me. The ladder seemed secure. Vowing not to look down, I ascended. The room above mine appeared to be full of shadows. Smoke oozed from the next and I glimpsed a man reading, a cigarette smoldering on a nearby table. Three floors higher I saw a middle-aged couple studying a map in their underwear. Worried they would see me, I hurried up the last few floors, never slowing to look in the windows.

The ladder curved over the top of the building. I followed its contours and dropped to the roof. The first thing I saw was a gathering of beer cans, dispelling any notion that my idea to climb here was even remotely original. Shards of a broken mirror also littered the roof. Impulsively picking up the biggest, I stared at myself. I didn't know how the prostitute could have compared me to Robert Redford. My hair was brown. No one envied my dark eyes. The passage of three decades had started to weather my face, faint wrinkles appearing like cracks in porcelain. A week-old beard hid dormant laugh lines and a new scar on my chin. Suddenly hating my reflection, wishing I had more scars, I dropped the glass and watched it shatter again.

Though hard to tell how high I was, I guessed it to be about twelve stories. A pulsating Bangkok encompassed me—music belching from bars below. I could see people, mostly foreigners, dancing on the streets. To the north, a sprawling apartment building obstructed my view. Though the structure looked fairly new, it had obviously seen neglect. Most of its paint had peeled away, green mold flourishing in its place. Chunks of plaster were also missing, and the building's windows were darkened with soot.

Ten balconies spanned each of the complex's levels. Clothes and sheets hung from lines and old television antennas. Below the garments were potted plants, bicycles, garbage bags, chairs, fish tanks, and anything else the mind could conceive. As I gazed at these possessions, a woman came out of an apartment directly across from me. She saw me and waved. I returned her greeting and then found a wooden crate to sit upon.

The unexpected encounter reminded me of Suchin and Ratu. I recalled how nice it was to hold her. I didn't know why I had done so, or why I found her so captivating, but I couldn't drive the sight of her from my mind. I remembered her face and its intricacies with surprising clarity, as if I'd seen it countless times.

Dismissing the thought, I recalled my first meeting with the boy and wondered why I'd been so indifferent to him. It would have been easy to have helped him, to have given him some food. Any decent person would have done so.

I wouldn't have hesitated a year ago. Fueled by my love for Sarah, I'd have done damn near anything for anyone. It had been easy to be generous when I was cherished, enjoyable to share my good fortune. But since her death so much had changed. My heart was no longer a heart, but a barren, soulless thing that simply pumped blood. In most ways I'd died with Sarah, and were she alive today, she wouldn't recognize the man I'd become—the same sort of desensitized jerk I would have despised a short time ago.

As I pondered the boy, I realized that I was so full of self-pity that I'd forgotten others suffered as well. Cursing myself, my entire existence, I stood. How could I have walked away from a homeless boy? How could I have become what I had? I swore again, hating myself for failing him, for failing Sarah, for living while she died. At that moment there seemed to be nothing in my mind save this hate of myself. No hope. No reason. No God or future or sanctuary. I felt alienated from the world, alone but for my parents. Yet they inhabited a realm of light. A cathedral I would never again enter.

"Four months," I whispered, feeling as if it had been four years since she died. "Only four goddamn months."

Looking back on those months, those endless nights, it seemed that I had been entombed within a Shakespearean tragedy. I still found it incomprehensible that everything had turned so. That I'd gone from dusk to dawn conversations with Sarah to pitiful days of self-decay. Surely it would be better to feel nothing than only misery. Surely I should have died as Romeo did—with the one I loved far more than myself. If only I'd possessed his courage. If I had, I wouldn't have let her go. I'd have fought longer and harder, and if she had to die then I would have died holding her.

As I descended the ladder, I moaned, closing my eyes.

Suddenly I could no longer tolerate the pain. It devoured me, searing my every thought as if a red-hot poker were being thrust through my face, my head, my very thoughts. Before the sobs could arrive, I let go of a rusty rung. I felt the world sway.

An image flashed as I drifted backward, swaying like a cut redwood. The scene was of my parents standing before my freshly dug grave. My mother's tears glistened in the sun. My father tried to pray, but instead damned whoever was listening. My mother collapsed into him and I knew their love would die as surely as I had.

I lunged for the ladder—not for myself, but for them. Steel stung my palms as I slid down. My knees and ankles smashed against the rungs, the clang of bone against iron resounding.

Only when I ceased to move did I see again. Dangling from the ladder, I wept, uncaring who heard me, oblivious to all but my woe.

CHAPTER 5

Inspiration

For the first time all day, I didn't feel scorched. I rarely did on the back of a motorcycle, with the wind massaging me like a billion microscopic fingers. On a motorcycle I felt a rare sense of freedom, as if I had the power and speed and agility of a peregrine falcon. Certainly this freedom was accompanied by an unquestionable danger. But in my current state of mind, the last thing I worried about was danger.

Even in Bangkok, at three o'clock in the afternoon the roads weren't overly congested. I sped down a boulevard lined with giant eucalyptus trees, darting in and out of the slower traffic. Earlier in the morning, I'd rented the Kawasaki for about three hundred baht, roughly ten dollars. The two-toothed man and

I'd done business before, and his face had brightened when I approached.

The deal was also good for me. Riding was always a rush, regardless of whether I was going six or sixty miles per hour. The exhilaration that accompanied the bike allowed me to forget my troubles, if only for a few minutes. It was as if the engine could somehow empower me, thrust me forward when all else failed.

Like most motorcycles in Thailand, this steed's speedometer was broken, stuck forever on zero. The gas and oil gauges twitched rhythmically, as if reading the bike's pulse. The headlight worked, a major coup considering all the dents and scratches encompassing it. I knew the light had never been broken, because if it had been, it still would be. Thais didn't fix things like headlights. Not when they'd only break again.

I merged onto a busier road. My destination was the Grand Palace. Located in the heart of Bangkok, it was the pride of the city—a massive and majestic complex of marble, golden, and ceramic temples. The colorful complex was one of the most impressive creations I'd seen. Despite the crowds, I wanted to gaze upon it once more.

I veered off the thoroughfare, passing the palace gates. A hive of parked mopeds dominated the sidewalk. I hopped the curb and pulled up beside them, locking the Kawasaki's wheel to a pole. Not that the two-toothed man would be sorry if it were stolen. But I would be, as he had my passport.

Since no one was allowed into the complex wearing shorts,

I pulled a pair of jeans from my backpack. I put them on quickly, aware of how heavy they felt on my legs. Sweat was instantaneous. Mingling with hundreds of locals and travelers, I paid a nominal entrance fee and was soon inside. The Grand Palace's name couldn't have been more appropriate. The grounds were bestrewn with temples, murals, fountains, and thousands of candles. Graceful statues of dragons, warriors, snakes, fish, Buddhas, and flowers stretched toward the sky. Each work of art was intricate—most inlaid with brightly colored glass and tile.

As I walked on white marble, I took several pictures that I would send to my parents, even though no camera would ever do this place justice. After all, few photographs capture wisdom, or beliefs passed from generation to generation.

Though all the temples were spectacular, I headed for the one containing the Emerald Buddha. As I reached its entrance I took off my shoes and dropped them next to scores of sandals and flip-flops. Stepping through a massive doorway, I marveled at how much cooler it was inside. The temple was surprisingly intimate. It might have been a hundred feet long and half as wide. Though its ceiling, walls, and pillars were ornate, my eyes were drawn to the green Buddha perched atop a golden throne at the far end of the room. Thais knelt before the Buddha, making soft intonations, swaying as they prayed.

The Buddha captured me. The statue was rumored to have been created six hundred years earlier in India but, inexplicably, ended up in Thailand a century later. Revering the statue, the

Thais built this temple for the sole purpose of housing it. I moved as close as possible to the priceless statue. Kneeling, I fixated on the Buddha's smile, jealous of the serenity it epitomized. I knew Buddhists believed that suffering was inseparable from existence, and that only by accepting suffering could one reach a state of illumination called Nirvana.

Sarah had always spoken highly of Buddhism. She'd believed in its doctrines, used them to justify her sorrows. I'd never understood her fascination, but now, in the wake of her death, I longed to find comfort in Buddhism's teachings. Maybe the ancient inhabitants of Asia knew something I didn't. Maybe they'd glimpsed the truth of suffering, realized that it made us human, made the joys of life much more profound.

Unfortunately, as much as I tried, as much I sensed the spirituality here, I couldn't accept my anguish as a by-product of life. Nor could I believe that there was a reason for Sarah's passing. She had everything to offer. Her death benefited no one.

I slumped, unable to embrace the doctrine. Nearby, Thais lit incense and uttered low incantations. A grizzled monk began to dust the Buddha with a bundle of peacock feathers. His movements were surely the same as those of generations of monks who had dusted the Buddha before him. The monk prayed as he worked, nodding rhythmically. Smoke from hundreds of incense sticks obscured him.

My eyelids drooped. I hadn't slept well the night before. Surprisingly, the usual nightmares of Sarah's death hadn't kept me up. Instead, too many thoughts of Suchin had circled within my head. Whether I was reading or taking a shower, I couldn't pry her from my mind. Her face was too familiar, as though I'd seen it in a previous lifetime. No, there was more to it than that. For some bizarre reason, I felt like I'd known her, cherished her above all else. The feeling was akin to deja vu but much more intense. I'd watched those eyes before—held them with my own, long into the night.

I tried to discount such feelings. Suchin was a homeless woman in Thailand, after all, beset with what seemed to be a serious illness. What we had in common I couldn't surmise. Perhaps I'd dreamt of her, or read about someone similar in a novel. Perhaps she reminded me in some way of Sarah. Or maybe in my desperation to feel something other than sorrow, I had subconsciously manufactured a connection between this woman and myself. Maybe a part of me thought such a linking would save me.

Surprisingly, no matter how hard I tried to let logic govern my thoughts about Suchin, I couldn't convince myself that she was of little consequence to me. Something told me that I didn't run into her by chance. I was meant to meet her at the canal, to see her once again. The longer I sat in front of the Emerald Buddha and thought of her, the more impatient I became. I had an urge to see her, to discover why she dominated my mind. Taking a final glance at the Buddha, I stood, spinning on my heels.

Outside the sun seemed brighter than ever, though it was

almost five o'clock. I scurried toward my motorcycle, which a Thai soldier leaned against. I nodded to him, unlocking the front tire. The soldier held a clear plastic bag that contained soda. A straw, secured by a rubber band through the bag's opening, ferried liquid to him. He took a sip, grinned, and pointed to the banyan tree above. As bulky as a three-story house, the tree was the product of a forest long since vanquished. The soldier must have appreciated the shadows this sentinel bred.

I smiled and said good-bye, gunning my motorcycle to life. It died, and I kicked down on the starter mightily. The engine spat, and I revved it to what must have been the red line. The soldier didn't flinch, as loud motorcycles were the norm here. The prevailing thought among Thais seemed to be that if a motorcycle didn't split one's eardrums it must be broken. I hated the racket but knew that if I didn't give my steed some gas the contraption would falter again.

Shifting into first, I let out the clutch. The curb fell away and I was on the street, which was now very busy, swollen with those returning from work. Decrepit but fast-moving buses seemed to come from every direction. They were packed with Thais, so encumbered that riders stuck their heads and arms far out the windows. Surrounding the buses and the clouds of diesel smoke they spewed were thousands of cars, tuk-tuks, mopeds, and bicycles. Every driver appeared to be in a hurry.

I felt like a soccer ball trying to avoid a field of strong-legged players. Whenever I slowed I heard a honk or a squeal of tires. Spying a side street, I turned, not bothering to signal. A child jumped in front of me, and I swerved to miss her. She looked up, waving as I passed. Though my heart skipped, I waved back, relieved I hadn't clipped her. The girl shrieked in excitement, happy to have made contact with a foreigner.

The traffic here was considerably thinner. I slowed, peering at the dozens of vendors I passed. Men, women, and children were selling live prawns, puppies, jade, umbrellas, ivory, orchids, pickled animal organs, and bicycle parts. The scents of saffron, curry, and incense permeated the air. Laughter rose from both old and young voices.

I stopped when I came upon a man making batches of chicken fried rice. Hatching an idea, I ordered three helpings. The vendor withdrew a homemade cigarette from his mouth and set it on the ground as if it were made of gold. He then pulled a squawking rooster from a bamboo cage. A machete fell and the bird's head spun. The man stuck a giant fork into the thrashing bird and started to yank off its feathers. The sight made me nauseated. Motioning that I'd be back, I jumped off my bike.

After locking the Kawasaki, I walked a few blocks, mingling with the hordes of Thais. It took me ten minutes to find a woman selling clothes from portable racks. Flipping through the garments, I searched for those made with the best material. I didn't care much what they looked like. It was only important that they stay intact a long time.

Settling on a dress embroidered with cranes, a red T-shirt, some coarse black shorts, and two pairs of sandals, I placed the goods before the woman. She scrutinized me carefully before producing a pad of yellow paper. On it she scrawled, "900."

Nine-hundred baht was about thirty dollars, not much if you were buying clothes in the States. But I wasn't in some overpriced mall, and I knew nine-hundred baht was too much. I held up five fingers. The vendor reached over and uncurled two more from my fist. I sighed and turned to leave, which prompted the woman to grab my arm. Now she raised six fingers. Though I knew six hundred baht was still too high and that I could talk her down further, I nodded, which caused her face to blossom. She took my crumpled bills, wrapped the clothes in newspaper, and handed them to me. I dropped the package into my backpack.

"Kob khun krab," I said, thanking her.

"Kob khun ka," she replied graciously, grinning and counting the money. I then retraced my steps, careful not to get lost in the labyrinthine network of stalls. In a few minutes I was in front of the rice vendor. We haggled intently, finally coming to a mutually satisfying price. After putting three bags of food in my backpack, I hopped on my motorcycle.

It started grudgingly, but soon I was again drifting down the streets. The pollution seemed thicker than ever, pieces of grit stinging my eyes. I used my left hand to hold my shirt over my nose and mouth. Breathing through the thin cotton helped a little. Though I was forced to let go of the material to grip the bike, I kept the cloth between my teeth. The air was so foul that I held my breath for as long as possible.

Mercifully, Ko Sahn Road wasn't much farther. Shifting into fourth gear, I accelerated, catching up to a bevy of mopeds. One of the scooters was loaded with a woman and three children. Though the driver was petite, hardly bigger than the kids, she guided the machine expertly. A naked boy of three or four sat in front of her, held in place by her thighs and knees. Behind the woman were two girls in matching gray school uniforms.

How four people could ride on a moped was beyond me. But the group was not an unfamiliar sight. Down south, Sarah and I had seen entire families on a single scooter. Clad in shorts and sandals they had sped about, dodging potholes and water buffalo.

The girls giggled as I passed. Waving excitedly, they cried out, "Hewwo! Hewwo!"

I smiled. "Hello! And good-bye!"

They shrieked as I left them behind. The chaos known as Ko Sahn Road was just ahead. Slowing, I made my way down the street, avoiding clusters of people and merchandise. Soon I parked my bike and started wandering about, looking for Suchin and Ratu. I hoped they would be nearby, as this was their hunting ground. Amid the thousands of people along the street, distinguishing familiar faces was like looking for a particular needle in a pile of needles. I first checked the alley where I'd seen them the other night. Finding nothing but heaps of refuse, I methodically peered into restaurants, stores, banks, and bars.

I couldn't help but wonder why I was looking for them. A

part of me intoned that I was trying to make amends for my earlier callousness toward the boy. Without question, I wanted to help him, and needed to redeem myself in his eyes. Yet I was also searching because voids existed in my life that desperately needed filling. By befriending this pair of strangers, by making their lives easier, perhaps I could feel a bit like I did before Sarah died.

I hunted feverishly. The crowds made me claustrophobic, and I bought a beer to calm my nerves. Drinking as I walked, I tried to ignore the constant barrage of sales pitches from hawkers. On most occasions, I simply passed them without a second glance. Other times I had to stop and refuse the more aggressive salespeople, my rudimentary Thai quickly marking me as someone who had been in-country for some time and hence immune to most any offer.

After an hour of painstaking searching, my efforts were finally rewarded. I found Suchin and Ratu in a pool hall. Smoke and a dozen stained pool tables dominated the squat building. Foreigners in tank tops played at two tables, drinking beer and high-fiving after successful shots.

Suchin was playing against a bald man with a gut so expansive he looked fifteen months pregnant. The guy was nothing but piercings and tattoos and attitude. Sitting down unobtrusively, I watched Suchin wield her cue. She shot with skill and surprising strength. Her opponent was worthy but drunk. It only took her a few minutes to dispatch him.

The man yanked a bill from his wallet, dropping it on the

table. "You're too damn good for me," he said in what I thought was an accent from the American South.

"One more game, mister? Maybe this time me not so lucky."

The man belched, then stumbled as he reached for a bottle of liquor. "You think?"

"Sure. You much better than me. I play like girl."

"I tell you what. Let's play again. You win and I give you ten dollars. I win and you come back to my room with me, give me a massage. Give me what I want."

She stepped away. "This I no can do."

"You too good for me?" he exclaimed, the sudden venom in his voice causing my pulse to quicken.

"No, sir. Only in pool."

He raised an open hand. "Only in pool?" he mocked. "Why, you ain't better than any other rice eater. And they do anything for money."

Suchin shrunk as if he'd hit her. I moved toward them, ready to help her if he grew more belligerent. Cursing, he pushed her aside and staggered toward a door with the word "RestRoom" painted on it. Though aware I should remain motionless, my bladder was full, and I followed him through the door. To my mild surprise it led outside to an alley. The man had already started to coat a nearby building. I moved about ten feet from him.

"Best goddamn bathroom I ever been in," he muttered, taking a pull from his bottle.

I ignored him and urinated willfully, targeting some overgrown weeds.

"You hear me?" he blurted. "Bathrooms is one thing Sin City got dead-on right. That and whores."

An image flashed in my mind of Sarah giving pens to grinning schoolchildren in the south—on an island as beautiful as any place on Earth. Despite its flaws, despite the horror of the tsunami, I liked Thailand and its people—and I quickly came to its defense. Or perhaps to Suchin's defense. "You know," I said, "Bangkok used to be called the 'Venice of the East.'"

"That so?"

"Yeah."

"Sin City's better."

"Hardly. But people like you sometimes make it appropriate." I zipped up my shorts as the man cursed and stumbled toward me. "I'm not interested in any trouble," I said, raising my hands. "But you should leave the girl alone."

He spat at my feet. "Not interested in trouble? Well now, that's good for you. Much safer. But if I was you, I'd mind my own damn business. A whore's a whore. I treat 'em as such. Why, this country's built on whores. Stacks of 'em. You want her? Fine. Warm her up for me. I'll break her tomorrow."

"You'll … 'break her?'"

"Dogs is meant to be broke, ain't they?"

It took me a few seconds to realize he was serious. As I stood in disbelief he licked his lips. Thinking of him hurting someone like Suchin made my head throb with fury. Everything but his smile grew dim. Since Sarah's death I had developed a temper that sometimes got the best of me. Now was one of those times.

"I've met only one dog tonight," I finally answered, staring at him.

Though the man's face was so flabby it might have been bread dough, I saw the muscles around his temple twitch as he clenched his jaw. He roared, swinging a fist at me as if he were trying to knock down a building. If I'd been slow, he'd have broken my jaw. As it was, I ducked, easily avoiding the blow.

"I'm gonna kill—"

His words stumbled as my fist disappeared into his ponderous gut. When he doubled over I brought my knee up hard, ramming it against his forehead. The man yelped, then crumpled unconscious to the ground. Grabbing his shirt, I dragged him to the side of the building and propped him against it.

"Damn you," I muttered, my voice quivering on account of my pounding heart. "Damn you to hell."

I waited a few minutes until he began to moan. Relieved that I hadn't hurt him too badly, I went back inside, locking the door. Suchin was chalking a cue as she leaned against a table. Her eyes rose to mine, and concerns for the man fled.

"You follow me?" she asked.

"Kind of."

"You see what happen with man?"

"I saw enough."

To my surprise, she shrugged nonchalantly. "It okay. I win ten dollars from him."

Unsettled by the fight, I took a couple of deep breaths. "I

brought you … you and Ratu dinner. Let's find someplace quiet to eat."

Though I thought she might argue, she smiled. Brushing sweat from her face, she called to Ratu, who came quickly from the far side of the room. He threw his arms up in excitement when he saw me.

"So sorry, mister. I forget yesterday, thank you for watch!"

"I'm glad you like it."

The boy spun it about his wrist. "It seven, four, four."

I looked at the cheap watch I'd bought this morning, nearly identical to the one I'd given him. "You're right."

"Seven, four, five now!"

I patted his back and led him outside. Suchin followed, watching me closely. I navigated the ranks of vendors and soon was at my motorcycle. As I put the key in the ignition, Ratu jumped on the bike's faded seat. I handed Suchin my backpack and she hung it on her bony shoulders. After I sat behind Ratu, she took her place behind me.

Though the bike felt cumbersome, I kicked it to life. Soon we were humming down the streets. I drove toward the Chao Phraya River, thinking its banks would be a good place for a picnic.

Ratu started to sing, and Suchin wrapped her arms around my chest. Though I knew she thought nothing of it, her touch felt reassuring. It made me want to drive faster, to feel her embrace tighten.

"I forget your name!" she yelled in my ear.

"Owen."

"Powen? That nice name."

I grinned and repeated it over the cry of the engine.

She squeezed my arm. "Powen sound more Thai to me. Better name. Maybe you should change."

"Thanks a lot."

She said something in return, but I didn't hear it. Normally I'd have asked her what she said, but I found the silence agreeable. Oddly enough, it felt like the kind of silence that years of companionship breeds, not the uncomfortable pause between the words of strangers.

Bangkok blurred around us. Traffic was thinning, and it didn't take long to reach the river. We passed over it on a modern bridge and turned down a trail along its bank. The bike was hard to control as we climbed rocks and muddy rises, but we made our way to a clearing of grass. Orchids and birds-of-paradise surrounded the grass. The air bore their perfume.

Ratu jumped off and Suchin dropped from behind. The bike wouldn't stand on the damp soil. I tried to lower it to the ground, but the machine was too heavy and fell from my grasp. My companions laughed as I leapt out of its path, banging my shins against the front tire.

Though the blow hurt, I couldn't help but grin. "Let's sit down and eat before I throw both of you in the river," I said, motioning for Suchin to open the backpack.

Her smile subsided as she spied the food and clothes. "You too kind," she said, holding the dress in front of her. Turning to the boy, she added, "Thank Mister Owen, Ratu. He good man."

"Kob khun krab, mister," he said, bowing to me.

I glanced up as a red balloon drifted above us. "Why don't you both change into these while I find us something to drink?"

My companions nodded happily. Energized, I walked toward the street behind us, which ran parallel to the river and bustled with activity. I soon came upon an outdoor market that sprawled as far as I could see. It didn't take long to find a man selling beer and juice. I bought several cans of juice and four cold bottles of Singha. After paying the man, I noticed that his cart was parked in front of a travel agency. Faded posters of Singapore, Hong Kong, Sydney, and Tokyo dominated soiled windows.

Next to the agency, music pulsated from a darkened building. I saw several older couples enter, dressed in clothes that would have been in style three decades earlier back home. Though the notes were muddled, I could have sworn the song was "YMCA." Whistling the tune, I hurried back to my newfound friends.

Suchin and Ratu were where I'd left them, holding hands, talking loudly. Ratu leaned against her shoulder as he spoke. She stroked the back of his head, giggling. Neither heard me approach, and I couldn't resist the childish urge to leap at them from behind, crying out. Both jumped up like startled cats.

Suchin stepped defiantly forward. "We only scared because you sound like pig," she squawked. "Only you not so good-looking!"

"Really?"

"No. And pigs is smart. Very smart. I think if I put you and pig in maze, pig find way out first."

Grinning, I set the drinks down and used my pocketknife to open two beers. One I handed to Suchin. The other I savored. "It's a good thing I didn't get pork fried rice," I said, unpacking our dinners.

Suchin and Ratu were reluctant to sit on the grass in their new clothes but, after I prodded them, did so. Ratu took a huge gulp of juice and hurriedly devoured his rice. Suchin ate much more slowly and seemed to take little pleasure in her food. She did drink most of her beer before setting it on the grass.

"Why you so good to us?" she asked. "Why you care?"

"I haven't done anything," I replied, not ready to tell her that she seemed familiar. "Besides, it's not like I had a lot going on tonight."

She tilted her head sideways, as if doubting my words. "When people give, they want. They want big thing."

"No, no, no. I've done nothing for you, so there's no reason for you to feel like you have to give me something back."

"That good."

As we spoke, Ratu shoved plastic spoonfuls of rice into his mouth at breathtaking speed. In a couple of minutes he managed to devour his food. When finished, he thanked me, and then hurried to the river. Soon he was skipping stones. In the distance, vessels of every shape and size drifted by—barges and tugboats and scores of water taxis.

"Is he always so hungry?" I asked.

"No, but this hard time for him. He too old to beg. Too young to work."

"What will he do?"

She sighed. "I take care of him now and he do okay. But when I die, he have to learn streets by himself."

The detached way she mentioned her death saddened me. Her face was stoic. Her words emotionless. If she had cried for herself, those tears were long since departed.

I opened another beer. "If you don't mind my asking, how old are you?"

"Twenty-five."

Shifting to my knees, I replied, "You can tell me … the truth." Though aware of Ratu's laughter and the distant groan of traffic, I concentrated fully on her, wondering how she'd react.

"I almost twenty-three," she said. "But why you need know?"

"Tell me your story. Tell me why you're sick and living on the street."

"Why? So you can feel sad for me and good about buying clothes? So you sleep well tonight?"

I rubbed my temple. "That's not why. Like I said the other night, I just want to understand."

Her nostrils flared, like a bull's before it charges. I readied myself to apologize, and to change the subject. But then her face softened, grew distant in the dying light. "It old story," she whispered. "As old as Bangkok."

"When did it start?"

"When I was fifteen."

"So young?"

"So I said. My family live in village to north," she began, her words running together. "My father was farmer. Mother wash people's clothes in river. I had brother, but he little, and sick—too sick to help in fields. One day man come from Bangkok, tell my parents if I go with him, I work in rich man's house. I will clean, cook, take care of children. The man put money on table. Big, big money. He say if I go to Bangkok my parents can keep money. He say more come every month. We thought it good deal. I knew I was problem for my parents. I was mouth to feed and they very poor. If I leave, I can help them."

Suchin paused. The sky was dimming, shadows growing bold. A convoy of tapered boats navigated the river. These were full of vegetables and fruits, returning from the floating market to the north. A single man stood at each stern, his hands gripping the long tiller that steered the boats. Women prowled their interiors, sorting through the remaining produce. The drone of the boats' engines was uniquely peaceful.

"So I left with man," Suchin continued, her voice growing unsteady, as if memories would make her mute. "He never speak to me on train to Bangkok. When we get there he buy me pretty skirt, new shoes, blouse. He even get me haircut." She hesitated, touching the embroidered cranes on her dress. "I never get such beautiful things before. I thank him … think how lucky I am. Man only smile. He then leave me at big house. It late. I think maybe I take care of children while parents gone. But only another man is home. No family.

When I ask where wife is, he laugh."

Suchin bit her bottom lip. I saw it tremble and reached out. "Don't go—"

"He take me to room and … then … he want me. And soon … my days of being a girl are over."

Suchin sipped her beer, set it down with a shaking hand. I longed to somehow save her, to spare her from the pain. I leaned forward to hug her, but she drew away and her voice began anew. "In morning other man come. He take me to house where there is many women. When they see me cry, they laugh, ask me how good it was. I cry all day on floor. Next night same thing happen. But then … I climb out window and escape."

"Where'd you go?"

"I try to find job, try very hard, but nobody help me. I no have food. I get thin, think maybe I die. I want to die. But then I remember family. If I die, they still hungry, brother no see doctor. Always be sick."

"What did you do?"

"I finally get job on Ko Sahn Road washing dishes in Irish pub. In few weeks I rent small room with another girl. I buy clothes, eat every day. Soon I can send little money back to parents. Send them more each month. I never tell them what happen, only that I fine and happy."

Suchin started to add something but stopped, looking westward. The sun was setting, illuminating nearby clouds with its crimson fire. The clouds hung like magical tapestries over the river, its waters ablaze with their reflections. Almost directly in front of the sun was the vast silhouette of the Temple of Dawn. Isolated and wondrous, the temple reached far into the sky.

"How long have you been sick?"

She looked away. "Four years ago, I got free blood test. Nurse say I have HIV."

"What did you do?"

"Start taking medicine. Go back to work. I work very hard, but they pay me little. I there for almost four years. Then my body get weak. I can't wash dishes for long hours. They make me go, and I live on street. Sometime I play game for dollar."

I found her composure remarkable. "You're so strong. Really, you're ... incredible."

Her smile was almost wasted in the darkness, but I saw it briefly. She touched her bottle against mine, the connection so gentle it seemed more a lover's caress than a clink of glass on glass. "Thank you, Mister Owen," she said.

"I won't ask you about the past again," I promised. When she didn't respond, I opened another Singha. I didn't usually drink so quickly but was nervous about being with her, nervous that I had asked too much. The previous beers had gone straight to my head, heightening my every emotion. Though I was immeasurably saddened by Suchin's story, I also felt blessed by our growing rapport.

"Is there anything you want to do before ... before you get even weaker?" I asked, averting my eyes, wondering how I could help her, wanting so very much to help her.

"I always hope to climb mountains and see snow," she replied matter-of-factly. "It my dream as young girl. Once I have boyfriend from South Africa. He say that he take me to mountains near his home. I even got passport." Suchin shrugged, smoothing out her dress. "But he never take me. I never see snow."

"Why the mountains? Isn't the sea as beautiful?"

"Maybe, but why not see two most beautiful things in world?"

I pondered her words. I'd always taken it for granted that I'd climb mountains, look upon lands from above. In fact, I'd almost gone to Nepal before returning to Thailand. Putting down my beer, I said, "I should really be taking you to a good hospital instead of talking to you about dreams."

I hadn't meant for the comment to sound harsh, but it had. For the first time since I'd known her, the wall Suchin had built around herself crumbled. She began to cry. At first she just sat and sniffed, but as her tears intensified, she stood.

I moved toward her. "I'm sorry," I whispered, leaning toward her, seeing her draw away. "That didn't sound right."

"Not your fault," she said bravely, wiping her tears. "Anyway, I hurt many times before. And I go to hospital. Nothing they can do."

"But there's new medicine. People are living much longer. People live normal lives."

"I get free medicine from clinic. Good medicine. Same medicine Americans get. But each day I get more weak. I get another infections. My HIV is very, very bad kind. I not live much longer. Doctor say six months."

"Six months? That's crazy."

"Four, five, six months. Maybe more."

"But why not see another doctor? I could get you—"

"I no want to spend end of life in hospital."

"It wouldn't be like that. They could help you. I could help you."

"Mister Owen, one of my friends at Irish pub is doctor. He doctor whose wife died and he came to pub many times after she gone. He so lonely. Anyway, he good, good man. He have a heart like Buddha's. When I learn about HIV I go to him. He help me. For years he help me, make sure I get best medicine. I see very good AIDS doctor in Bangkok many times. But there is not so much he can do for me. My body is difficult. Not like yours."

"If this other doctor is so nice to you, if he has such a good heart, why are you sleeping on the street?"

She scowled at me. "Don't think people are always bad, Mister Owen. People are better than you think. This man give me money. He always give me money. But I send it to my parents. They need it for my brother."

I glanced skyward and then looked at her again. "But we should take you to another hospital. Maybe an American doctor would do something different. Maybe you don't have to … to die so soon."

She sniffed, stepping away, fresh tears staining her face.

"Dying in hospital not for me. There still too much to see. Too much I want to do. Yes, people living longer now with HIV. Of course, I know this. But people still dying. Many, many people. And soon I die too. And I no want to die in hospital. Even American hospital."

"Not everyone is dying. Most people are living."

"But not everyone, Mister Owen. Not people who are same same as me. We still dying. Every day."

"Please, just go with me to—"

"No."

"Why not?"

"Because I try everything. Every medicine. Every combination. Nothing work. Everything just break my hopes."

Frustrated to the point where I couldn't respond, I again looked above, staring at the few stars visible over Bangkok. In such a brightly lit sky they seemed distinctly out of place. The nearby moon was almost ripe, clouds drifting before it. Unexpectedly, a shooting star sprang to life, streaking with incredible speed, covering a great stretch of sky before disappearing into the skyline. I'd never seen such a meteor above a large metropolitan area. With so much background light, it must have been massive.

As I pondered the sight, I became convinced that it was an omen, a sign that somehow I was supposed to help this woman. I could never have explained the feeling. It reminded me of an instinct—something intangible and unknown, but remarkably powerful.

I thought of the dreams I'd dreamt just a year earlier. Not unreachable visions, but simple aspirations of happiness and love. They'd have been realized if only we'd been somewhere else, anywhere else, when the wave hit. Sarah would be with me right now, sharing a walk along a beach or a quiet cup of coffee.

But the wave had found us, and I wasn't strong enough to save Sarah. Nor was anyone around to help us. Not a Thai fisherman. Not God. Not luck. Help would have been worth more to me than any possession, any amount of money, any smile to ever grace a face. Help was all this stranger needed. I questioned why she shouldn't get it. Why should her dream go unfulfilled when I could make it happen? Why should she experience nothing but pain?

As I studied her, it occurred to me what I must do. Though the idea was ludicrous on the surface, I was weary of having my life dictated by a fear of consequences. Every significant decision I'd ever made had been the result of intense scrutiny. Reason and logical paths, once so crucial, were now like shackles I wanted to cast away. Reason mandated that I leave Suchin, but then she would die terrified and alone, much like Sarah had. How could I abandon her, as I had Sarah? How could I live another day if I said good-bye instead of helping her? I couldn't. If I left her, I would die before she did.

"I'll take you to Nepal with me," I said, suddenly desperate for her to stop crying. "First we'll get you the best medicine, and then we'll go to Nepal."

She looked at me as if I were mad, sputtering, "You drunk!"

I smiled. "Maybe. But I want to take you with me. I want you to see the most beautiful mountains in the world."

"But we just meet. I not know you so well. How can I trust you? How can you trust me?"

"I don't know ... how to answer that. Maybe you should just trust your instincts. If you don't believe me, if something about me doesn't seem right, I'll say good-bye. I'll wish you good luck and walk away. But I really do want to help you. Helping you would help me."

"I have no money."

"Nepal isn't far from here," I replied. "And plane tickets aren't expensive. Why, we could leave in a day or two if you wanted."

She gasped in excitement, coughed from the sudden intake of air. When her shudders ceased, she took my hands in hers. "I think too much beer is in your brain, Mister Owen. It little to begin with."

"I'm serious, Suchin."

"What about Ratu?"

I looked at the boy, who was chasing fireflies. "You'll be back soon. I'll leave him the key to my room and some money."

"What if?" she paused, collecting her thoughts. "I not so strong. What happen if I die on mountain?"

"That won't happen. We'll get you the best medicine there is. We'll see a new doctor tomorrow. You've got a lot of life ... so much life ahead of you."

She pulled me toward her, hugging my torso. "I do trust you. Maybe that crazy. Maybe stranger no understand. But living on streets teach me to learn who to trust and who not to trust. I see good people and bad people, and I know who is who. And you good person. My heart tell me so."

"Thanks."

"I never have such wonderful news. Never, never, never, never."

"I wouldn't lie about such a thing."

"I know. Other people make promises they no keep. So many promises. So many lies. But I believe you."

"Let's go buy the tickets," I replied. "There's a travel agency not far from here."

"No, no, you go. I stay with Ratu."

I winked, running into the night. Though the alcohol made me stumble, my feet felt unnaturally light as I sped toward the agency. I wanted her to hold the tickets as quickly as possible.

The shop was still open. Hurrying inside, I pulled out my credit card, setting it on the table. A woman behind the counter looked up from a magazine, smiling when she saw the plastic. She said hello in Thai.

I returned the greeting and pointed at a sun-bleached poster of Everest. "Kathmandu. Two tickets for the day after tomorrow, please."

The woman looked bewildered. Sighing, she said, "Very difficult."

Several airlines flew from Bangkok to Kathmandu, and I didn't think tickets would be a problem. She was just trying to up her commission. When she shook her head again, I turned to leave. "Okay, I'll find another travel agent," I said. "Bye-bye."

The woman called at me to stay. We then haggled on a price. Finally agreeing, she made two calls on a rotary phone shaped like a car. She yammered in broken English with an agent for about ten minutes. Holding the receiver against her belly, she told me that she'd arranged a flight on Majestic Nepal Airlines.

Wanting to make certain the tickets were legitimate and that they'd be waiting for us at the airport, I asked to speak with the agent. The woman worked for the airline and answered my questions succinctly—her voice thick with what I thought was a British accent.

Finally satisfied that I wasn't getting scammed, I paid for the tickets. They weren't as cheap as I'd initially hoped, but I was pleased to have secured them. After thanking the woman, I returned to Suchin and Ratu. His head was on her lap, her fingers stroking his forehead lovingly. He appeared asleep.

Grinning, I sat down beside her. "I bought the tickets. We leave the day after tomorrow at one o'clock."

"Do I really go to mountains?"

"You're going."

Her smile grew. "Thank you, Mister Owen. You save me."

"I'm saving myself, just as much as you."

"How so?"

"I just … I just need to do something like this." I moved next to the boy and lay down. Though my mind raced, my body was spent. The cool grass felt wonderful against it. Glancing at my watch, I saw that midnight had passed some time ago. "Let's sleep here."

"Good idea," she said, stretching out next to Ratu.

For a long time we lay in silence, staring into the blank sky. The nearby city was somewhat quiet, nothing more than background music. The moon had shifted and was much lower in the horizon. I stared at it until my lids grew heavy and I closed my eyes.

"Is this real?" Suchin whispered.

"I hope so."

She replied, but her words came to me jumbled, like distant memories. Then sleep overtook me and I knew no more.

CHAPTER 6

RESOLVE

I woke with a throbbing head. The sun towered in the sky, torturing me with its brilliance. From a nearby rock, Suchin watched Ratu chase frogs at the river's edge. Their voices rose and fell with great speed, and bursts of laughter separated conversation.

I slowly recalled the events of the night before. My chest tightened when I remembered the tickets. "You're an idiot," I muttered to myself, panicking as I thought about the implications of my promise. As much as I liked Suchin and wanted to help her, I'd clearly gone too far. Thailand was her home, and I had no right to take her from it, even if she wanted to go. The thought of bringing her to Nepal made me cringe. It wasn't a very safe country at the moment, for I'd read that government troops were hunting down bands of rebels in the mountains. Moreover, May was about to unfold, and I knew it was almost too late to trek. Soon the rainy season would begin, making passage through the mountains an arduous task. Such a journey might be fatal to someone so sick.

I hit the ground, angry that I'd let the beers and my overwrought emotions cloud my judgment. As wonderful as Suchin was, I shouldn't have promised her the impossible. How could I put her life in danger just to make myself feel better? How could I use her as so many others had?

Suchin must have seen me move, for she jumped from the rock. I sat up, preparing to tell her it was all a mistake. But before I could mutter a word, she ran to me, wrapping her arms around my neck. "Today my dream come true!" she said, beaming. "You number one man in world!"

"Suchin, I don't think—"

"You make me happy for first time since I left parents!"

"I … really?"

She nodded, holding me tight, as if afraid of letting me go. "I not feel like this for many years, Mister Owen. I forgot how it feel to be happy. I really did. Now I remember how it feel so good. I feel like child again. Same same." Her eyes ripened with tears.

"Those mountains are many, many times taller than Bangkok's skyscrapers," I said softly. "Do you think you really have the strength to climb them?"

"No problem. Me not have big muscles like you, but still very strong. I never give up."

I exhaled slowly and deeply, realizing I couldn't destroy her euphoria. Destroying it would destroy her. I'd kill her as surely as the virus would. Stepping away from her slightly, I still held my hands on her shoulders. "Well, I tell you what I'm going to do. I'm going to postpone our trip for a day or two if we need to. Because before I take you to any mountain, you're going to see a different doctor. A few of them. I have to be sure that you're getting the best care that you can."

"Mister Owen, I already tell you—"

"That's the deal, Suchin," I interrupted. "We see doctors before we do anything else."

I felt a minor sense of relief when she finally nodded. As she walked over to Ratu, I began to pick up the area, my mind in a thousand places as I stuffed bottles and plates into a trash barrel. Near the river, I saw the two friends hug. Then they ran toward me. I expected Ratu to be sad that I actually might take Suchin to the mountains, but quite the opposite was true.

"Thank you, mister," he said, beaming. "Thank you for making sister so happy."

"Will you be okay for a few weeks?"

"No problem, mister. I have many friends. We live together."

I suddenly wished—not for the first time—that I had a little brother. Tousling up his hair, I said, "You're a good kid, Ratu. The best. If we do leave, I'm going to see that you stay in my guesthouse until we get back. It's not much, but at least you'll be off the street. Eat all the food you want in its restaurant. I'll pay for everything in advance."

"Advance?"

"Don't worry about it. Just sleep and eat in my guesthouse. Bring a friend if you want."

Ratu clapped. Unable to contain his excitement, he started to babble in Thai. "He think we lucky to find you," Suchin interjected. "He really think you angel."

"I'm no angel."

"He think you are. Me too."

"Are you sure he'd be all right if we leave?"

"He be fine. He know I love him."

I dropped to the boy's level. "If we do go, we'll be back soon. And when we return we're going to get you off the streets. I'll buy you some clothes and make sure you go to school."

"But I no like sch—"

"That's another conversation," I interrupted. Pointing at the motorcycle, I said, "Let's get this thing off the ground."

I bent down to grab hold of its seat while Suchin and Ratu moved to the front. We lifted hard, muscling the bike to an upright position. Mud fell in clumps from its dirty side and we briefly scraped it clean. The bike soon supported our unlikely trio and, earth churning beneath us, we wheeled around. I took one last look at the Temple of Dawn, and then we were in traffic, darting about like the dragonflies I'd seen at the river's edge.

*

About two hours later, after phoning the U.S. Embassy to inquire about the best health care in Bangkok, I drove Suchin to the Royal Thai Hospital, which was located at the city's periphery and sat among fields of well-manicured orchids. As in any developing country, cash opened doors for us, and what would have normally taken days took hours and in some cases minutes. Suchin was seen by one of the best AIDS specialists in the country. Her blood was taken, and multiple tests were run.

After a long lunch in the hospital cafeteria, we met with the specialist again. His face was somber as he studied the lab results. Though his office was beset with windows and a shimmering river snaked into the distance, my eyes didn't leave his face as he started speaking to Suchin in Thai. Almost immediately, she interrupted him. "Please talk in English. My friend want to hear these things."

The doctor studied me for the briefest of moments. He then looked at Suchin and sighed. "Your T-cell count is very low, and your viral load is quite high. As you know, this is a bad combination. A most deadly combination."

"Tell me how bad, please."

"Your meds are not suppressing the virus. And … and we can't stop it at this point. You have a particularly aggressive and drug-resistant strain, and we can slow it, but we can't stop it." The doctor spoke matter-of-factly, but he shook his head slightly in frustration. I noticed this reaction, and as I watched him, I felt myself growing light-headed. I didn't want to be hearing these words.

"Can we change medicine?" Suchin asked.

"Yes, yes, we will. But that won't change the outcome."

"What you mean by … outcome?"

"I mean that, ultimately, the virus will win."

"How soon?"

The physician shrugged. "Impossible to say. Three months. Six months." He set the lab results down. "I'm very sorry."

I shook my head, trying to somehow deny what I was hearing. "Isn't there anything else we can do? Some new study? Some new drug? There must be something."

"I wish there were. Believe me, no one wishes this more than I. But in this year alone about fifty thousand Thais will die from AIDS. Unfortunately, nothing can be done for these people. Nothing other than to make them comfortable."

The doctor continued to speak as he wrote out a prescription, but I hardly heard him. I watched Suchin as she listened, as she tried to act brave. She'd heard these words before, but I think that she'd hoped to somehow hear differently today. She bit her lower lip as the doctor spoke. I slumped in my chair—sad and angry and confused. I couldn't understand why so much suffering existed in the world, why such suffering was fact rather than fiction.

After the doctor left, Suchin turned toward me. "I'm so sorry," I said, putting my hand on her arm.

She sniffed. She took a deep breath, appearing to steady herself. "Look at me, Mister Owen." I glanced in her direction, but she placed her hand under my chin. "No, look at me." When my eyes met hers, she spoke again, "I know this for long time. You no be sad. I ready for this, for what will happen to me."

"But … but I want a miracle."

She nodded. "You give me miracle. I meet you one night, and you promise to take me somewhere different. Somewhere I dream about. Somewhere I be close to Buddha. Where I think about the future, not past. That is miracle."

"That isn't the miracle I'm talking about."

Her eyes sharpened, honed in on me. "Mister Owen, you make me one more promise. One more promise and then I never ask for another."

"What?"

"You take me to mountains. And when you do, you be happy. If you take me to mountains and if you are happy, then I will be happy. My last time in this body will be good time, if you do this for me. Can you do this for me? Can you please, please do this for me?"

Could I? I wondered. Maybe I should push harder, try to find another doctor, another outcome. "I'll try," I finally replied, still debating if I could do more. "I want you to be happy. You … you deserve to be happy. And I'll do whatever I can to make that happen."

"Good," she replied, playfully swatting me on the knee. "Now we get new medicine and we leave. We have much to do. No time to waste."

CHAPTER 7

KATHMANDU BECKONS

Mornings in Bangkok are unique. The city is like an old woman awaking from a deep slumber. It stirs. It groans. It quiets. It stretches and moans and slowly rises. Vendors douse sidewalks with water, sweeping cement clean with thatched brooms as sunlight filters down. Monks light sticks of incense. A rare coolness pervades the air. Everything, whether man or beast or machine, moves slowly, as if reserving its strength for the chaos ahead.

The previous night, after we'd found Ratu in my guesthouse, we'd gone out for dinner and much later retired to my room. Ratu and I had slept on the floor while Suchin slumbered on the sagging mattress that had known only my body for so many weeks. I hadn't slept much, my mind consumed as always with

Sarah, but now also encumbered with Suchin. I didn't know if what I was about to do was right or, for that matter, if I had any right to do it.

That morning, as the city roused itself, we said good-bye to Ratu. I gave him more than enough spending money to last a few weeks and paid for his room and meals in advance. I was happy to see a friend of his appear, as it seemed that this friend would stay with him in my room. Suchin hugged Ratu more times than I could count. As much as she wanted to travel to Nepal, she had a nearly impossible time prying herself away from him.

After we'd said our final good-byes, we collected our few possessions, returned my motorcycle, and were soon crammed in the back of a tuk-tuk. The machine's diminutive size contrasted starkly with the racket it made. The tuk-tuk sounded more like a chainsaw than a vehicle, revving up and down in short bursts of noise. The driver kept both hands on the steering bar, nimbly guiding the machine through traffic. We were nearing the airport, and my pulse quickened. This was the point of no return.

I tried not to think of all that could go wrong. Anything could happen in the mountains. I might twist an ankle, we could get caught in a mudslide, or she could grow weak and die. There were no doctors high in the Himalayas. If Suchin took a turn for the worse, there'd be little I could do.

Knowing that somehow I was going to have to resign myself to whatever fate demanded of us, I stared blankly ahead. I'd made the mistake of telling our driver to take us to the airport quickly. The youth, undoubtedly thinking of a big tip, was intent on proving he ought to be in Daytona racing stock cars. His tuk-tuk's engine was loud and obstinate as we accelerated through the muddled traffic. He seemed to dare buses and trucks to squash us, apparently somehow convinced that his three-wheeled tuk-tuk would obliterate these behemoths upon impact.

A rare stretch of open road loomed ahead and our driver floored it. Department stores, markets, skyscrapers, and thousands of pedestrians merged into a torrent of sight and sound. So many colors, smells, and noises abounded that it was almost overwhelming. Never had I seen a city so alive.

Suddenly we lurched to the right, as if our tuk-tuk were drunk instead of, as I suspected, our driver. A massive shadow fell upon us. I looked up in time to see an elephant in our wake. Atop it was a man from one of the hill tribes to the north. Goods were draped over the elephant, which was presumably his only means of transportation. When we wheeled crazily around a corner, the elephant disappeared.

"Big elephant," Suchin yelled over the racket.

"Incredible! Do they come into the city often?"

"Not as much as when I young. Then they come every day."

That didn't surprise me. Everywhere I looked, I could see construction, evidence of relentless expansion. Frankly, I was surprised elephants were still allowed in the city. "Did your father use one?" I asked, yelling in her ear.

Suchin giggled. "No, silly. Only rich farmer buy elephant. My father very poor. He have nothing."

Our driver pulled onto the city's main highway. Soon Bangkok receded. A 747 streaked overhead, coming down not far in the distance. I glanced at Suchin and saw that she was smiling. "Are you sure Ratu will be okay?" I asked.

"Please no worry about him. He never better."

"And you? Will you miss Bangkok?"

"A little. But I very happy to see mountains. To walk with clouds. To feel like a giant."

"It might be cold."

"Good. I never be cold before." She paused, tightly gripping my arm. "Thank you, Mister Owen. You make me happy."

I should have been warmed by her words but experienced a pang of guilt. "It's been awhile since that's happened."

"What you mean?" she asked, her brow furrowed.

"The only person I've really made happy is gone."

"Where to?"

"I wish I knew."

Flustered, I turned away from her, watching our driver slow as he approached the airport's main terminal. After pulling up to the curb, he hopped out of his seat. It had no back and only a bottom of uncovered springs. I pulled my traveling backpack, which was the size of a small desk, from the vehicle. Grunting, I threw the pack on my back. I fastened its thick belt about my waist and adjusted its shoulder straps until it hugged me. The pack contained most of our possessions. A few essentials were in a fanny pack that I wore in front for easy access.

I paid the driver, giving him a handful of coins. I wanted to get rid of them all and tipped him well. After counting deftly, he bowed. "Kob khun krab," he said, his smile revealing tobacco-stained teeth.

"Kob khun krab," I replied, turning to catch up with Suchin. Our plane was leaving in little more than an hour, and even though she'd never flown before, she understood the implications of being late. She squeezed through hordes of people, her thin legs pushing her forward with surprising speed. Maybe she was stronger than I thought.

Suchin made a few wrong turns, but finally found the Majestic Nepal Airlines ticket counter, which was surprisingly empty. Without saying a word, she unzipped my fanny pack and withdrew our passports. The attendant looked at me and said hello in English, but before I could respond, Suchin peppered her with questions in Thai. Grinning, I watched my companion hand over our passports. Their conversation seemed to unfold at the speed of light. Though I understood the occasional phrase, I stopped listening. If Suchin got us on a plane to India, so be it. I wasn't going to interfere.

In no time at all, the attendant handed us our passports and boarding passes. Suchin nodded to me and, taking my hand, led me down the corridor. "No problem. Our plane fly in sixty minutes. But we go there now."

I found it ironic that after spending so much time abroad I was being led about like a puppy by someone who'd probably never been in an airport. It was certainly nice, however, not to have to worry about where I was going. Deciding to trust her, I pulled my pack higher up on my hips, adjusting the weight.

Nearby, a uniformed taxi driver was telling three Americans he'd take them to Ko Sahn Road for only five hundred baht. When they quickly agreed I couldn't help but smile, knowing they could have easily talked him down to half the price. As the driver glanced at me I winked. He paused in surprise, then laughed unreservedly, aware that I was on to him.

Suchin pulled me ahead. She took another wrong turn, and as we backtracked, she muttered to herself in Thai. Still, in a few minutes we came to the security area and I threw my pack down upon the X-ray machine. After retrieving it, I once again followed her lead.

"Slow down, will you?" I pleaded. "This thing's heavy."

"We no miss plane. You better get more strong if you want to climb big mountain. Maybe I have to train you."

"Train me?"

"Sure. I make you run down street, climb steps, maybe jump a rope. With me as number one boss you get very strong."

"I bet you'd like that."

"Why not? Mother boss for my father. She train him every day, in many things. And she very, very happy."

"And how about him?"

"He fine. He understand that training good for him. Without training, he be very bored."

I avoided some spilled water. "You know, you're certainly a sassy little thing."

"Sassy?"

"It means … you like to be the boss."

She laughed. "Yes, I very sassy. Father tell me so many times. Same same as you. But if we miss plane, I be more sassy."

I hurried to match her pace, groaning. We proceeded to the immigration counter, got our passports stamped, and then walked by several foreign planes. I didn't think our gate would be far. Sweat streaked down my face and I wiped my brow. "Man, it's hot," I muttered.

Suchin paid me no heed, as she was busy staring at a blue plane a few gates ahead. People were already boarding it. Jumping up, she yelled, "That our plane! It look like good one. Like lucky one."

Moving closer I could see that the Majestic Nepal airplane was actually rather humble. "I've never seen such a lucky plane."

"Very good, Mister Owen. I happy you like it."

"Owen. Just call me Owen."

"What a beautiful plane, Mister Owen. Thank you so much."

Her smile was infectious and I grinned. Watching her was like seeing a child blow out her birthday candles. Her happiness was so genuine that I found it somewhat disconcerting. When was the last time I'd felt that way?

The walkway seemed to vanish behind us. Soon we were at the plane's entrance. Only now did I realize how many years it had truly witnessed. Paint peeled from its aluminum skin, which was pockmarked, as if it had suffered from horrible acne as a youngster. Inside, the carpet was stained and torn. Taking a deep breath, I followed Suchin to our seats, wondering how a drunken impulse had so quickly become reality. Once at our seats, I crammed my pack into an overhead bin, provoking a few disapproving stares from fellow passengers.

I offered Suchin the window position and she took it gladly. I then grabbed my seat belt and prepared to latch it. Unfortunately, it had no buckle of any sort. The two straps' ends were frayed, as if the buckles had been torn off. Looking at the seats on either side of me, I made sure I didn't have someone else's belt. To my surprise, I saw that several passengers had the same problem. I followed the lead of a teenager and tied the two ends of my belt together.

Suchin had probably never used a seat belt, and I buckled her in, tightening the strap almost as far as it would go. When the pilot started the engines, she gripped my leg. The prop outside the window spun to life. The cabin filled with its drone.

Soon we slowly taxied toward the runway. Suchin seemed as nervous as she was excited. Grabbing my hand, she squeezed it tightly and with surprising strength. The plane swung to the left, lining up with a runway. For a moment, we sat idle. Then the pilot revved the engines and we rolled down the tarmac. Though we were soon going very fast, we merely bounced along the ground like a ball thrown down a hill. The plane convulsed with effort, yet gravity still defied it.

"Come on, you old bird," I whispered.

The plane lurched upward, back tires bumping the pavement six or seven times before losing contact. Suchin's grip tightened on me as the Earth fell away. Though her head obscured most of the window, I watched the airport growing smaller. Soon it vanished, and all I saw were rice fields. Where Bangkok was I had no idea.

Much later, when we were among the clouds, I touched Suchin's shoulder. "Say good-bye to Thailand."

When she looked at me, I didn't know if her tears stemmed from joy or sorrow. "I already have."

CHAPTER 8

CITY IN THE CLOUDS

Handing our meal trays to the stewardess, I shifted in my seat. The captain had just announced that we'd soon begin our descent. After he'd signed off, Suchin quickly turned and gazed out the window, as if we'd be landing in three seconds.

"It takes a little while to get back down," I said.

"Oh. But we went up so fast."

"Well, going down is … it's slower."

She twisted toward me. "Maybe he should wait to get people excited until we are closer to ground. He tell people too early."

I grinned. "How excited are you?"

"I feel like bird."

"When we come down over Kathmandu, I think the view

will be even better. My guidebook says mountains surround the city."

"What else in book?"

"Well, it talks about the different treks. There's a map and an explanation for the easiest to the most difficult."

"What trek we do?"

"I think we'll do one of the five-day treks. The book says they're really pretty."

Her eyes narrowed. "But in Bangkok I hear from many foreigners that Annapurna is most beautiful trek. They love it and always talk about it. We must do Annapurna."

I shook my head, wishing she'd never heard of the Annapurnas. Sarah and I had researched the Annapurna trek and I knew the route was difficult. "That'd be way too hard for us," I said. "It takes more than two weeks to complete, and you'd have to climb to almost 18,000 feet. And it's getting too late in the year to be trekking. Soon the rains will come."

She looked at me intently, her brow furrowed. Finally, she said, "I think you sad because you give up too easy. You no fighter. If you want to do baby trek, okay. But I think you give up before you try."

"Suchin—"

"Mister Owen, what you quit in America?" She leaned closer, pressing me. "Why you traveling with no job?" An uncomfortable silence filled the small space between us, the drone of the props suddenly grating. I didn't want to talk about Sarah, about the voids in my life. "Why you here?" she asked again.

Rattled, I took a drink of apple juice. "Not now."

"Why not now? Again, why you here?"

"It's not—"

"You ask me questions. So many that my head spin like a tuk-tuk looking for passengers. Now it time for me to ask you."

I set the juice down. "Suchin, I was in Phuket when the tsunami hit. I was there with my wife." I paused, collecting my emotions, holding them back with great effort. "We were on our honeymoon."

"Oh. So sorry, Mister Owen."

"The wave ... well, it took her from me. I tried to save her. Maybe I could have. But it took her and she's gone." I closed my eyes.

As I felt Suchin's hand squeeze mine, Sarah's face flashed in my mind. Oddly, I recalled how she'd introduced herself at our blind date. She'd told me jokingly that if the night turned out as badly as her last such date that she'd never again listen to her best friend when it came to the opposite sex. I'd laughed, not knowing what to say but enjoying her candor.

Remembering our seemingly instant connection, how her eyes didn't flee from mine, I flinched, forcing Sarah away. I didn't want to walk through memories right now. Those paths were too trodden. "Anyway, after her funeral, I returned to Thailand. I came back because I felt like ... I hoped I'd be returning to her."

"Then why you not go to Phuket? Go back to where she

died? Maybe you can help people rebuild. I think she would want you to do this."

I nodded. "Someday … someday I'll go back. But I'm not ready for that beach." I paused, unsure of myself, of how much to say. "I think I'd crumble there."

"Take your time, Mister Owen. But the more soon you go back, the more soon your heart can start to heal. I can go with you, if you want, though I think maybe you should go alone."

The sincerity in Suchin's words touched me. My hurt seemed to make her hurt. "I should go alone. But thanks for offering."

"Of course. You help me. I help you. Same same. Right now I think we need each other."

Even though our fellow passengers appeared asleep, and I didn't have to worry about anyone eavesdropping on our conversation, when I spoke next my voice was barely more than a whisper. "Sometimes, I feel like quitting. I want to give up. Maybe I have already. Maybe that's why I've been in Bangkok for so long."

"If you quit, you waste gift of life. You help nobody. You think Sarah would want you to quit? To throw away your life? Of course not. She love you and she would want you to be happy."

"Yes, yes, she would. But that doesn't make anything any easier."

"Mister Owen, you think you only one in world with problems? With hurt?"

"You don't know my problems. You don't know anything about me."

"I know—" Suchin's face contorted as the plane suddenly shook, lunging downward as if it were a duck shot from the sky. While the captain announced we were encountering turbulence, I told Suchin not to worry, even though I'd read that Kathmandu had one of the most dangerous airports in the world. After all, winds constantly ricocheted off the mountains surrounding the city, causing terrible flying conditions.

The pilot angled the plane down. The white world about us parted, revealing a city besieged by the elements. Bordering substantial mountains, Kathmandu looked to be in the throes of a storm. Dark, angry clouds hovered above it, flashing as lightning spat below.

"We try not to fly through clouds in Nepal, as the clouds here have rocks in them," joked the pilot over the intercom.

I don't think anyone thought the comment was particularly funny. The air was very choppy. The plane acted like a skiff in a violent sea—dropping crazily, fighting its way up, falling again. I looked out the window in time to see a bolt of lightning strike a barren stretch of land just outside the city. Other passengers must have also seen it, as a great deal of nervous chatter suddenly dominated the stale air between us all.

Suchin didn't look good. Her eyes seemed unfocused, and she had broken out in a cold sweat. I shoved an airsickness bag in front of her just before she threw up. Patting her back as she heaved, I tried not to get sick. Foolishly, I'd left my juice unfinished, and it toppled from my tray, spilling on my lap. I swore between clenched teeth. Patting Suchin with one hand, I continued to hold the airsickness bag with the other.

Mercifully, the ground was growing closer. The city didn't look as large as I'd expected. There were no sprawling suburbs or tall buildings, just multitudes of homes and stores. When we passed over a temple, I found myself asking whatever god dwelled there to let us land safely.

I heard the familiar sound of landing gear locking into place. Suchin finished throwing up and handed me the reeking bag. I held it closed while dumping out the contents of a plastic sack we'd been carrying. Putting the soiled bag in it, I tied it shut, hoping to contain the stench. After setting the sack under my seat, I made sure her belt was tightly fastened. Our wheels smacked the ground an instant later. Though the plane shuddered on impact, the pilot pulled off a decent landing, and several passengers applauded his efforts.

Looking out the window, I tried to locate the great Himalayas. I only saw an old airport, however, covered in mold and flaking paint.

But I knew the mountains loomed in the distance—vast worlds of rock that we'd soon be climbing.

*

Sitting in our bicycle taxi, I stared at Kathmandu, which was a claustrophobic place, dominated by narrow streets and thin buildings. An infinite network of electrical and telephone wires ensnared structures as if they were insects caught in a spiderweb. Rain was coming down hard, and I saw few people.

Those outside carried newspapers or massive leaves over their heads.

Our driver pedaled relentlessly, his muscled calves knotting in effort. The cobblestone road rose and fell like ocean swells. Suchin and I exchanged smiles. Under the taxi's canopy we were quite dry, and even though the going was slow, I suspected neither of us had experienced a more interesting ride.

Several children selling knives ran toward our taxi, but the driver motioned them away. One ignored him and approached me, stopping only when I shook my head. The knife he held was as long as his arm. Its thick blade was curved and its hilt full of fake jewels. I wondered why anyone would buy one.

Many other signs of tourism were present. Though I saw few travelers, every block seemed to have at least one hotel, photo lab, and restaurant. Each had several signs. One boasted Kathmandu's best pizza. Another announced the presence of a Western doctor. A third declared, "We have Internet!"

Occasionally, a cow slept in the middle of the street. I knew that many Nepalese were Hindus and therefore took pains to honor these creatures. They didn't eat their meat and allowed them to roam the city. Our driver—and every car that passed—widely circumvented the cows, as if reluctant to infringe upon their space.

As our creaky machine approached the crest of a hill, the city grew more congested. Traffic congealed, vehicles with two, three, or four wheels belching smoke as they lumbered past. Our driver seemed to take the chaos in stride. His sandaled feet pumped steadily, his stare always straight ahead.

"Where can we find hotel?"

The flight had taken a toll on Suchin, and I was glad to hear her speak. "I don't know. I think we're in the center of town. Really just about anything would work."

Pointing ahead, she said, "That look like hotel."

The place was called the Everest Hotel. For anyone to name the frail, droopy building after the tallest mountain in the world was amusing. However, the hotel looked oddly inviting, and I asked our driver to pull over. He must have been tired, for he didn't try to talk me into a longer trip.

After coasting to a stop, he helped us out of our seat. It was a good two-foot drop to the ground, or to the water, for a massive puddle encircled the taxi. With no option but to jump into it, we landed with a splash. Ankle deep in the brown water, I strapped on my pack while asking the man how much we owed. He asked for a pittance and, liking the quiet determination he'd displayed, I doubled his request. When he smiled, I saw that his teeth were metal studs.

Suchin and I hurried into the hotel, wiping our feet on a frayed welcome mat. Besides being ancient, the building was in decent shape, its tile floors clean and polished. The lobby was unadorned, save for wooden chairs and a smoke-stained fireplace. A Nepalese woman peeling potatoes sat behind a desk. When she saw us she dropped her knife. "Namaste," she said.

Though I knew only three words in Nepalese, this heartfelt

greeting was one of them. "Namaste," I said, bowing slightly.

"You want room?"

"How much?"

The price she quoted seemed fair, and I didn't bother to haggle. Suchin was sagging, and I wanted to get her to bed. I was tired and could only imagine how she felt. After paying, we walked down the hallway, stopping at room sixteen. The door had no knob, just a latch with a padlock through it. Opening it, I flicked on the room's only light and went inside. Twin beds were pushed close together in the center. The beds sagged like old skin, but the blankets looked clean. A faded poster of Everest adorned the biggest wall.

After testing the toilet and shower, I put my pack down. "Suchin, why don't you take a hot shower? It'll make you feel better."

Though she was terribly tired, her smile wasn't forced. "I hardly ever take hot shower. Always cold."

"Enjoy it."

"What will you do?"

"Unpack our clothes."

Her sudden hug caught me off guard. Before I could say anything she twisted away, shutting the bathroom door behind her. I listened to her undress, slightly uneasy about us sharing a room. I didn't know what to expect and wasn't sure how to act. Only when she turned on the shower did I step from my trance, unzipping my bag. Our clothes were damp and I hung them around the room to dry.

Finished, I lay down and closed my eyes. Though I felt as if only a minute or two had passed, when I next experienced conscious thought Suchin was asleep in the other bed. Glancing at my watch, I saw that it was midafternoon, which because of the time change, meant that it was almost dinner time in Bangkok. Getting up, I went into the bathroom and stripped, uncomfortable with the thought of her seeing me naked. I then draped my wet clothes over the showerhead and changed into a fresh outfit.

The sky seemed lighter as I moved to the room's only window, gazing at unfamiliar sights. It had stopped raining and the sun beat down, chasing the clouds away. The temperature was rising. Soon heat and humidity would prevail.

I sat on the corner of my bed, glancing at Suchin. Her eyelids shifted as she dreamt. I studied her for a few seconds and then turned my attention to the photo she'd rested on the windowsill, reaching over to pick it up. The plastic frame was cracked—though not from careless hands but old age. The black and white shot was what I'd seen in Bangkok, but now that I was closer, I could study the picture intently. A young couple stood behind a girl and boy. In the background was a thatched home, which drooped awkwardly upon stilts. Though everyone was dressed in worn clothing, their faces were bright and unburdened. Suchin's smile must have been hereditary because her parents and brother displayed it with equal zeal.

"What you doing?" she asked sleepily.

I set the frame down. "Sorry. I just wanted to see who you came from."

The corners of her mouth rose. "From the best."

"How old were you in the picture?"

"About six. Maybe seven." She started to speak but was interrupted by a yawn. "This only photo I have of them. Every night I sleep next to it. That way, I watch over them. They watch over me."

"Just like when you were young."

"That right," she said. "Sometimes I afraid I forget their faces. But with picture next to me, I always remember."

"Your mother's beautiful. I see her in you."

"You do?"

"In your eyes, in your smile."

"Thank you, Mister Owen."

"You're welcome." I rose from her bed and pulled the curtains closer together. "Listen, I want you to go back to sleep. I'm going to buy us some things. I'll get you clothes and boots, and we need good sleeping bags."

"How you buy me boots when I no there? I need to try on."

"True. But you also need some rest. If the boots I find don't fit you, I'll take them back for another pair."

I thought she was going to debate the point further, but after I carefully measured her foot against my hand, she nodded. "Okay, this time you boss. Next time I boss. I be better boss than you. More experience."

I grinned. "I'll be back in an hour or two. Then we'll clean up and have a good dinner. Tomorrow we can buy anything else we need."

"No start trek tomorrow?"

"We should wait a day to let our bodies adjust to the altitude. Then we'll be stronger for our climb."

When I stepped away, her hand darted from the covers, grabbing my knee. "Mister Owen, you must understand. I no get stronger next day. Maybe I stay same. Maybe I get more weak. Resting do me no good. It waste of time."

"But we—"

"Please," she beseeched me. "Already rain start to come. It better if we leave tomorrow. I be strong in morning. Then we can do Annapurna trek."

Though I disagreed with her logic, I didn't want to argue. "All right. But you go back to sleep. If I return and find you out of bed we'll wait another day."

"You boss."

"Really?" I said, not unkindly. "You know I'm not the boss. Now get some rest and don't let me catch you awake."

"Okay, number two boss."

I glanced at her photo, thinking of the happy family, wishing that she could go back in time. "Sleep well, Suchin. I'll be back soon." As she said good-bye, I pulled the door shut, wondering if she'd look at the photo and whisper to her family of the adventure she was about to embark on.

*

Much later, after the sun had vanished and the world had been painted black, Suchin and I sat in a dim restaurant. "Charlie's" was famous in Kathmandu for its lasagna and chocolate cake. The rambling building brimmed with trekkers from every continent. Though I understood little of what was said, I often heard the words Everest and Annapurna.

These were the two most popular treks in Nepal. The Everest trek took you all the way to the mountain's base camp. The two-week hike was so demanding that people often opted to take a small plane back to Kathmandu once they reached the base camp. Though the view of Everest was purported to be spectacular and well worth the difficult journey, the Annapurna trek was slightly more popular. It took more than two weeks to finish and skirted some of the highest mountains in the world. Halfway through, trekkers had to climb Thorung La Pass, which was about 17,500 feet high.

I'd skied the Rockies several times and knew that as awesome as those mountains were, they stood at only about 13,000 feet. I found it hard to imagine that on the eleventh day of our trek, when we tackled Thorung La Pass, we'd climb from 14,500 to 17,500 feet. That same day, after reaching the summit, we'd have to descend six thousand feet to the nearest village.

My guidebook said many trekkers were forced to turn back as they climbed Thorung La. The air was so thin that people suffered from acute mountain sickness—meaning that fluid had formed in their lungs or brain. Incessant coughing and headaches were the first signs of AMS. Trekkers who experienced these symptoms were told to descend as quickly as possible. If they didn't, the fluid could fill their lungs, drowning them.

Because the trekking season was drawing to a close, I suspected that many of the people around us had just come from the mountains. Most of the travelers were sunburned and had cracked lips. Seeing how fit and strong and tired they looked, I wondered if we would ever complete the circuit. Suchin was in no shape to begin such a journey. I'd have to carry all of our gear and knew it would be a struggle for me as well.

If things got bad in the mountains, I promised myself that I'd force her to turn around. With any luck, her desire to see the Himalayas would be satiated after a week or so. Then we could descend slowly and enjoy Kathmandu's sights before our return flight to Thailand.

I had to admit that Suchin had recovered amazingly in the past few hours. When I had come back to the room with an armful of new clothes, maps, medicine, boots, and two sleeping bags, she'd literally leapt out of bed. She had tried everything on and found all the goods to her liking. The boots were her favorite, as they were light and waterproof. She'd tested this claim by stomping in puddles on the way to Charlie's.

Glancing down, I asked, "Do they feel okay?"

"Wonderful," she said, sucking up a strand of spaghetti. "It fun to jump in water."

I was pleased her appetite had returned and lifted my glass of red wine. "To puddles."

"To you, boss number two."

We laughed and sipped the cheap wine.

"Close your eyes, Suchin," I said. "Just for a moment."

She gave me a puzzled look but did as I asked. After pulling a necklace from my fanny pack, I leaned across the table and draped it around her neck. On my solo excursion, I'd bought the piece from a girl selling silver jewelry at the side of the street.

"Go ahead and open—"

She blinked, immediately reaching for the necklace. Its slender chain carried a trumpeting elephant. The rendering was the size of a quarter, intricately engraved.

"Just because your father never had one doesn't mean that you can't."

She squeezed my hand. "Owen, he so beautiful. I never get such gift. Thank you."

"He looks at home with you."

"I love him," she replied, her eyes tearing. "I … I don't know … he's perfect."

"That's the first time you've called me Owen. Without the mister."

"That true."

We shared a smile and sipped our wine. I was about to ask if she wanted anything else for the trek when the lights suddenly flickered and went out. Conversation wavered as waiters lit thick candles on each table. When our waiter approached, I looked up at her. "Excuse me, but why did the power go out?"

"Kathmandu doesn't always have enough electricity," she

said smoothly. "So sometimes they turn off the power in different parts of the city."

"Often?"

"As often as they like," she replied. The woman was obviously proud of her command of English. Like all Nepalese who dealt with foreigners, she had to be fairly fluent in the language or she would never have gotten her job. "Enjoy your evening," she said, lighting the two candles on our table.

With the electricity off everything was much more intimate. The same people who'd been talking loudly now leaned forward, their voices soft, their laughter muted. The pulsating reggae music from a bar outside was gone, replaced only by the occasional drone of a car.

Suchin pushed her plate aside. "Owen, I know you worry about me. But I happy now. More happy than in long, long time. And when we climb mountains I be free."

"Free?"

"So whatever happen in mountains, no be sad. You make my dream come true."

"I'm glad. But I still wish you'd agree to a shorter trek."

"Please, Owen, no talk about baby trek again. I many things, but not baby."

I watched the candle flicker in a sudden draft. Then I watched her. "You're no baby. That's for sure." As she went back to her spaghetti, I envisioned the weeks to come. Despite my reservations, I looked forward to our journey together. Everyone I talked to on the street had told me how the mountains had moved them, made them feel both insignificant and significant. Listening to their tales, sensing their excitement, was thrilling.

Though the trek would be physically demanding, I hoped it would transcend any experience I'd had. I also hoped it would pull me from the bowels of depression. "Suchin," I said over the quiet breeze of conversations, "I want you to know that this trip is as much for me as it is for you. I brought you here, but I wanted … no … I needed to come."

She winked. "I understand that, Owen. And I think we be good team."

I smiled and dug into my lasagna. She took a sip of her wine, then wiped a crimson drop from her lip. Suddenly, I experienced the familiar sensation of having been with her before. No matter how hard I tried, I couldn't shake the feeling.

Leaning forward, I asked, "Why do I feel like I've met you before?"

She didn't answer me immediately, merely staring into my eyes. It seemed as if she was looking through me. "Owen, Buddhism say everything born again and again and again. You and me, we are very, very old souls. As old as mountains. And old souls stay together. Maybe in past life we brothers or sisters. Maybe we once lovers."

A chill ascended my spine. Though I wasn't as spiritual as I used to be, her words shook me. Could they be true?

I thought I'd only asked the question to myself, but she nodded. "Yes, Owen. Maybe we meant to come here. Maybe once, long ago, this our home."

CHAPTER 9

THE ROAD TO BAHUNDANDA

The lurch of the truck jarred my brain. Sitting on the vehicle's ravaged flatbed, I nudged a nearby goat aside. Its horns looked sharp, and I didn't want one going through my neck when we hit the next pothole. The goat's owner gave me an indifferent shrug, making no effort to pull on the nylon rope about his hand and rein in his animal. Slightly frustrated, I waved my finger at the beast, warning it to stay away.

Suchin saw my look and laughed. Sitting comfortably on a pile of hay with her back against my pack, she was in an enviable position and hardly seemed to notice the truck's jolting.

Though at some point the road had been paved, potholes the size of kitchen sinks littered its surface. Some of the bigger craters were at least a foot deep, and from a distance the road resembled the face of the moon. I'd have thought our driver might do his best to avoid the potholes, but he never adjusted his course. I could see him through the broken window in the cab's rear, casually sipping from a thermos while the truck bottomed out every minute or so.

Tall, perhaps ten-foot branches had been tied vertically to the edges of the flatbed. Ropes and smaller branches crisscrossed these, creating two walls that looked quite strong. A huge sheet of canvas ran from the top of one wall to the other, protecting those below. Creatures of every sort sat within its shade. Aside from three goats, a handful of baby pigs, several dozen chickens, and some ducks, about thirty Nepalese were on the truck with us. Some clung to the walls, while others sat on haphazard piles of hay. One man had tied each end of a sheet to a branch, creating a hammock for his two children. Though it swung madly from side to side, the kids slept as if they were still in the womb.

Leaning back on the hay, I closed my eyes. I had a heartbeat's worth of peace before we hit the king of all potholes and I was thrown several feet up. When I landed, the air was hammered from my lungs. I tried to breathe, but only when my chest felt as if it would burst was I finally able to draw air. Swearing, I stood, unwilling to go airborne again.

In a transmission-destroying lurch, the truck stopped at a crossroads. Nearby, under the shadow of a gnarled tree, stood several dozen people. They bore bags, wood, chickens, goats, and wide-eyed babies in slings. When they started to climb into the back of the truck, I was pushed from my spot. Bodies pressed Suchin and me forward.

Soon the situation grew comical. When it seemed the truck would hold absolutely no more people, a dozen others hopped aboard, then a handful of children, then a woman and her roosters. Within a few minutes, people were clinging to the walls and dangling out the back. Although counting faces was impossible, I guessed there to be at least sixty passengers.

For a heavenly moment, all was still. Then the truck lunged ahead. Everyone was thrown back, and many passengers grabbed at each other to keep from being hurtled out the rear. Amazingly, no one fell, and people gradually found places to sit. The younger Nepalese let their elders have the choice locations. Soon about half our contingent was no longer standing.

By now it was exceedingly hot. Feeling a little light-headed, I looked for a place to rest. Not a single square inch of space seemed available, however, and I was forced to stand, clinging like a lizard to the network of branches. Then a man next to me nonchalantly dropped his bag and climbed up the backside of the cab. Glancing up, I saw that a wooden railing surrounded the top of the cab. Calling out to Suchin, I followed the man, hoping that no one would stop me. The climb was easy. After dropping over the railing, I leaned down to help Suchin. She was all smiles, moving with surprising agility. When she reached the top, she gave me a hug.

The wooden barrier encircling the cab's roof was waist high.

Grasping its planks, we were able to stand in relative security. Turning around, I saw that Kathmandu had vanished. The sky was cloudless and brilliant blue and I could gaze for miles. To the north, the Himalayas rose almost straight up. They were the color of ash, as jagged as a serrated knife.

A tap on my shoulder caused me to adjust my gaze. I followed a man's dirty finger as he pointed to the front of the truck. At first I didn't understand what he was pointing at, but then I noticed that an electric wire hung ominously across the road. The wire wasn't very high, and I wondered if it would clear the truck. As I was still wondering, the native swiftly dropped to the roof of the cab. Suchin and I followed his lead, and a few seconds later the wire flew over our heads by a foot. Thanking the man profusely, I stared ahead, searching for other wires.

Suchin tugged on my shorts. "Very exciting ride!" she exclaimed, as if a kid on a roller coaster. "Mountains more beautiful than anything I see before."

"I can't believe how steep they are!"

"Yes, they very big. Much bigger than I ever dream."

I nodded, the sun warm on my face. "Your English gets better every day."

"I need practice. Many, many practice."

I spotted more wires in the distance. Now we were ready and crouched down long before they sailed by. Soon Suchin and I were able to judge which ones we'd have to duck and which were high enough not to worry about.

The road was full of switchbacks and hills. Whenever

we reached a crest, our driver threw the truck into neutral. Attempting to save gas, he was very hesitant to brake, and more than once the truck rose up on two wheels as we rounded a particularly tight corner. Suchin laughed hysterically. She often let go of the railing and threw her arms in the air. Concerned about her growing carelessness, I sat on the cab's roof, pulling her down beside me.

"You no fun, Owen. Why you such a baby?"

"Because I don't want to see you go flying off this truck. If you broke your back it'd be hard to do much mountain climbing."

Suchin put her thin legs between a gap in the railing, dangling them off the side of the cab. "Maybe you right," she said, smiling at me. "But I not be surprised to see my baby go down below with the other children. It very safe there."

"What did you say?"

"Baby's ears no good? I say—"

Lunging forward, I tickled her. Trapped beneath the railing, and unable to turn around, she begged for mercy. I gave her none, laughing as she squirmed in my grip. "Who's the baby?" I interrogated.

"Owen, he ... number one ... number one baby."

"Wrong answer!" I tickled harder and Suchin shrieked. Our fellow rider howled in laughter, the wrinkles in his face deepening. I smiled at him as I dug my fingers into her stomach.

"Owen no baby!" she screamed.

"Who is the number one baby?"

"Ow ... no, Suchin number one! Suchin number one!"

Nodding, I stopped, moving away from her. Still giggling, she threw my hands aside and stood. "Why you do that? You know I boss. You be in big trouble."

"Terrible trouble, I'm sure."

"You bad man, very bad man. Maybe I climb faster than you and leave you behind for good."

I pulled her down when a wire appeared from nowhere. Glancing ahead, I saw that we were rapidly nearing the mountains. "Damn, they're big," I whispered, even though these were foothills compared to what would soon surround us.

Soon the pavement ended. A pair of heavily rutted tracks lay ahead, disappearing at the summit of the next hill. We weren't far from Besisahar, the village that served as the launching point for the Annapurna trek. As it was already one o'clock, I was eager to begin hiking. My guidebook said the next village was about a four-hour walk from Besisahar. Though we should arrive well before sunset, I was concerned Suchin would slow us down considerably. If we didn't make decent time, the trail would grow too dark to proceed. I knew trekkers occasionally slept on the side of the trail, but that was about the last thing I wanted to do. Surely Suchin would fare better with a full belly and a decent bed.

When we rose to the crest of the next hill, I spied Besisahar. The village was miniscule by any standard, nothing more than a half-dozen wooden homes surrounded by pigs, crops, and junk. Against the magical Himalayan backdrop, Besisahar was an eyesore.

Even as we careened toward the village, our driver hesitated to brake. Casting aside mud like a giant plow would snow, the truck barreled and bounced down the road. Chickens scurried for cover and pigs squealed as we approached. Only when the village was dead ahead did our driver downshift into first. The engine wailed hideously as it redlined and we lurched to a stop.

From our perch, I counted people as they unloaded. I'd tallied sixty-two when I saw a man toss a slew of bags to their owners. When he lifted up my green pack and looked around for someone to throw it to, I called from above. But I was too late. My pack sailed into the air, splattering in a sea of mud.

Cursing, I climbed down to retrieve it.

*

Eating a boiled egg, I followed Suchin down the trail. We'd been walking for just over two hours, and after climbing out of Besisahar, we now descended toward a river far below. The trail was narrow, well groomed, and cut into the side of the mountain like an enormous wrinkle. I hadn't seen anyone on it since we'd left the village.

The mountains to the north were black, cold, and barren. I guessed them to be about half the height of what we'd see in a week's time. My guidebook, which was extensive, didn't even mention them, as if they were too insignificant to ponder. The dusty pages did note that this range was relatively young, created fifty million years earlier when the Indo-Australian plate collided with the Eurasian continent. Prior to that upheaval, there was nothing here but the Tethys Sea.

Looking at the trillions of tons of rock rising into the sky, I found it hard to believe that this was once a shallow sea. "They make you feel a bit small, don't they?" I asked, pointing ahead.

"They as big as Bangkok."

Though her voice was stronger than I might have expected, I detected a slight weariness. "Are you tired?"

"No problem. I walk all day in these boots."

"How about a couple more hours?"

"This trail no problem. I get more tired walking up stairs."

The going had been fairly easy, probably since we were only at an elevation of 2,500 feet. Once we started rising, I knew the days would get progressively harder.

"You hear me, Owen?"

"I'm sorry," I replied. "I was thinking of something else. What did you say?"

"I say if you want, I sing you song."

"Sing me a song? Sure, I'd—"

Suchin nodded as if vindicated. "Good. This Thai love story. It about man in jail who love his wife very much. You listen and maybe you learn something."

"But I don't speak much Thai."

Ignoring me, she began to sing. I quickly recognized the tune, having heard it in a dozen different bars and restaurants. Though her voice often cracked and was terribly off-key, I found it easy to imagine a man sitting in a cell, dreaming of his home and lover. Perhaps I could relate to the song because I was in the Himalayas, a land as lonely as it was beautiful. Or it could have just been Suchin. Like the man in jail and his lover, I knew that no matter how much I grew to care for her, a wall would always separate us.

Her voice preceded our footsteps as the trail dropped to the bottom of a sprawling valley. To our right was the Marsyangdi River. Boulders dotted its surface, water pounding against them. Though a good half mile away, the river seemed crazed, its roar filling the valley. Gazing ahead, I could see that the trail soon climbed an undersized mountain. The going didn't look too tough. To my delight, we were making great time, having already passed the walk's midway point. Suchin was faring better than I could have hoped. She'd set a fairly brisk pace, and encumbered with all our gear, I struggled to keep up.

My companion started to belt out a new song, which was much faster paced. As Suchin sang, she shook her shoulders and hips as if dancing. I joined in, swaying as I grew familiar with the beat. Singing quietly, I followed her lead, mimicking her every rise and fall. Turning around briefly, she clapped, congratulating me on my efforts.

Suchin made a game out of it. She'd sing something new and I'd try to repeat it. At first, she gave me simple lines to follow, but when I had no problems doing so, she sang longer and faster. Not surprisingly, I began to falter. Suchin giggled after most of my mishaps. I found myself laughing with her.

"You speak very funny Thai," she said, rolling her eyes.

"Well, my teacher isn't very good."

She swatted me playfully. "Try again."

This time her words were barely comprehensible. I did my best but was quickly overwhelmed. Though out of my league, I asked her to repeat the line. She did again and again. I worked hard to perfect it, knowing the game was a good way to pass the time.

The trail, which was only two or three feet wide, rose sharply after a series of switchbacks. Long ago, stone steps had been carved in the steepest areas. These were worn smooth with age and the passing of countless feet. Climbing here was hard work, and we stopped singing. The sky grew somber, and I found myself hoping it wouldn't rain. Surely the steps would be dangerously slippery if wet.

"We be smart to walk more quickly," Suchin said. "When we get to top we slow down."

"Don't tire yourself too much. We've got a long way to go."

"No worry."

I wondered what her true feelings were. Hesitating, I asked, "Will you tell me if you have any problems?"

"Yes, I tell you and mountains."

"Good, because to make this trip work, I need to be able to trust you."

"You can trust me, number two boss."

As if to prove herself, she increased her pace, her boots kicking up clouds of dust. We neared the summit of the diminutive mountain. From here the river's thunder was less intense, though it raged only several hundred feet below. I traversed the valley with my eyes, following the granite-colored water to where it disappeared in the north.

"It's amazing that the river's cut so deeply into the valley," I said.

"How water cut rock?"

"Well, it's had a lot of time. Water has been flowing down from these mountains for millions of years." Pointing to a particularly white stretch of rapids, I added, "Imagine all that power. It never stops pounding against those rocks … doesn't stop for a second. Give it enough time and that water will beat those rocks into oblivion."

"What oblivion?"

"It means destruction. Those rocks will become grains of sand that the river will carry to the Indian Ocean."

"Oblivion wrong word. Rock become sand and sand become ocean. Rock become part of everything, not nothing."

I picked up a smooth stone, wondering if it had once been caressed by waves. "That's true."

The trail began to flatten. Finishing the last of the steps, we hurried triumphantly forward, hardly noticing the yellow flowers bordering the trail. In a few minutes we reached the summit. Even though the mountain was unimpressive, truly a pebble compared to its nearby brethren, it felt wonderful to be on top.

"We climb our first mountain!" exclaimed Suchin.

Her words echoed and, inspired, I shouted at the top of my lungs. My cry reverberated eerily in the narrow valley, startling a group of gray birds in a nearby crevice. They took flight as one, wings so close they seemed to kiss.

"They're so lucky," I said, imagining what it would be like to fly here. Not far to the north, dominating the world around us, stood Himalchuli and Ngadi Chuli. According to my guidebook, each mountain was almost 26,000 feet high. Trying to put their size in perspective, I did a quick calculation, estimating that two dozen hundred-story buildings piled on top of each other would rise to the same height.

Cold and unforgiving, the mountains rose steeply skyward, peaks disappearing into the clouds. The Himalayas here were barren of almost any kind of vegetation. The only sign of life was the group of birds we'd startled. Circling for prey, they hovered on air currents, rarely flapping their wings. One bird squawked, its voice loud and clear despite the distance separating us.

Throwing up my arms, I yelled in reply. But the world was silent. I heard nothing but the wheezing of my lungs.

*

Five hours later, in the village of Bahundanda, I lay on a frightfully narrow bed. Upon closer inspection, I'd discovered the bed frame was once a door. An arm's length away, Suchin slept on a similar slab of wood. Though I thought the room was stifling, she had her sleeping bag pulled up to her chest. I was in my boxer shorts and nothing else, sweat seeping out of me. A thin mattress atop the door did little to appease my body. Gazing about our hotel room, I absently fingered my wedding ring. The room was essentially a wooden box with one window—more like a coffin than anything else.

Despite all that left to be desired about the room, I'd have been a fool to complain. A glance outside revealed that the stunning Himalayas encompassed the village. Besides, the room was only costing me twenty rupees a night, which was the equivalent of about a quarter. When the woman had told me the rate, I had to ask her to repeat it. I'd heard that prices plummeted in the off-season and had expected them to be especially low now that the Nepalese government was rooting out pockets of rebels from their mountain havens. Still, I never expected a quarter to get a room.

I sighed, closing my eyes. I found it slightly amusing that the dilapidated, two-story shacks were called hotels. From what little I'd seen, most had wooden planks for floors, a single bulb for lighting, and a hole in the back for a toilet. Running water was nonexistent, room service a fairy tale from another land.

To my knowledge, we were the only guests in the hotel. While the silence was wonderful, I wasn't comfortable with the isolation. My pack alone was worth more than most of the locals made in a year. What would happen if someone just came in here and decided to take it? The door to our room had no lock, so I'd moved my bed in front of it. If someone tried to rob us, they'd at least have to come through me.

A decade earlier, crime was unheard of in the highlands. I'd read, however, that in recent years solitary trekkers were increasingly preyed upon. Bandits occasionally roamed the trails, as did the rebels who sought to oust the ruling monarchy. One woman in Kathmandu had even told me about a couple who'd had everything, including their clothes, stolen just two weeks before. The unfortunate travelers had walked into the next village completely nude.

What a nightmare, I thought, my mind growing dim as sleep claimed me. My last conscious image was of running naked down the trail. Then I began to dream. At first scenes flashed before me like strobe lights in slow motion. But soon I was in the ocean. Sarah swam next to me, her hair spreading like a golden fan behind her. Her indigo eyes seemed somehow enhanced and magnified by the ocean. Behind Sarah and the slice of beach that bore our bungalow, limestone cliffs rose like monoliths to tower above the turquoise sea. The ancient cliffs were topped by brilliant foliage. Sandwiched between the sea and sky, the cliffs looked as if they were stubbornly keeping the blue tones from merging.

Sarah stopped swimming and lay still, her body somewhat buoyant in the warm water. Floating, she closed her eyes. "I could stay here with you forever," she said. "Maybe we should."

Thinking of the food, the people, the beach, and the weather, I replied, "You wouldn't have to talk me into it."

She playfully splashed a handful of water my way. "Since when do I have to talk you into anything?"

"Well, how about since now?"

"Come again?"

"Talk me into something."

Sarah reached for me and, as our bodies intertwined, I savored the fullness of her lips, the suppleness of her breasts. I kissed her cheek, her eyes. I smelled her salt-laden hair and drew her scent deep into my lungs. We kicked rhythmically as our lips met again, Sarah quietly moaning as my hands eased their way into the backside of her suit. Suddenly I wanted to kiss her neck, her shoulders, her belly—all of her. Drawing away, I said, "Let's go back."

She nodded hungrily and soon we were kicking for shore. At first we swam leisurely, gulls wheeling above. But things changed—mutated with the swiftness of a falling kite. The shore seemed to shrink, and we kicked harder. Unseen forces clutched at our feet, our hands, dragging us into the deep. We clung together as the surging sea swelled menacingly beneath us. Then we saw it reaching toward us—a wave of froth and fury and fire. It moved like the wind and was upon us in a blink, hammering us apart, mocking me with the deafening roar of its voice as I screamed to Sarah.

In the black, bitter depths of the sea, I twirled and twisted. Alone. Torn. Broken.

And I felt myself dying when I realized that Sarah was gone forever.

CHAPTER 10

SACRIFICE

My pack felt heavier than it had the day before. My heart did as well. Struggling to keep up with Suchin, I tried to force Sarah's death from my mind. I knew of no trick, though, no way to give myself any sort of respite from the memory that plagued me. Time and time again I saw her vanish into the darkness. I could still hear her muffled scream, still sense her terror.

I always felt like this after the dreams—dirty and disconnected. The memories smothered me in guilt—guilt that I hadn't been able to save her, that I had survived when she hadn't. Why didn't the wave take me? If one of us should have died, it should have been me. Sarah was the survivor. She was the one people turned to in their darkest moments. People turned to me for a game of cards, a debate about politics. I occupied people. I kept their minds from their problems rather than solving them the way Sarah had. I was a fake.

Picking up a rock, I threw it far into the distance. It sailed over the precipice to our left, disappearing without a sound. I wished I could have thrown it harder, to the other end of the world, no, through the other end of world.

"Why you cry last night?"

Suchin's question caught me off guard. When I didn't respond, she waited for me to catch up and then grabbed my hand. I found her touch strangely reassuring.

"Tell me when you want to," she said.

Her voice was soft, but mine softer. "I haven't spoken about it for a long time."

"It good to talk, good to get weight off heart."

I proceeded to tell her the story—how Sarah had understood me like no one else, how love had been only a meaningless word until I met her, how the sea had stolen her from me. As I spoke, Suchin listened carefully, never uttering a sound. Even when I described the tsunami, she remained calm.

Only when I was silent did she look up at me. "Why you think it your fault?"

"I should have never let go of her. And been stronger. Or died trying to save her."

"You ... spoil her memory, Owen, by thinking like that."

"You weren't there. And everything is spoiled."

We walked a few paces in silence. Then she asked, "Do you have picture?"

I reluctantly produced the passport, which Suchin opened with a sort of reverence.

"She very beautiful," my companion said, and then turned the pages of the passport until she came to the few strands of hair. She studied the hair but made no comment. Finally, she asked, "What she like?"

"Oh, I could never really describe her. She was … she didn't like to see people get hurt—whether a drunk in the park or a friend at work." The corners of my mouth rose as I recalled her temper. "She wasn't anyone that you'd want to argue with. When we did, she'd just … crucify me."

"I wish I met her."

"I'd have liked that. You'd have been friends."

"Nothing more important than friendship. My mother be poor in money but rich in friends. She lucky."

"She is."

"And Sarah? Were you friends before lovers?"

"We were friends from the start—even from our first date."

Suchin stuck the passport back in my fanny pack. "Owen, was your love strong?"

"Our love? Our love … it … it inspired me. It made me want to be a better person. I know it sounds silly, but I … I used to write her little poems. I was never any good at it, but she always carried her favorite ones with her. She'd read them on the bus, at the back of the bus where no one could see. So, yeah, our love was strong. Strong enough that I didn't like being away from her; that I thought I'd be with her forever."

"Then you lucky, Owen."

"Lucky?" I replied, bewildered, seeking her eyes. "Luck isn't a word I'd use to describe what happened. How can you even say that? It's like … like saying you're lucky to have AIDS."

"Maybe I am."

"That's a strange thing to say," I replied, increasing my pace. "Nothing good will ever come from her death, or from you getting AIDS. Never."

Suchin hurried to keep up with me. "Many people not know what love is. They the unlucky ones. You know, and you better person because you know, and you can have again."

"You don't walk into a bar find someone like Sarah. It just doesn't happen."

"No shut out world, Owen. I did once. I did for more than a year. My friends tried to help me, but I forced them away. I shut them out. But shutting out world only make me feel more alone, more afraid. It big mistake."

Suchin's words failed to register. For the first time since I'd known her, I wasn't interested in what she was saying. I found it irritating that she could see virtue in what happened to Sarah. Though I understood that Suchin needed this outlook to move beyond her own problems, I wasn't able or willing to share her beliefs. I didn't even want to discuss them.

Glancing at her, I knew that she was aware of my frustration. She was biting her lip, something she seemed to do when upset.

"I'm sorry," I said somewhat reluctantly. "I know you're just trying to help. But I don't see things as you do. I can't." When she didn't respond, I added, "Sometimes, after the dreams, I wonder if I'd be better off having never known her. I mean, my life was so good with her. So complete. How can I not be bitter when today everything is so … incomplete?"

"Most people never get so high, Owen. You think street people in Bangkok feel so complete? They beg every day so their children have food. How do you think it feel to watch your children starve? To watch your little boy or girl cry all night because they hungry?"

I'd seen such children, and her words connected with me. "I feel for all of those people. I wish I could help them."

"You can, Owen. You start soon. When we get back. Immediately. Then you understand why I tell you not to shut world out."

"Maybe I will," I replied, hopping as I pulled a rock from its perch against my ankle. "But just let me say this—after having such contentedness it's hard to not envy those who have it now. It's like … pretend you were blind and I gave you sight, let you get used to it, savor it, and then took it away. How could you live again in blackness? How could you not be bitter?"

"People learn. They find pleasure in other things. You must push past away from present. Maybe if someone becomes blind again they go back to doing what they liked when they were blind before. Maybe you can take that small step, and then later you can take bigger ones."

"I've tried to tell myself that. But it's a lot easier said than done. My life used to make so much sense. We had plans, goals. Each day seemed to have a purpose. Now that I'm alone, they just blend together, kind of like reruns."

"Reruns?"

"Old TV shows that they play over and over and over."

Suchin stepped sideways to avoid a grasshopper. "Owen, look around. These mountains not reruns." She placed her hand on my forearm. "And you never alone. I with you. And though you no believe it, Sarah still in your heart. You take her anywhere you go."

I stopped. Though my eyes avoided her, my words didn't. "I want to believe."

"Then believe."

Turning about, I studied the mountains that rose like the bows of battleships above us. We were encompassed by this convoy of peaks and ridges, surrounded so completely that in all directions the horizon was jagged. This was a beautiful place—no, a sacred place, so magical that I tried to imagine Sarah here, seeing everything with me. "How do I know if you're right?" I asked.

"She here, Owen. Helping to show you the way. She always next to the one she love. But you must, must let her show you. If you do, you no longer be blind anymore."

*

Thousands of steps later, after a long descent, we neared a suspension bridge. Anchored in slabs of cement, twin cables dropped from the mountain's base, arching gracefully over the Marsyangdi River. Wooden planks comprised the floor of the bridge. Looking across the river to the west, I could see that several of the planks were missing. Others dangled, swaying like socks on a clothesline. Ten stories below, the Marsyangdi raged—pounding patiently against rocks that were both seen and unseen. The valley was narrower here, a thin chute through which the water poured. The river was obviously full, fueled by melting snows in the highlands.

"I go first," said Suchin, or at least I think she did, for her words were hard to hear amid the river's tumbling. I started to protest, but she took a tentative step forward. Following her footsteps, I wondered how old the planks were. Many were splintered, others clearly rotten. Fortunately, the bridge was narrow enough so that I could hold the cable on either side— each a scarred strand of woven wires as thick as my arm. The cables must have each weighed as much as a truck, and I shook my head in awe as I envisioned Nepalese somehow stringing them across the river. Surely the task must have been brutal.

In the middle of the bridge were several missing planks, though each gap was bordered by an intact board. Despite the river being so far below, the wood here was slick with moisture. I walked very carefully, never putting too much weight on a single board. Suchin was even more cautious. Several times I had to stop to keep from passing her, especially when she came to the eight-inch gaps where planks had fallen.

The day had turned hot and the spray felt good. I was tempted to climb down the other bank and dunk my head in the water. Glancing below, I searched for a suitable place to descend. One didn't exist, however, and the slick, serrated rocks at the river's edge looked treacherous. Only a fool would venture down there.

Suchin took a final step across the bridge. I followed, glad to be off the contraption. Ahead I saw a village, which appeared to be in about the same shape as the bridge. Consulting my dog-eared guidebook, I saw that it was Syange, located at about 3,600 feet.

"Should we eat lunch here?" I asked, my stomach empty and restless.

"If we see good restaurant."

I doubted we'd see anything resembling a decent restaurant. I'd heard that the higher one climbed in the mountains, the worse the food became. Much of what trekkers ate had to be carried up the trail. In fact, we'd already passed a half-dozen Nepalese with huge crates of soda on their backs. The crates were anchored to the men and women by loops of straps that ran from atop their heads to below the crates. Each man and woman carried well over a hundred pounds of soda, I'd guessed. Even barefoot, the Nepalese had maintained a steady pace, almost keeping stride with Suchin and me. Struggling up the rocky trail in my high-tech gear, I'd found myself astonished by their fortitude.

Syange's main street was paved with flagstones. A handful of dilapidated shops and restaurants crowded each side, leaning like tired drunks over the street. To my left, a few children played in the mud. Spying us, they dropped what they were doing and ran over.

"Candy! Candy!" they shouted.

Seeing that the children were well fed and not wanting to encourage their begging, I smiled but shook my head. The children continued to plead for a few steps more but, realizing I wasn't going to give them anything, ran back to their mud. I yelled good-bye in Nepalese and hurried to catch Suchin.

She was peering into a restaurant called "Buddha's Kitchen." Inside were dirty tables and an old woman rubbing dried corncobs together. At her feet was a tin bucket, full of kernels.

"Popcorn," she proclaimed proudly, as if answering one of life's great mysteries.

"Are you open?" I asked.

"Good, good popcorn."

Suchin giggled, sitting down at the cleanest table. I nodded and joined her as I said, "Do you have a menu?"

Thrusting a corncob at me, she asked, "Where you come from?"

"America."

"U.S.A., U.S.A.," she spat out, machine-gun style. "Nice country. Big house, big ocean, big popcorn."

I had to pinch myself to keep from chuckling. "Could we please see a menu?"

"Never mind, never mind menu. I cook you best food in Kathmandu."

"Kathmandu?"

The old woman looked at me as if I were mad. Dropping her cobs, she scurried to the kitchen. Suchin and I smiled at each other, our grins lengthening when the woman started babbling to herself in English, her words a stream of incomprehension.

Suchin whispered, "You think she cook okay?"

"I have no idea."

"I think she cook like you sing."

"Look who's talking."

"What you say?"

I laughed, ignoring her. The woman was making quite a racket in the kitchen. Aside from her constant yammering, it seemed she took great pleasure in banging pots together. Several times during the next few minutes I glanced longingly at the door. Tired from the morning's trek, Suchin and I put our heads on the table. It felt good to close my eyes, so good that I wanted to lie down on the dirt floor and sleep.

I don't know how long we dozed before the woman set two plates down. Her voice was like a hammer, smashing into my brain. "I know American like pepperoni pizza. So I cook you potato and egg."

My mind groggy from the quick nap, I looked at my plate, which brimmed with three potatoes and three eggs. All appeared to have been boiled. Massaging my eyes, I muttered, "Potatoes? Eggs?"

"Very good for strength. Get you up big mountain no problem." Adding something I didn't understand, the woman left.

Suchin studied her plate, which bore two potatoes and two eggs. "What happen to pizza?"

Our laughter was instantaneous. The woman must have heard us, for she joined in, her cackles incessant. Any passersby would have thought they stumbled upon a trio of old friends. Suchin was doubled over, giggling so intensely that she shuddered. Our hostess once again banged pots together, apparently bent on adding to the noise. My eyes tearing, I stuck an egg in my mouth and touched Suchin on the shoulder. When she saw it protruding from my lips she howled, pounding her fists against the table. Somehow I managed to chew and swallow it. To my great surprise the egg tasted fairly good.

Suchin ate as well, though still laughing. Taking a bite out of a potato, I said, "We should come here more often."

"Yes. Next time we order special."

Our chuckles ebbed as we ate. We still had about nine miles to walk, and I wanted to get going as soon as possible. Though the food quickly lost any appeal, I forced myself to eat. Suchin didn't have my willpower, and I had to beg her to finish half a potato and one egg. When we could swallow no more, we rose, our chairs creating furrows in the floor as we moved them backward. "How much do we owe you?" I asked, unzipping my fanny pack.

The woman quickly emerged from the kitchen. The upper

part of her torso was covered in flour. Taking a quick look at what she'd served us, she said, "Two pizzas cost one thousand pesos." When I didn't respond, she added, "I like pesos."

Not knowing what to do, I thanked her and set a few Nepalese notes on the table. Immediately the woman smiled. "When you get to top of mountain, please say hello to Buddha. Ask him if he like my cooking."

"We'll say hi to Buddha for you," I said, strapping on my pack. "Thank you for opening your restaurant to us. Your food was delicious."

"If Buddha want good popcorn, tell him to come to Buddha's Kitchen."

"We will," interjected Suchin.

"Good. I cook many, many popcorn. Best popcorn for him."

We turned, leaving her there. She started to babble about pesos, and Suchin and I shared a smile. Outside, a few townspeople milled about. As we walked past, they studied us with a strange sort of curiosity, as if wondering why we'd gone to see her. Impulsively, I turned around and saw that the woman was watching us from a window that bore no glass or shutters. I waved to her and bowed slightly—a gesture of respect in Nepal. As I did so, I noticed Suchin smile, though she said nothing.

It took about a minute to get to the other side of the town. I had to admit that my body felt rejuvenated. The prospect of several more hours on the trail didn't seem as daunting as it had a short while ago. Outside Syange, the trail turned slightly to the east. It followed the contours of the river, bordered by purple flowers and knee-high stalks of marijuana plants. With nothing to do, I looked for a walking stick. I'd seen several for sale in the village and thought it'd be a good idea to have one. Though great pines towered above, virtually no branches were on the ground. The area had been picked clean.

Wood was precious in the Himalayas. Without an ample supply, the villagers could never survive the brutal winters. I'd read somewhere that they'd walk for days to buy or scavenge it, stockpiling as much as possible. Most homes, in fact, had a three-foot layer of quartered logs atop their roofs.

"What do you think winter is like here?" I asked, still searching for my stick.

Suchin looked at me strangely. "I not know. I never see snow. How I know what winter like?"

"Use your imagination."

"What 'magination?"

"Imagination means to … to think about what something looks or feels like without ever having seen it."

She didn't reply, but I noticed her glance around, as if measuring the elements. "I think winter very beautiful, but also very difficult."

I was about to respond when I noticed the sun-bleached bones of a dead cow not five feet from the trail. Weeds grew amid ribs that pointed upward. Looking closer, I saw twin horns protruding from the skull. Clumps of dried flesh clung tenaciously to the stump of each horn.

"Why they no bury or burn it?" Suchin asked quickly.

"I don't know. But it's natural that—"

Taking my hand, she said, "Let's go now. I no like this place."

As she turned I glimpsed her eyes. Usually so bright with life, they were suddenly filled with fear, with the dread of being one day, one step closer to death.

*

My body on autopilot, I followed Suchin through a forest. Vegetation here was thick—hanging like green curtains around us. Tall ferns and flowering trees rose from every patch of soil uncovered by boulders. I'd never seen most of the plant species, and it seemed as if we were suddenly in a prehistoric era. I half expected to see a saber-toothed tiger come charging through the brush. At some point, an avalanche must have lost steam here, for car-sized rocks were strewn everywhere. Occasionally, they lay in piles, forming discordant caves. I glanced into several caverns and saw droppings and bones but no animals.

As my feet fell upon the moist trail, a gentle roar in the distance grew to occupy my ears. After a few dozen more paces, we rounded a corner, coming upon a waterfall. About sixty or seventy feet above us, water surged from an overhang. The waterfall wasn't wide, but it fell with power, assaulting the ground below. The boulders and trees closest to the waterfall were covered in moss. As we walked past, spray engulfed us. The water felt so good that we slowed, quickly growing soaked. Wiping my brow and face, I sighed in pleasure, thinking it was the best shower I'd experienced.

Though I wanted to linger, we had to press on. Soon the waterfall was but a memory. The trail rose, offering a series of switchbacks. The town of Chyamje was close, and we walked with a purpose. My pack assaulted my shoulders, and I could hardly wait to be rid of it. A few miles back, in a poor, broken village, I'd given some T-shirts and an extra pair of jeans to a group of children. Though the gifts had lightened my load, my pack was still much heavier than it should have been. I intended to empty it that night of everything nonessential.

Upon reaching an unnamed summit, we saw Chyamje directly ahead. The village was in better shape than most we'd passed. Each of its approximately two dozen homes had plenty of wood atop it. Most had gardens surrounded by loosely stacked walls of rock. Though I saw several hotels in the center of town, an older one on the eastern periphery intrigued me the most. Suchin and I headed toward it, our steps longer than they'd been all day. Like all the structures, the hotel was fashioned of stones. It had a few tiny windows with blue shutters. Behind the building stretched a large field of wheat.

Our approach was witnessed, for a man opened the hotel's blue door. "Namaste," he said, beaming.

I smiled and asked him to show us a room with two beds. Bowing graciously, he spun, motioning for us to follow. We passed a dark dining room with a massive wooden table and then came to a corridor filled with about twenty doors. The proprietor opened the last, walked inside, and flicked on the light.

"You will sleep well here tonight."

"It's perfect," I said. "Thank you very much."

The man bowed again and left. Suchin and I sat on one bed, untying our boots. We then unpacked silently. Suchin withdrew her picture frame from a silk pouch. She kissed the photo of her family and placed it on the windowsill. After throwing on our sandals, we rested for a short time. The room felt hot and stagnant, however. A fly buzzed relentlessly against the only window.

I reached into my pack and withdrew a Frisbee, which a friend had given me before I left. "Can you throw it?"

"Of course," Suchin answered. "Better than you."

I pinched her arm playfully. "We'll see about that."

We walked out the hotel's rear entrance, listening to the tired wood creak under our weight. Outside, a wonderful blue gazebo was filled with empty chairs. So far, I reflected, trekking in the off-season couldn't have been better, despite the small threat of the rebels. Behind the gazebo sprawled a clearing, and we moved to it. Suchin stood at one end, while I walked to the other. When I was about fifty feet away from her, I turned, tossing the Frisbee. Immediately, I could tell that my toss was too hard. The disk sailed above her, smacking into the top of the gazebo.

"It must be the altitude," I said to myself, remembering that we were about 5,000 feet high.

Suchin's throw was much better. I caught it and tossed it back. It was a windless day, and the flight of the disk was perfectly flat. A group of children in mud-stained clothes noticed us and gathered near me. They'd probably never seen a Frisbee and clearly were in awe as we hurled it back and forth. After each throw and catch they cried out in glee.

Wanting to impress them, Suchin and I stepped farther apart. Unfortunately, we were soon restricted by the village's narrow confines. Throws drifted over us and thudded into stone houses and wooden shacks. Apparently worried that we'd break something, Suchin walked out of the village and onto the path from which we came. Now nothing lay between us but the edge of a wheat field, the trail, and a steep, rocky rise.

Though we were a good hundred feet apart, I could toss the Frisbee to Suchin with no trouble. She had a harder time, but her throws sailed to some part of the clearing and I was able to catch most of them. In the distance, I spied a group of kids coming down the trail. They were nearly a football field from me, at the edge of the wheat field. When they saw me and waved, I impulsively heaved the disk in their direction. The children shrieked in joy, jumping frantically. The Frisbee's trajectory was straight and true, covering the long stretch of ground. It landed directly among them. A boy picked it up and ran toward me.

By now adults were congregating around the gazebo. In no time it seemed that the entire village was present. Old men and women stood idly. Farmers sat on a table. Dozens of children ran madly about. Though he'd come far, the boy wasn't winded when he handed me the Frisbee. Immediately, the children far down the trail yelled, motioning for me to throw it again. Taking aim, I flicked it as hard as I could. The Frisbee sailed high, catching a current of air and riding it far into the distance, landing well beyond the kids.

The nearby children jumped about, too excited to remain even remotely still. Even the adults joined in, clapping and hollering loudly—their pleasure at watching their children play as tangible as the dirt beneath my feet. Four hundred feet away the kids were scrambling up the rocky rise, each trying to reach the disk first. A girl claimed it and started toward me, her skirt billowing like a parasail behind her.

The girl soon handed me the prize, giggling hysterically. I thanked her in Nepalese. My words caught her by surprise and she smiled, running behind a woman. The child's shyness provoked chuckles from the adults gathered about me. As they nudged each other and grinned, the group of distant children shouted. They had moved even farther down the trail and were probably out of range. Twisting to my left, I threw the Frisbee with all my strength. For a few seconds it looked as if the disk might reach them, but then it drifted to the left and plunged into the wheat below. Screaming happily, the children ran into the field.

I watched in horror as they trampled the precious grain. Around me, parents cringed and turned away, as if unable to watch the desecration. And yet, incredibly, the parents and other village elders said nothing. The Frisbee was found and was soon in my hand. Children shrieked with anticipation in the distance. Unsure what to do, I set the Frisbee down, which provoked the children to shout even louder. Turning to the mothers and fathers about me, I pointed at the trampled section of the field. "I should stop."

Our hotel's owner was nearby and said something to his peers in Nepalese. They chatted excitedly, pointing often to the children. "Don't worry," he said, "they want you to throw it."

"Are you sure?"

"Everyone says so."

"But the wheat?"

"The children's happiness is more important."

When I hesitated, the adults urged me to throw again. A woman permanently hunched over from decades of hard labor and malnutrition motioned for the children to move back even farther. Knowing that I couldn't possibly reach them, and that more of the wheat would be damaged, I smiled at the villagers and heaved the disk. My Frisbee left my hand straight and true, and seemed to sail forever, soaring among the Annapurnas. And though it was nothing more than a circle of green plastic, the Frisbee's flight was as perfect and beautiful as anything I'd ever seen.

Yet its journey was too short, and the wheat was again trampled as dozens of children raced after the disk. All moved with speed and agility, fearlessly leaping down high walls separating the terraced sections of the field.

Glancing about, I studied the villagers around me. One didn't need a psychology degree to see that they were in pain over the wheat. These people had almost nothing, and undoubtedly the crop was the result of weeks of backbreaking labor. Although most of the wheat was out of danger, two distinct trails marred the field's otherwise perfect surface. Yet remarkably, when the Frisbee was again in my hand, the villagers said nothing. Several motioned for me to throw it as hard as I could.

As the Frisbee and laughter filled the sky I couldn't help but think that the children's euphoria had overwhelmed their elders. Apparently the adults would rather suffer than stop the proceedings. A part of me understood. I'd seen how difficult life was for children this high in the Himalayas. Many were malnourished, scarred, and knew little but work. A carefree afternoon such as this one probably occurred a few times a year. None of the villagers—not a single soul—was willing to end this moment.

For the remainder of the day, Suchin and I threw the Frisbee. A great, muddy trail was carved into the wheat, but no one stopped the game. When dusk settled, the elders' faces were etched with broad grins. They laughed quietly, sipped their tea, and smiled like their children smiled. Some of the parents, and even grandparents, stepped forward to try a throw or two. I left the Frisbee with the villagers, and it sailed over and into the wheat until long after the sun had dropped behind the mountains.

To all of us, the children's happiness was intoxicating. And on this day, that mattered most.

CHAPTER 11

SEPARATION ANXIETY

The trail crossed a broad, flat valley I'd read was once a lake. The seemingly out-of-place valley was filled with fields of corn, barley, and potatoes. A stream gurgled nearby, as clear as the sky above. Staring into its pools, I wondered what species existed at this altitude. As we followed the stream's contours, I leaned upon a walking stick Suchin had found the night before. I didn't know where she'd discovered it, but when I awoke, it was propped against my pack. A knob the size of a cue ball crested the wrist-thick pole. Suchin must have used my pocketknife's file to sand the stick, for it was fairly smooth and free of snags. She'd wrapped several strands of red fabric just below the knob. These fluttered in the wind.

The thought of her toiling over my present made me feel closer to her—as if the shoulder-high stick somehow physically connected us. After dinner, she had disappeared for an hour while I studied my guidebook's maps and researched the coming days. While I rested she must have worked, forcing her tired muscles to shave and sand the stick, to tightly tie the fabric around the wood. Though I felt somewhat undeserving, I was pleased that Suchin thought enough of me to make such an effort. Her affection meant that I was doing something right— at least in her eyes.

The night before, after we'd each visited a stone bathhouse and washed ourselves with a bucket of water, we'd talked for a long time from within our sleeping bags. Periodic bouts of coughing had kept her up, interrupting the gentle words between us. Her coughs were brutal, wracking her entire body. She told me they were nothing new, but I thought they sounded slightly more ominous than what I'd heard in Bangkok.

"Why you no speak of parents?" she asked suddenly, moving to my side on the trail. "You no like them?"

Appreciating her directness, I smiled. "They're wonderful."

"How do they meet?"

"Searching for stars."

She tugged at a snarl in her hair. "Stars? I no understand."

"They were both astronomers, I mean, people who study the stars. After working on a project together, they fell in love and got married. I came two years later."

"You have big family—many brothers and sisters?"

"No, it was just the three of us. I grew up with stars, learning about constellations and comets."

"What constellation?"

"Groups of stars that ancient people thought looked like men, women, and animals. They prayed to them."

"You show me sometime. I like to see beautiful thing. Maybe there is constellation of me up there."

I grinned. "We could create one. It wouldn't be difficult. Maybe we could find some stars that looked like you leading me around by a leash."

"That be good. Very nice idea, Owen. You smarter than I think before."

A beetle dropped from the air to land on the dusty trail before us. I stepped over it, turning again toward Suchin. "What's the most beautiful thing you've ever seen?"

"These mountains. If you no count them, I like Ko Phi Phi."

"Yes," I said, remembering how its cliffs jolted from the sea. The butterfly-shaped island, which rose from turquoise waters, could have highlighted a fairy tale. It bore no roads— only bungalows on the beach and a few hotels. Of course, the tsunami had torn into Ko Phi Phi on a colossal scale, and I feared that much of its beauty had been destroyed. Distracted, I asked without thinking, "Did you go there with your family?"

"No, I go with my Thai boyfriend. He take me for two weeks."

"Was he good to you?"

"Yes, many times. He take me fishing with him far out in sea. We catch big tuna that we eat for dinner."

"That sounds fun."

She wiped her brow, then rubbed her temples. "I think he the one … who made me sick."

"Why?"

"Because he get sick too."

I started to speak, but then stopped. "Are … are you angry at him?"

"You ask strange question, Owen."

"But—"

"And yes, in beginning…" She paused, nipping at her lip. "In the beginning I angry at him."

"But now things are different?"

"Now I understand that hate give heart only problems. It help with nothing. It not help me with today or tomorrow. It not help with anyone else, either."

"Forgiveness is a lot harder for me."

"But Owen, I no have much time left. Why I want to think about bad thing or why I no like someone?" She sighed, her nostrils flaring a bit as she stepped over a boulder. "It better to think about how many good people I meet in this life, how wonderful world sometimes can be. How beautiful. That why you always so sad about Sarah. You hate yourself because she die. You hate world. You hate your god. And so much hate means that a big part of you died with her. Maybe your body no die, but most of your soul died that day."

I avoided her eyes, walking steadily forward. How she could be so intuitive I'd never know. "How do you know these things?"

"Because I go through them, Owen. Because I hate world and myself for long time. But then I listen to what Buddha says and I accept my fate. I think there must be reason for what happen to me. Maybe that reason was to find Ratu and help him survive. Maybe someday he discover cure for AIDS. Maybe he save many, many peoples. But for him to save people, I have to first get sick and then find him. That why I no longer hate … at least for the most part."

"I don't … how can you be so strong?"

"You strong too, Owen. If you no strong then you no take me to mountains. Don't forget that." She squeezed my hand, grinning. "But still, you very lucky to have me."

*

I'd experienced a lot of things in my life, but never the sound of beaks tearing apart flesh. The eight griffons didn't seem to mind us as they picked the dead cow clean. The birds—Himalayan versions of vultures—were huge, boasting nine-foot wingspans. They mostly ate in silence, occasionally hissing at each other when one got too greedy.

Sitting on our heels, we watched them for a good five minutes. "I bet they be much more beautiful in the air," Suchin said softly.

"I'm sure you're right," I replied. Wanting to see them take flight, I stood and approached them with my walking stick held threateningly. The giant birds turned at me, strips of flesh dangling from their saber-like beaks. They seemed to scowl at me for an instant. Then they hissed, spreading their wings as they ran toward me. As they attacked me, they appeared to transform into winged dinosaurs—bloody beaks agape, talons kicking up the soil. The croaks that spat from their throats certainly sounded prehistoric—warnings that screamed at me that these birds would rather be clubbed to death than leave their food.

Cursing, I stumbled backward, wildly swinging my stick. I didn't want to harm the griffons and pulled back on my weapon as it approached one's head. The bird sensed how close it came to getting smacked, stopping to glare at me malevolently with oversized eyes. Suchin moved to my rear. Dragging my pack, she whispered for me to walk backward. And so I did, never taking my eyes off the hissing, enraged creatures. Only when I'd moved a few paces away did they unfold their wings and return to the mangled corpse.

Moving back onto the trail, I put my pack back on, and we hurried ahead as the griffons fought over the flesh, pulling it apart among them. Three more dropped from the sky, roughly shouldering the lightest birds aside. The fearless creatures huddled around the cow, their hisses relentless.

"I thought maybe they eat you," Suchin said, her eyes swollen with fright.

"So did I."

"My walk stick save you."

I eyed the strong wood. "Yes, I think it did. It might have saved you, too. You're small enough that one of those damn things might have carried you away."

Suchin giggled, slowing her pace. Ahead, bordering a small pond at the edge of the trail like giant tufts of hair, were groves of bamboo. Brown rings segmented the emerald trees, which were about fifty feet tall. Their trunks creaked eerily as the wind forced them together, reminding me of the sound an orchestra creates when its members tune their instruments. I suspected that hundreds of generations of bamboo trees had rubbed against each other in this spot. The trees were beautiful, and I found myself wishing we had more in America. I studied them as we passed, turned to watch them fade into the distance.

As I turned, my right foot struck a rock, causing me to yelp in pain. Earlier, my feet had started to throb. I'd taken off my boots a few hours before and had seen the telltale signs of blisters. Now I could only curse my stupidity for not breaking in the boots enough. Fortunately, Suchin didn't seem to have the same problem.

The trail was steep, and each step made me want to remove my boots and immerse my feet in a bucket of ice water. Having no choice but to continue, I leaned heavily upon my walking stick. Fortunately, I had medicine and bandages in my pack. With any luck, I could tape up my feet the next morning, and they wouldn't trouble me too much.

Pulling the guidebook from my fanny pack, I read as I walked. It looked as though we had a 1,200-foot climb and an eight-mile walk ahead. After crossing three suspension bridges and passing through two villages, we'd reach the town of

Bagarchhap. Given the state of my feet and Suchin's condition, another eight miles seemed like a long way to walk. The sky was utterly cloudless and the sun beat down. Surprisingly, despite the heat, I wasn't sweating much. Reaching into one of my pack's many pouches, I pulled out a bottle of water.

"I don't think we're drinking enough, Suchin," I said, handing her the water.

She took a swig from the bottle as she walked. "Thanks, Owen. But I not so hot. Remember, I from Bangkok. This like a cold day for me."

I smiled. "I'd rather have the water in our stomachs than on my back."

"Is my baby tired?"

"Baby's feet hurt. How about yours?"

"No problem. Why not let me carry pack?"

I had to give her credit for asking, but glancing at her lean frame, I knew it'd be a terrible idea to give her anything. "I'm fine," I said. "We'll be there in another two hours. I can rest my feet then."

"Okay, number two boss."

I nodded, opening and drinking from a second water bottle. The bottles went back into the pouch. An hour earlier, a group of children had asked for our empty bottles. When I'd handed them over, the kids had shrieked in glee, running off with their prizes held high. I didn't know how the children would use the bottles but was glad to make them happy. They were a sad-looking lot, many with the bulging bellies that signified malnutrition. The younger ones went naked, while their elders dressed in ragged clothes.

"Owen?"

I noticed an unfamiliar trepidation in Suchin's voice. Quickening my pace, I moved beside her. "Yes?"

"When I die, you no bury me. I no want to be like cow. I no want animals to eat me."

"You're not going to die for a long—"

"Burn me," she blurted. "If I die in Thailand, burn me in hills of my village. If I die here, burn me in mountains."

"Suchin, you've got a lot of time ahead of you. Months and months and months. Let's not talk about—"

"You know that not true."

"It could be," I muttered, looking skyward.

"Promise me ... please promise me that when I die, you burn me."

Silence dawned and lingered as I thought about what she was asking me. "I'll take you home," I said softly, "to the hills of your village. And ... I'll do what you ask. But not for a long time."

She nodded. "Thank you, Owen. I will sleep more easy knowing that. You burn me and let my ashes stay on ground, blow in wind. That better than being eaten by animals. That way I can still travel to new places."

My eyes teared. The thought of her ashes blowing about struck me like a thousand tiny fists. I didn't want her to leave, didn't want her to travel to new places with the wind. "Maybe

… maybe this medicine will be better," I finally said, without conviction.

Suchin looked at me, and certainly saw my glistening eyes. "I'm sure it will be, Owen. Of course it will be. But still, thank you for your promise."

*

Annapurna II beckoned from the distance. Staring through the cracked window, I studied its every contour. Like most of the bigger Himalayas, Annapurna II was the shade of coal. Its upper third was colored in white—a deep white that mirrored the hues of the fading light. Even though I was miles away and no breeze stirred here, I could see snow being blown from its peak—a peak that seemed to rise forever, as if it were still growing, still seeking to dominate the sky.

"It too big," whispered Suchin.

I nodded, taking a bite of my rice. "I know. It doesn't look real. It really doesn't."

Though my tea was weak, I savored a mouthful. It felt good to swish around my teeth. I hadn't showered in four days and felt distinctly unclean. Though we could have bought a bucket of hot water, so far Suchin and I had resisted the temptation. Wood was far too limited here to waste on heating water.

Cutting into a malnourished potato, I continued to stare at Annapurna II. In awe of its incredible vastness, I thought how comical it was for climbers to speak of conquering these giants. A flea might as well scale the head of a horse and claim immortality.

Intent on asking for more food, I turned, banging my foot against the table. Pain assaulted me. Cursing my clumsiness, I glanced at the quarter-sized blisters on each of my ankles. Though the skin hadn't broken, I suspected it would tomorrow.

The old woman saw me turn. She shuffled to the fireplace like a crab in a tidal pool. Suspended from thick chains above the fire was an iron cauldron. The woman used a ladle to scoop soup into a bowl. After filling the bowl to the top, she slowly made her way back.

Our hostess placed the steaming bowl on the table. Tonight we would eat dal baht—the most common meal in Nepal. Though somewhat tasty, dal baht was nothing more than broth filled with rice, lentils, and few spices. Sipping the soup, I nodded at the woman. "It's very good."

She smiled like my grandmother might and went to get Suchin a bowl. I found myself hoping that our hostess had boiled the water for a long time. The nearby river, though it looked clean, was certainly not suitable for drinking water due to herds of yaks in the highlands. My guidebook said that most hill people didn't understand the concept of germs, and boiled water only to appease their customers. Many believed Westerners simply liked hot water. Unfortunately, since wood was in such scarce supply, water purported to be boiled was often not.

The soup was actually quite good. Having consumed a fair

amount of rice and potatoes, I was surprised at how hungry I remained. Suchin, on the other hand, barely touched her meal. I knew she thought that Nepalese cuisine was terribly bland, but I wondered how much she'd have eaten if she had liked it. After all, she was gaunt when we'd met.

In a few minutes, the dal baht was gone. Sipping my tea, I watched the sky darken. The sun was falling behind a row of mountains to the west. As it dropped, Annapurna II was inundated with amber light. Soon the color deepened, and the mountain glowed as if aflame. Though I wanted to remain and behold the scene, my feet throbbed. Nodding to Suchin, I said, "If you want to stay and watch the sunset, go ahead. But I'm going to try and deal with these blisters."

Pushing her bowl of food aside, she replied, "You miss me too much if I stay."

The floor felt cool against my toes. As always, I followed her. Unlike the other hotels we'd stayed in, this one contained another group of trekkers. I could hear them speaking German as we passed a room on our right. A few paces later we came to our door. Suchin pulled a rusty key from her pocket and undid the padlock.

Once inside, I lay down on one of the beds. Groaning in pleasure, I stared up at the pockmarked ceiling, wondering if it would ever get fixed.

"Where your foot medicine?" Suchin asked as she unzipped my pack.

I told her where to find the bandages and ointment, and

she withdrew the sock containing my first-aid kit. Moving to the bed, she held the sock aloft, dumping out its contents. I rummaged through small bottles of vitamins, laxatives, malaria pills, pain killers, and antibiotics before I found what I was searching for.

Suchin took the tube from my hand. "What I do with this?"

"Are you going to be my nurse?"

"Of course, Owen. I do anything to heal you."

"Well, just rub that stuff over my blisters. It'll help them heal."

She lifted my foot gently, placing it on her lap. I flinched as she massaged the ointment into my skin. Fortunately, the medicine felt like shade—cool and refreshing. I sighed in pleasure and put my other foot on her lap.

"You greedy, number two boss. Very greedy."

"I know. But it's been a long time since I've felt a woman's touch. I want to make the most of it."

Suchin finished with the second foot. Carefully moving up the bed, she motioned for me to lie on my stomach. After I complied, she pulled off my T-shirt, playfully casting it aside.

"What this?" she asked.

I twisted my head and saw the gold of my ring between her dark fingers. "My ... it's my wedding ring."

She nodded understandingly. "Relax now."

Her fingers probed my back. Moving them in circles, she used her thumbs to press deeply along my shoulder blades. Her fingers kneaded me as well, locating and manipulating knotted muscles as if they were strands of bread dough.

Four days of carrying the overloaded pack had taken a toll on my back, and I found myself cringing as she deeply massaged it. Though Thais were legendary for their prowess as masseuses and I knew I'd benefit from her expertise, the thought was of little solace. The process was just too painful.

A thumb found a particularly sore stretch of muscle, and I moaned.

"Stop being baby," Suchin chided.

Grimacing, I clenched my fists, vowing not to cry out again. But when she put her weight behind a sore spot above my kidney I couldn't help but squirm.

"With so many big muscles, I thought you strong man. Why can you no sit still?"

"Because you're killing me!"

She giggled. "If massage no hurt, it no good. You feel much better tomorrow. Then you thank me for my kindness."

"Kindness?"

"Yes, kindness. Now be quiet or I push more hard."

For the next half hour or so she tortured me. At one point she actually stood on my back. Carefully shifting her weight, she dug the balls of her feet into my sore spots. It took a great amount of willpower for me to remain somewhat still. But I did, for once happy she was so thin.

"Okay, Owen, now please wipe away tears and lie on back."

"Thank God," I muttered, rolling over. Suchin sat on the bed and motioned for me to put my head on her lap. I did, smiling as she began to rub my temples. She used her thumbs, moving them in unison.

"What happen on chin?"

I touched my scar. "Oh, I was showing off to Sarah and a bunch of kids."

"What you mean?"

"It happened when we were first in Phuket. Some children were climbing coconut trees. They'd scurry up the trees, knock coconuts down, and put them in a big pile."

"I love taste of coconut milk," Suchin interjected, her fingers pausing.

"I know. It's fantastic. Anyway, the children started daring me to climb a tree. When I wouldn't, they all laughed and pretended to be afraid of the trees. Well, after a few minutes of being tormented, I climbed the tallest of the bunch. Somehow I got up the thing, but when I reached for a coconut I lost my balance and fell."

"You hurt bad?"

"Well, kind of bad. I cut my chin open, but it could have been a lot worse. Of course, the kids, being as tough as they were, thought my fall was really funny. They all started climbing halfway up the shortest trees and jumping to the ground. They laughed so hard that a couple of the little ones wet their shorts."

"Sound like good memory."

"It is."

My companion used one hand to caress my brow while the other pulled softly on my hair. This felt good, so good, in fact, that I groaned in pleasure. When her fingers dropped to my eyes, I closed my lids. She hummed as she rubbed, her voice serene. Incredibly relaxed, I found myself drifting to sleep. The sound and feel and smell of Suchin seemed to carry me away. Soon I was somewhere distant, my thoughts and pains suddenly meaningless.

I don't know how long she held me. Only when she stopped humming did I awaken. I thanked her quietly, savoring the moment. She smiled and disappeared into the bathroom as I forced myself to stand. After stripping, I put on a fresh pair of boxers and climbed into bed. The fabric of my sleeping bag was cool. Though we were only at about 7,000 feet, I could already feel a difference in the air. How much colder it would be in a week I could only guess, but I suspected we'd walk through a fair amount of snow.

Suchin came out of the bathroom in the flannel pajamas I'd purchased in Kathmandu. "I like sleeping clothes," she said, tugging at the price tag, which was still attached behind her neck.

"I'm glad. They get more comfortable every time you wear them."

"Really? They already nice."

Suchin grunted, casually pulling off her top so that she could get at the tag. I glimpsed her brown nipples and turned away. "Sorry," I muttered.

She laughed. "Why you sorry? Nothing wrong."

"Well, I shouldn't see you … I shouldn't see you like that."

The floor groaned beneath her. I heard her put her top back on and turned to face her. "Because I too thin?" she asked, a slight edge to her voice.

"No."

"Because I sick?"

"No, because we're just friends. And friends … friends don't see each other naked."

"Why not?"

I looked at the ceiling, wondering how this conversation had unfolded, how I was going to get out of it without upsetting her. "Because, like it or not, if I see you naked, I might … well, I might think about sex."

"So? That natural. Of course, you should think about sex."

"But I don't want to think of you that way, Suchin. I don't want to see you and think about sex. That's not why I'm with you."

She tossed the price tag into an old paint can, which now collected trash. "I no believe you. Maybe you worried that I am thinking of sex. That I take off my shirt, jump naked on you and ask for ten dollars."

"That's ridiculous."

"Ridiculous?" she retorted angrily. "Many foreigners think that because I work on Ko Sahn Road that sex is all I want. They think that if they wave money in my face I do anything. Japanese, French, German, Americans. Even Thais."

"I've never thought about you that way," I replied, rising from the bed.

"Not when you first see me? Not when we become friends?"

"Never."

Suchin started to reply but stopped herself. She touched the elephant I gave her, staring at it thoughtfully. "I never have man as good friend," she said, her voice softening. "The only men I ever with all want to sleep with me. I not know how to act, how to think, with you."

"Don't do anything different," I replied.

"Nothing?"

I shook my head, smiling. "You're a handful. I'll give you that. But I wouldn't change anything about you."

"You sure, Owen? Maybe you give me blond hair and big boobs and—"

"No, no, no," I interrupted, grinning. "I like you just the way you are. You're perfect."

"I bet you like me better if I have—"

"Suchin, can we just go to sleep?"

My companion hopped into the other bed, squirming into her bag. "If you say so."

"Thank you."

"No problem."

"Good night, my friend," I said quietly, relieved that I hadn't made her more upset. "Thanks for my wonderful massage."

"You welcome."

"I'm glad you're here with me. Very glad."

"That smart thing to say. That what my father might say to my mother after he make her angry. You baby, but you no dummy. Maybe you find way out of maze faster than pig."

"Good night, Suchin."

"Have a nice dream."

A few minutes passed. As my mind slowed, I could hear her restlessness, her whisperings in Thai. Though I knew she wanted to talk, we needed rest. And so I pretended to sleep.

Later, as a dream unfurled, I heard her hop to my bed in her sleeping bag. She then eased down beside me, her back facing my belly. I stroked her shoulder with my thumb, smiled when she snuggled closer.

CHAPTER 12

THE MOUNTAINS AWAKEN

P ines loomed above us like giant Christmas trees, permeating the air with the sweet scent of sap. The trail was soft, covered with what seemed to be an inch of decaying needles and pine cones. Only an almost imperceptible slant of the ground upward hinted that we were still climbing. Today we had a relatively easy 1,500-foot ascent to the next village. Having consulted my guidebook, I didn't think the hike would take all day. With any luck we'd be at Chame by early afternoon.

So far, at least, my feet weren't hurting too much. Suchin had bandaged them this morning while I'd sipped tea in bed. Waking up next to her had been marvelous, and while she slept, I'd remained motionless for an hour, more content than

I'd been for a long time. Feeling her hand upon my shoulder, her breath upon my chest, was reassuring, almost sheltering, in fact. I don't know what was so potent about her touch, but it had made me feel as if I'd started the journey toward reincarnation, as if I was somehow growing complete again. During breakfast, we'd exchanged intimate smiles, as if we had explored each other's bodies all night instead of slept side by side.

We'd been rejuvenated by our lengthy slumber and had gotten an early start, leaving the hotel just as the Germans came in for breakfast. I'd been tempted to ask if we could trek with them in case something went wrong, but Suchin was adamant that we continue alone. She'd argued that we could take care of ourselves. Though I hadn't agreed with her, I succumbed to her wishes, telling myself we could always walk with them the next day.

Now, as we rounded a sharp corner, we came upon a mule train. I counted a dozen animals—each tied to the one before it with a purple cord. Beneath the wooden boxes they carried, the mules were covered with brightly colored blankets. Red plumes had been strapped about their heads. These were about a foot high and swayed like dancers as the mules walked.

The trail was only a couple of paces wide, and Suchin and I had to step aside to let the convoy pass. A boy leading the first mule smiled as he walked by. When the animal paused to sniff at me, the boy swatted its rump with a thin stick. Unperturbed, the mule moved ahead. One of the animals urinated as it passed, and Suchin and I moved back so as not to get sprayed.

Though some of the mules were more elaborately decorated than others, each bore the plumes. I wondered if practicality dictated the use of these. Perhaps the plumes obscured the beasts' peripheral vision, keeping them in blissful ignorance as to the many precipices bordering the trail.

At the end of the mule train walked an older boy. He might have been in his late teens, though guessing his age was tricky. His hair was matted thickly, as if he were trying to grow dreadlocks. His clothes—torn and faded and full of patches— could have clad a scarecrow.

"Namaste," I said.

He bowed, clasping his hands before him. "Namaste."

I liked it that the greeting was used for both hello and good-bye, as if even words were too precious to waste in the Himalayas. Vowing to learn more Nepalese, I stepped back onto the trail. Suchin hurried ahead of me. I grinned, finding it funny how she liked to lead. Even when she was tired, she kept a decent pace, never slowing enough for me to pass. Of course, I had no desire to overtake her. If she wanted to show me the way, so be it.

Thinking that I should take a picture of the mules, I pulled my camera from a pouch and turned around. But the creatures were gone, with only droppings of dung marking their passage. So instead I captured Suchin as she moved ahead, her little frame surrounded by mountains in my viewfinder.

*

Watching the sky darken and feeling the wind pick up considerably, I told Suchin to hurry. We were still a couple of miles from Chame, and I had no wish to be caught in the open if a storm hit. I stuffed my camera and other valuables into a waterproof bag. I also put on an extra shirt, as the temperature had fallen considerably.

Pines gyrated in the wind. Howling gusts rolled down the narrow valley and struck us head-on. My baseball cap went flying, and I quickly backtracked to retrieve it. Pulling its strap tighter, I hurried to catch Suchin. I looked for the blue skies that had accompanied us all morning, but instead of the sun I saw dark, swirling clouds. Instead of warmth against my face I felt a cold, stinging wind. In short, the world had turned angry.

I knew we were in trouble when the rain suddenly hit, falling with a fury I'd seldom seen, assaulting us in thick, driving sheets. I yanked a poncho from my pack and threw it over Suchin, snapping it about her with clumsy fingers. I'd once read that many AIDS victims ended up dying from pneumonia, and, above all else, I wanted to keep her dry and warm.

I slipped on my poncho. Though it had a hood, water ran down my back, drenching my shirt. The rain fell even harder, pelting us relentlessly. The cold wetness made me shiver despite my pumping legs. Lightning cracked overhead, followed by a terrific boom of thunder. I took three steps and lightning flashed again and again. Thunder exploded like bombshells.

Recalling how many charred trees I'd seen in the past few

days, I worried that a bolt might strike us. I felt terribly exposed, though there were towering pines everywhere. "Shit," I said, my boots filling with water.

"This big problem!"

"I know!"

"How far to next village?"

"An hour if we hurry!" I yelled over the growing tumult of the storm.

"Let's go," Suchin muttered as she quickened her pace. Keeping up with her in the downpour nearly pushed me beyond the limits of my strength. The trail was muddy, and several times I fell to my knees. It was always painful to rise, to move ahead on my throbbing feet. With nothing better to do, I repeatedly swore.

I'd read that every year mudslides killed hundreds of Nepalese and knew that trails such as this one were quite dangerous during a rainstorm. We needed to arrive at Chame soon. Eyeing the mountains that rose almost straight up on either side of the path, I wondered if we could dodge a mudslide. I imagined one coming down at us, picking up speed, dragging trees and boulders and animals along with it.

Ankle-deep rainwater rushed down the trail, obscuring rocks and other obstacles. "Don't lose the trail!" I yelled. "If we get lost we're screwed!"

She didn't reply, her boots spraying mud. My teeth chattered incessantly. My soaking clothes dragged me down. I hurried after her, not believing how dark it had become. We might as well have been teleported to the back side of the moon. This world was one that I had never seen.

Growing increasingly worried that we'd lose the trail, I called ahead, "Suchin, you've gotta slow down!"

A bolt of lightning seemed to rip the sky asunder. I cringed as if physically struck. Though hard to tell for certain, it appeared that the bolt had hit the ground a few hundred yards ahead. I couldn't decide if it'd be safer to find shelter under a tree or to keep moving. Though I wanted to seek sanctuary, it had grown frighteningly cold, and I feared that if we stopped for any length of time, Suchin would be in trouble. Deciding not to rest and risk hypothermia, I followed her closely, making sure she didn't stray from the trail.

A dozen freshly created waterfalls cascaded from cracks in the mountains. The dirty water fell in torrents, what felt like millions of gallons. This obscene amount of water tore down from the heights, filling my ears with its fury and the air with its spray. I could have been standing on the bottom of an ocean and seen less water.

We rounded a bend and were forced to climb over a tree that lay splintered across the trail. The pine's trunk was smashed, as if it had fallen from a great height. Gray rock rose around us on all sides. The tree could have toppled from anywhere. Most of its branches had been sheared away, though several limbs had impaled themselves into the ground at various angles.

The unfolding scene would have been magnificent were I not so worried about Suchin. We moved as quickly as we could, slipping in the mud and water. Several times unseen objects tripped us, and we toppled in ungainly heaps. Amazingly, we kept a good pace. I guessed Chame to be a half hour ahead, assuming we were still on the trail.

In the distance I heard a sudden cry. Suchin heard it too, and ran faster. Soon we rounded a hill and stopped dead in our tracks. The land before us had been wiped clean of trees by an immense mudslide. Debris and mud rose at least twenty feet high on what I presumed was the trail. Near the edge of the quagmire, standing knee deep in the mud, a man dug fanatically. He screamed, his body convulsing with sobs. At first, I didn't understand what was happening. Then my mind cleared.

"No!" I exclaimed, dropping my pack to the ground. Running up the mud, I dropped to my knees beside him. As I dug, he babbled in Nepalese. He cried and shrieked and shuddered. Suchin fell next to me. Her small hands burrowed into the misplaced earth.

The mud was so wet and full of stones that it felt like fresh cement in my hands. How anyone could survive beneath it, I couldn't fathom, but I dug with a reckless fury. Boulders and shattered hunks of timber were also a part of the slide. When we uncovered large pieces, the man and I hurled them aside together. We never paused, never stopped to wipe the mud from our eyes or to utter a word to each other. With adrenaline surging through me, I didn't notice the cold, the rain, or even the lightning. There was only the mud in my hands. I wanted it gone, away from whomever it suffocated.

A tenacious boulder tore off the tops of two of my fingernails, yet I hardly noticed the pain. Cursing the boulder, damning it to all eternity, I yanked it loose and heaved it down the slope. Glancing at Suchin, I saw that she was digging just as hard. The local was a madman, attacking the earth as if it were his mortal enemy. He did the work of ten men, tossing debris aside with what seemed superhuman strength.

When Suchin uncovered the wheel of a wagon we all cried out. The man and I dove to where she struggled. I picked up a splintered branch and used it as a shovel, paddling through the mud. The villager was a blur beside me. He cried out a name repeatedly as he dug with hands both battered and bloody. It soon became clear that the wagon was upside down. Though it was small, I allowed myself a glimmer of hope. Someone could be alive, trapped under or within it.

I found something and pulled hard. A hoof, ripped from the leg of a mule, came up with my hand. Dropping it, I moved closer to the wagon, digging down along its wooden side. The man joined me. We worked as one, creating a foot-wide hole between us. Leaning down, I reached under what was the wagon's top. As I did, I heard a whimper.

Crying out triumphantly, the man thrust his head into the hole. Suchin and I dug around him, widening the hole as he searched. Soon the opening was big enough to accommodate his shoulders. From my vantage point, it looked like space existed below the wagon. The man reached into this area, groped for a moment, and pulled hard.

I shouted in triumph when he dragged a crying boy from beneath the wagon. Suchin and I helped lift the child from the hole. Though he had two black eyes and a bloody nose, I didn't see any other injuries. The father pushed himself up from the hole and hugged the boy ferociously, weeping in vast relief, trembling as he stood. After a few seconds, the child spoke excitedly. When he saw me he smiled, pointing to the mudslide.

The man let go of his child and hugged Suchin, lifting her off the ground. He then embraced me, his grip crushing. I laughed, grabbing the back of his balding head. He bowed repeatedly to both of us, continuing to do so long after I motioned for him to stop. Finally, he turned and hugged his child again, his hands leaving streaks of blood on the boy's shirt. Then the man pointed to my pack and toward Chame.

Though my pack lay in several inches of water, I didn't care, happily sliding down the mud to retrieve it. The man waited for me to return and then took his boy's hand and walked down the other side of the slide. Though they sank to their knees with each step, the going seemed easy for them. They stomped on the mud like a pair of children.

Soon we were back on the trail. The rain still came down hard and cold, but I was no longer afraid—far from it, in fact. The man started singing. Though Suchin and I found his words incomprehensible, we joined in, our voices rising above the storm.

*

The stone home was surprisingly comfortable. Several logs burnt in the fireplace, and though Suchin and I had changed into drier clothes, the heat felt wonderful. Our muddied garments had been rinsed and hung from a rope that our hostess had strung across the room. The boy we'd helped save sat on his father's lap. In the nearby kitchen, his mother busily cooked dinner. When the father had told her what happened, she'd pulled Suchin and me into her house, tears streaking down her face. Unlike most Nepalese, it appeared that the couple had only one child. Infant mortality was notoriously high in the Himalayas, and I'd wondered if they'd lost a few babies.

Thick blankets of every color covered the floor. The fabric was by no means clean, but I had seen far dirtier. Stone walls bordered the room. In many places the mortar between the rectangular slabs of rocks was missing, yet the rocks were large enough that they clearly weren't going anywhere. I suspected that before winter's arrival, the couple would fill the holes with mud.

The home's roof was flat, surprising because of all the snow it surely collected. From the rafters hung an assortment of tools and kitchen utensils. There was also a loft, which contained more blankets, a harness of some sort, and a limited supply of firewood. Though the room was completely unadorned, I felt quite comfortable. Leaning up against Suchin, I watched the man and his child. Ever since the ordeal, the father had clung to the boy as if he hadn't seen him for years. He stroked his head, speaking quietly into his ear. After some time, the child laughed and stood. Smiling at Suchin, he vanished into the kitchen.

The father turned to us. Bowing, he spoke slowly. Opening my guidebook to the language section, I found out how to say that I couldn't speak Nepalese. I butchered the words and had to repeat the sentence several times before our host understood. When he nodded, I asked him if he could speak English. He clearly didn't comprehend what I was saying, shrugging his shoulders noncommittally.

Realizing our impasse, the three of us laughed. I think everyone found it funny that despite the bond we shared, talking about the afternoon's event was an impossible feat. As we grinned, our host motioned for us to pay attention. He then used his hands to show what had happened. Two fingers walked down an imaginary trail, followed by a hand that I presumed to be a wagon.

The man growled, threw one of his hands up and then smashed it down onto the wagon. The two gnarled fingers frantically ran about the now motionless hand, trying to look beneath it. Suchin bent forward, and two fingers from each of her hands ran to the top of the imaginary mudslide.

The man threw back his head and laughed. Suchin giggled, coughed, then giggled again. Slapping me hard on the thigh, our host rose. He muttered something and strode into the kitchen, which was really nothing more than a fireplace surrounded by short stone walls.

"You were wonderful today," I said, turning to Suchin, impressed by her courage.

"Anyone do same thing," she replied, trying to straighten her tangled hair. "But I very, very glad we save him. I no save anyone before. It feel so good."

"Yes, yes, it does." I shifted closer to her, enjoying her warmth. "Do you think we were meant to be there today? I mean, if we'd waited for the Germans like I wanted to, the boy probably would have died."

She suppressed a cough before saying, "I not know. Maybe Buddha give us gift. Maybe we just lucky."

"You think it was a gift? Many would say it was a nightmare. We could have died."

"They wrong. It was gift. One we always remember."

I nodded, knowing she was right. Unwrapping the bloodied cloth about my two fingers, I gazed at the torn flesh that recently anchored the tops of my fingernails.

"Do you feel pain?" asked my companion.

"It hurts like hell."

"Can I help?"

"I'll be okay. If the boy had died it'd hurt a lot worse." I was about to add something else when thunder boomed overhead. Listening closely, I could hear the wind howling.

Suchin shifted, sitting on her feet. "Were you frightened today?"

"Absolutely," I answered. "Frightened. Terrified. Whatever you want to call it."

"Same same for me."

A flurry of activity drove our thoughts toward the kitchen.

The boy approached us with a battered table in his hands. Bowing, he placed it on the floor between Suchin and me. As we thanked him, he happily spun on his bare feet and went back into the kitchen. He came out with two steaming cups of tea. These he carefully placed on the table.

Next came his mother. Though she was stooped over from a lifetime in the fields, her eyes and smile were quite beautiful. She bowed to each of us, setting down a steaming dish of rice and vegetables.

Our host came next, his hands wrapped in bandages from my first aid kit. He carried a plate that bore a steaming bird. It had been baked and appeared little different than a Cornish game hen. Brimming with pride, he set the bird on the table.

I'd never seen or even heard of such a meal so high in the Himalayas. Understanding what the family was sacrificing, I bowed deeply to the mother and father. Immediately, they reached down, pulling me up. Shaking their heads, they motioned for me not to bow. Apparently it wasn't my place to honor them.

The man pointed to the food and handed us each a fork and knife. Taking the instruments, we watched the family sit down. The couple often looked to their child, smiling as they muttered silent prayers. The boy was infatuated with us, his bloodshot eyes following our every move.

The bird, whatever it was, tasted marvelous. The woman had basted it in fat and sprinkled it with sweet herbs. Its meat was juicy and tender, as good as any Thanksgiving turkey I'd ever tasted. The rice and vegetables were also delicious. The fact that the vegetables were probably grown in their garden made me appreciate them even more.

The evening would have been perfect if I hadn't heard Suchin coughing quietly. We'd been caught in the rain for more than an hour, and I worried that the storm had been too much for her. The more I thought about her, the more concerned I became. Setting down my fork, I said, "I'm worried about your cough. It sounds worse than before."

Nibbling on a carrot, she replied, "Owen, you no worry about me. I just tired. We work very hard today." Her smile was genuine, but her voice sounded weak. "I okay."

"I don't believe you."

Her face softened, took on a look I'd never seen. "Please, this wonderful day. No end it by worrying about little thing. Today we saw miracle. Think about that, not me."

"I think you're the miracle."

She giggled. "Now you say stupid thing. Me only young woman. My body weak. And I know nothing about world. You much better than I. You smart, have education. Maybe someday you be famous man."

I reached out to touch her. "You know, you've taught me things. I've learned from you."

"Maybe a rock hit you in the storm and now you forget who I am."

"I love who you are."

She looked at me oddly, as if she didn't know what to think.

"Just eat food, Owen. We talk more tomorrow."

I wasn't ready for silence, but she averted her eyes, casting them on the boy. Deciding not to press her, I picked up my fork. Though my belly was full, it would be impolite to leave anything on either plate. And so I finished the rice and picked the bones clean of meat. Between bites of food, I sipped on the tea. Whenever I drank, the boy's mother immediately filled my cup.

Finally nothing remained to consume. Setting her fork and knife down, Suchin smiled at our hosts. "Very good," she said, rubbing her stomach. The couple beamed, pleased she'd enjoyed the meal.

I thanked our hosts in Nepalese, bowing despite their protests. The woman then motioned for Suchin and me to follow her. Remembering I was taller than the low ceiling, I rose carefully, ducking as I moved. Our hostess pulled back a curtain and pointed to a narrow mattress. I could see it was the only one in the home. Realizing that the couple slept here, I smiled, shook my head, and started to reach for my sleeping bag.

Our hostess said something and grabbed my hand, pulling me to the bed. When Suchin hesitated, the woman prodded her over as well. Reluctantly, we sat down. Clapping her hands together several times, our hostess grinned. Her husband and son moved behind her. All three bowed to us before the mother closed the curtain. I heard them walk away, saw their silhouettes sit down by the fire. Though they were only a few feet distant, the red fabric provided some semblance of privacy and we quietly stripped to our underwear.

Suchin crawled into bed. Curious what our hosts were doing, I peeked over the curtain. Huddled on the floor where we'd eaten, the mother and boy were nibbling on the few scraps of meat still on my plate. The father sat nearby, sipping on what remained of my tea. When he started to turn in my direction, I ducked below the curtain. I didn't want him to realize I knew they'd nothing to eat. Shame was the last emotion he should encounter tonight.

Crawling into bed, I curled up next to Suchin. Comfortable and full, I thought about our hosts and the sacrifices they were making.

CHAPTER 13

DOWNTURN

Though the color of the sun's light had already changed from rust to amber to gold, we'd only been hiking for two hours. It had been hard to get out of that warm bed, tough to resist drifting back to unconsciousness. Upon waking, I was so awash with aches and pains that I could hardly move. My blisters were worse than ever. My fingers throbbed so badly that I felt like chopping them off and being done with them.

Our farewell had been memorable. The boy's father had given us each a stone Buddha, pressing it into our hands as he hugged us good-bye. His wife had cried, stuffing our pouches with nuts and hard bread. All three family members had followed us to the edge of their village. When we were far away they were still bowing.

Now, as we struggled up the slope, these memories seemed very remote. The valley was steep and narrow and full of thick forests. Ahead, a long suspension bridge dangled over the Marsyangdi. I found it amazing that, after so many miles, the river was still our companion. Though it carried less water here, the river was as fierce as ever—probably because it dropped so steeply from the highlands.

The suspension bridge was in better shape than most. All of its planks were intact, and we hardly had to slow our pace to cross. Not far in the distance was the Paungda Danda rock face—a colossal slab of slate jutting more than 4,500 feet straight out of the river.

After crossing the bridge we came to a set of prayer wheels—a chest-high wall about twenty paces long that was inset with dozens of engraved iron cylinders that were shaped like large coffee-cans. The cylinders were centered on spindles. Nepalese spun these prayer wheels as they passed, praying for a final release in Nirvana.

The prayer wheels looked as ancient as the mountains surrounding them. The elements and the touch of countless hands had worn down the intricate engravings on the iron cylinders. I spun them, praying for Suchin's health and for the good fortune of these people. The wheels wobbled as they turned, squeaking like streetcars.

The obvious age of the prayer wheels intrigued me. I pondered how long they had been here, how many generations of callused hands had swept over them. If only the wheels could tell the stories of those who'd passed.

After spinning the last wheel, I quickened my pace to catch up with Suchin. "What did you pray for?" I asked.

"My prayer already come true," she replied, her stride unfaltering. "But I now pray for something else."

"What?"

"Someday maybe you find out," she said, coughing softly. "Then you thank me."

I was about to reply when a sudden commotion caught our attention. Glancing over my shoulder, I saw a pack of monkeys scampering down an almost imperceptible trail. Behind the animals ran a girl who wielded a long stick. Screaming wildly as she chased the monkeys, she scampered through the foliage. Only after a few hundred yards did she stop and turn around. Though I didn't know why she had scared them off, I suspected it had something to do with food. Perhaps the monkeys had been in her family's garden or were troubling their chickens. Whatever the case, I admired the girl's tenacity.

"She strong woman," Suchin said, waving to her.

The girl lifted her stick and yelled. Her bare feet blurring, she spun about and ran down the trail after the fleeing animals. Suchin and I shared a laugh. "I'd hate to be those monkeys," I said, watching her fade away. "I don't think they're going to outsmart her."

"No, if they come back, they have big problem."

I offered Suchin a handful of nuts. She took three, popping them into her mouth one by one. I ate the remainder, knowing they'd give me energy—which I'd certainly need. According to my guidebook, the next few days would be quite taxing. I could already feel the higher elevation slowing me down. Sometimes, during a particularly steep stretch of trail, it seemed that I could never get enough air, and when I got too much, I experienced a quick bout of light-headedness. Suchin was having an even tougher time, though she tried to hide it. She'd been coughing steadily since we woke up that morning. Her eyes were bloodshot and weary, despite her sleeping for ten hours.

Thoughts of doom circled my mind like the preying griffons we'd encountered. An hour earlier, I'd told Suchin that we should turn around and enjoy a few days in Kathmandu. I hadn't even finished speaking when she grimaced at me and said that she'd go on alone if necessary, that she wanted to climb higher and closer to Buddha. I'd argued my point for a few minutes, but my words—regardless of my good intent—seemed to sting her. I'd felt her hardening toward me, felt her joy at being in the mountains wither into a sudden and acute sadness. In the end, I'd relented.

Trying to force thoughts of the future from me, I scanned the sky. Fortunately, yesterday's clouds were nowhere to be seen. In fact, the only reminder of the storm was the muddy trail, which in places was entirely covered in water. In such instances, we could do nothing but walk straight through the murky puddles, hoping we wouldn't sink too deep. Caked in mud, my boots felt like lead weights. I'd stopped scraping them long ago, realizing the mud's tenacity outclassed my resolve. I was tempted to walk barefoot but decided that cutting myself was a risk I couldn't afford.

We were now trekking in a holy area. Yellow, green, blue, and red prayer flags bordered the trail. Tied to slender poles sunk into the ground, the flags rippled in the wind. Suchin had asked me what they meant, and I'd told her Nepalese believed the wind would blow prayers written on the flags to the heavens.

Studying the faded writing on the flags, I wondered what they said. Did these people pray for health, good crops, love, or happiness? Were their hopes as humbling as mine? I liked the idea of the wind acting as a chariot, ushering dreams to the sky. I wanted to take my own prayers, scrawl them down on a yellow flag, and place it next to the others. Perhaps the wind would bring me answers.

With nothing better to do, Suchin and I debated if the Nepalese took the flags down during the winter months. She thought they must leave them be, but I found it hard to believe the flags weren't stored somewhere. Certainly the snow here got quite deep and probably would bury the head-high poles.

Reaching into my pack, I pulled out my portable CD player, which had traveled with me for months and bore the scars of many falls. Amazingly, the thing still worked. It had a Doors album in it, and soon I was listening to the desolate cries of Jim Morrison. I suspected he'd have liked it here, a land where the mind and the soul were stretched in new directions.

For the second time this day, Suchin slipped in some mud, falling to her knees. Only this time, when I bent to help her, she reached out and pulled hard on my ankles, sending me sprawling backward. I landed in an ungainly heap and slid down the trail. Because of the music, I saw rather than heard her laugh. Pleased to see her playful side again, I grabbed a fistful of mud and threw it in her direction, grinning when it splattered across her leg. She retaliated, her attack striking me in the face. Spitting out the foul earth, I used both my hands to fling round after round of mud balls at her. She fought even harder, shrieking in laughter.

Empowered by her smiles, I dove at her and pinned her to the ground. Though she struggled nobly, I was far too strong. Listening to Morrison rage, I held her motionless, using a finger to write my name in mud on her cheek. She swore at me in Thai when she realized what I was doing, writhing like an alley cat beneath me. Her curses made me laugh, and impulsively I bent down and kissed her forehead. Immediately, she pushed me aside and jumped up. A ball of mud splattered against my chest. As she reached for more mud, I hurried up the trail, suddenly eager to put some distance between us.

As I walked, I pretended not to notice the mud balls striking my pack. Whistling to the music, I swung my walking stick as if it were a conductor's baton. My indifference seemed to motivate Suchin. Her barrage grew so intense that I was finally forced to run ahead.

Only after a few hundred yards did I stop. Winded, I pulled out my disintegrating guidebook to find our location. According to its map, we were at about 9,500 feet. The day's destination of Pisang was still a good three hours away.

The mud fight gave me hope that some of Suchin's strength had returned. As she approached, I studied the way she walked, how high she held her head. She appeared to be in better shape than she had a short time before.

Pulling off my headset, I asked, "Are you feeling better?"

"Don't talk so loud. You sound like drunk American."

Quietness did prevail here. Not even the wind breathed, and I heard no birds or wildlife of any kind. When I spoke again, my voice was much lower. "I asked if you were feeling better."

"I know what you ask, you ridiculous man. You think I no hear?"

"Well, I just—"

"I much better, Owen. Stronger than before."

"Good."

"Why good? So you can push me to ground, hurt me like sister?"

I nudged her playfully. "Just when you're sassy."

"Maybe I be more sassy. Maybe I give you massage, hard one this time."

"No, no thank you. My back's feeling much better. Keep your feet to yourself."

Suchin kicked me playfully. "You be careful, Owen. I no want to make you cry again."

A lone house appeared after a bend in the trail. Really nothing more than a stone shack, the home's walls were so tired they seemed to lean against each other for support. The skull of a yak had been tied to the door. Dangling from its horns was a sign that read, "Fresh T & Food." Though my watch had cracked during the previous day's rescue, it still worked. Seeing that it was almost noon, I motioned to Suchin to head for the house, speculating as to what kind of food its owners might serve. The front door was open and we walked inside.

A young woman sat against a wall, breast-feeding a baby. Seeing me, she smiled, withdrawing the child from a swollen nipple. "Hello. You want food? Some tea?"

Feeling like an intruder, I replied, "Well, we're both … I think we're both a little hungry. Is this a restaurant?"

"Only restaurant open before Pisang. All others closed because this is the off-season. My food is very good and I'll give you cheap price."

"Your English is really good," I said.

"Soon I teach my baby. She must learn English. Now I get you food."

I dropped my pack on the dusty floor and we sat at the nearest table. If the woman thought it odd that we were covered in mud, she chose to hide her feelings. Instead she smiled, carefully placing her child in Suchin's arms. "You take my daughter."

My friend didn't seem to know what to do at first. She held the baby away from her, arms rigid and face perplexed. Though I had assumed the baby would cry, she closed her eyes. Drool dropped from her chin.

"Owen, give me clean shirt."

Nothing in my pack was totally clean, but I did my best, withdrawing a Cubs T-shirt. Suchin carefully wiped the baby's chin. She then asked for a bottle of mineral water. After pouring a little on the T-shirt, she started cleaning the child's face. The girl didn't stir, her diminutive chest rising and falling with surprising speed.

"She's beautiful," I said, reaching forward to toy with her dark locks.

"She beautiful and wonderful and perfect," Suchin replied, looking at the child. "Her mother very lucky."

I watched Suchin pull the girl closer. My friend began to rock back and forth, humming softly. In the background, the Nepalese woman busily prepared our food. Only then did I realize how young she was, even younger than Suchin. She might have been seventeen, though the mountains had aged her prematurely.

Deciding to be productive, I pulled a postcard from my pack. The card was of Thorung La Pass. A half-dozen trekkers were below the pass, tiny dots on an undulating white canvas. As my pen danced on the card, I felt acutely distant, as if my parents dwelled in a world I'd visited in a previous life. I told them that I'd come to the Himalayas with friends and was now in the middle of a long trek. Because I knew they'd worry, I wrote that I was with a group of travelers—four Canadians and three Brits, to be exact.

When I finished the card, I thought about how it would journey down the Himalayas on the back of a mule. I had my doubts about the local postal service. My guidebook said Nepalese often peeled the stamps off envelopes, later selling them to the next group of trekkers. Thus I couldn't help but wonder what the chances were that my parents would ever receive the note. Figuring they wouldn't, I stuck two stamps on the card and set it on the table.

Turning my attention to my companion, I noted that Suchin was completely engrossed with the baby. She stroked the child's head, still humming softly. All traces of worry had fled her face. She didn't look tired or sick, and any passerby would have thought her to be the girl's mother.

I wondered how much it hurt her that she'd never know the joy of giving birth, never feel the rich and pure love that a mother must feel for her daughter or son. Surely now, as she comforted the baby, her emotions must be rampant. I was tempted to ask her what she was feeling but decided not to intervene. I'd be foolish to break such a spell.

For the next five minutes, I sat and stared. I don't think Suchin was ever aware that I'd stopped writing. She had eyes and thoughts only for the baby. Her illness and past were gone, replaced by awe and beauty. Maybe the child reminded Suchin of her youth, withdrew her to distant memories. Maybe she imagined that the girl was hers. Whatever the case, I didn't want the woman to stop cooking. When she finally approached with our food, I subtly shook my head, telling her to wait. But she didn't understand and set the food on the table. She thanked Suchin and then bent down to retrieve her child. My companion looked lost for an instant, her face tightening. She tried to smile while handing the girl back to her mother.

A pair of tears raced down Suchin's cheeks, gaining speed, falling into her bowl of dal baht.

*

Night descends in Nepal like a black curtain drops upon a stage, swift and resolute. The Himalayas are vast walls that glorify and then suffocate the fleeing light. Death follows life, day after day.

As Suchin and I made our way down the stone steps, I gripped a flashlight in one hand and her arm in the other. The steep steps dropped from the darkened village like an endless spiral staircase. The land was quiet, the only sound the steady fall of our feet upon the stones. Down and down we went, our knees and backs aching from the day's arduous climb.

Just as I began to think the night's journey was a mistake, I spied the hot spring. Tucked into the rock near an ancient riverbed, the spring steamed contentedly. My guidebook said Nepalese claimed it healed bodies and cleared minds, a magical elixir that natives traveled miles to visit.

Anxious to feel its embrace, we increased our pace when the steps leveled off, and hurried a short distance to the water. We were the only people around, fortunately. I'd read that the pool was quite crowded during the trekking season and found myself marveling again that more travelers didn't journey this time of year.

Suchin's cough interrupted my train of thought. She hadn't eaten anything at dinner and had been shivering since the sun went down. I was cold as well. A chill dwelled in the air that we hadn't experienced at the lower elevations. It was an eerie evolution, as if we were climbing into winter.

Taking off my sandals, I placed my feet in the water, which wasn't as hot as I'd expected but pleasantly warm, nonetheless. Hoping no one wandered down the trail, I stripped, sliding into the pool. The water felt refreshing, and I plunged my head beneath it. When I broke the surface, I glimpsed Suchin as she carefully stepped down. Her thinness made me think of the scarecrow I'd seen earlier in the day. Frustrated, I closed my eyes, vowing to make her eat tomorrow.

Seeing me cringe, she asked, "What problem?"

I stared at her before replying, "I just don't like to see you so skinny."

"Maybe my beauty gone, but my mind still same, even better than before."

"You're still beautiful, Suchin. Really beautiful."

"You not uncomfortable, seeing me naked?"

"No," I replied truthfully.

She splashed some water on my face. "That good. Because if you uncomfortable maybe I have to walk all day naked. Then you get used to me. Are you used to me?"

"Yes, yes, yes."

"That good."

Reaching outside the pool, I pulled a miniature bottle of

biodegradable shampoo from my jeans. "I've got a surprise for you."

"I already have beautiful elephant," she replied, stroking the necklace. "I no need another thing."

"Just close your eyes."

"Okay, boss number two."

I edged toward her until our thighs met. Cupping some water in my hands, I gently poured it on her head. I repeated the move until her locks were matted and heavy. Unscrewing the lid of the shampoo, I rubbed some onto her head. She moaned as my fingers sprouted lather. My hands twisted languidly, caressing her scalp and long tendrils of hair.

"That feel good, Owen."

"Don't talk," I whispered, tracing the contours of her brow, sweeping my palms across her flesh. I gathered her hair and held it aloft, wringing it as I might sodden clothes. Suds slithered down my arms to her back and chest. I could see the outlines of her breasts in the starlight. Despite her thinness, Suchin radiated beauty, and I had to force myself to concentrate on her head. I massaged her scalp with great care, my fingers moving in tiny circles, constantly probing and kneading. Not until my injured fingers ached did I rinse the shampoo from her, letting the warm water trickle down her face. She groaned in pleasure and slid deeper into the pool. I slipped below its surface and proceeded to quickly scrub my hair. When I finished, she moved closer, kissing my cheek.

"I know why Sarah love you so much," she said.

"Why?"

"Because you romantic."

I set the shampoo aside. "It's easy to be romantic when you care about someone. You and Sarah make it easy."

"Before Sarah you never have another girlfriend?"

"I had a few. But Sarah was different."

"Why you no like these other girls?"

"It wasn't that I didn't like them. But I didn't dream about them either. I think that even when I had a girlfriend, I was searching for someone else. I just never really thought I'd find her."

"But you did."

"I did. And I found you."

She grinned shyly, then pointed up. "Tell me about star."

For the first time I truly noticed the sky's rapture. The moon hadn't risen, and the Milky Way glimmered in stark contrast to the darkness. With no light from nearby cities to obscure them, multitudes of stars flickered. I'd never seen so many, never half of what I did now.

"You're looking into the past," I said.

"What you mean?"

"The light you see from those stars is millions, even billions of years old. It's taken that long to reach Earth. What's really cool to think about is that some of those stars don't exist anymore. They've died, but their light still reaches us. And other stars are up there, thousands of them, that we can't yet see. Their light is still traveling through space, moving toward

Earth. It just hasn't gotten here."

"So in future, there be different sky?"

"Long after we're gone. But yes, someday the heavens will look totally different."

"But no more beautiful than this," she said, subduing a cough.

"I don't think that would be possible."

The sky was so clear that every few minutes a shooting star streaked across the blackness. If I searched carefully I could see a half-dozen satellites slowly drifting. These moved in subtle arcs, crisscrossing the heavens.

"Please show me pictures in sky."

Pointing to the west, I said, "Orion's my favorite. The ancient Greeks honored him as a great hunter, a guardian from above. Do you see the three stars in a row? They make up his belt. The two above are his hands and the two below his feet. You can see his shield to the left."

When Suchin was finally able to picture him, she laughed in obvious pleasure. "He so handsome. Why I no see him before?"

"Well, it's hard to find Orion in Bangkok, because of all the lights. But he's always there, hunting in the sky."

"Please show me more."

And so I did. I pointed out Hercules with his club raised above Draco the Dragon. I showed her Pegasus, smiled when she spied him and clapped her hands. I told her of Cassiopeia's beauty, made sure she saw her face. The Gemini twins were next—the proud sons of Zeus. Finally we looked at Hydra the sea serpent, the longest constellation in the sky.

After memorizing each set of stars, Suchin moved to the next, asking questions about her or his significance. We marveled at them all. The shooting stars were of constant interest, flaring like bottle rockets across the sky. We counted them for a while, stopping at fifty. I found myself wishing my parents could be here. They'd find it a sacred place, full of the wonder that had fueled them for three decades.

"Do you think Sarah is up there?" I asked, gazing at Orion.

"Yes. But I also think she here with us."

"Why?"

"Because people never leave the ones they love."

I sighed, wiping a drop of water from above her eye with my finger. "How can you comfort me so easily? How do you always know what to say?"

"We all want same thing, Owen. If I know me, I know you."

I pondered her answer. When the moon finally initiated its climb into the sky, I rose, stepping from the water. After a brief bout of dizziness, I put on my pants and shirt. "We should go. We've already stayed too long."

When she pulled herself from the pool, I didn't look away. As she dressed, I watched her face, studied how the starlight reflected off it. Only when she was ready did I turn on my flashlight. Its beam drifted a few hundred feet into the distance, woefully insignificant.

Holding hands, we began the long ascent to our hotel.

Despite the incomprehensible magnitude of this night, I felt strangely empowered, as if the old gods were reaching down to give me strength.

CHAPTER 14

COOKIES AND ASPIRIN

Pretending to sleep, I listened to Suchin suffer. She'd been coughing quietly for almost two hours. The coughs came in waves, wracking her body. To her credit, she fought them well, often holding her breath in an attempt to keep quiet. Though I longed to comfort her, I knew she'd be even more miserable knowing she was keeping me up. And so I just lay there, close enough to feel her warmth, but not quite her skin. Suddenly wanting to feel her, I groaned as if dreaming and rolled over, my hand coming to rest on her shoulder. My touch seemed to drive the coughs from her, and all was still. But then her body tightened; her lungs exhaled.

As she convulsed, I wondered about that night in Bangkok. Was I right to bring her here? Was this trip an answer to her dreams or would I become her executioner? I knew how she'd answer but wasn't certain if mine could be the same. Opening my eyes a fraction, I focused on her face. She was wide awake, with her hand cupped over her mouth. Though in obvious pain, she looked surprisingly calm, as if the pain had been her companion for many years.

Light began to filter through the room's only window, initially so dim it hardly seemed present. But as the Earth twisted, the light grew pale and then golden—patiently filling the room, inexorably driving the darkness away. Though I was at an angle to the glass and couldn't see much outside, I glimpsed a cloudless slice of sky.

A fit of coughing consumed Suchin. She put a white shirt over her mouth, muffling the noise. Only after she held it there did I realize my worst fear had come true. I watched in horror as the shirt darkened with blood. When the fit passed, she pulled the shirt away, looking at the quarter-sized circle of crimson.

"How much does it hurt?" I asked quietly.

She slyly dropped the shirt off the side of the bed. "Not bad. Only when I cough."

"But you're starting to cough a lot more."

"So?"

"I saw the shirt. Don't you know what it means?"

"It mean nothing. It happen to me before and then go away after few days."

"Suchin, please, please don't be so stubborn. You're probably catching pneumonia. We can start you on those antibiotics, but we really need to turn around and get you to a hospital before you get any sicker."

"Hospital can do nothing!" she retorted. "I go there before. Many times. All they give me is bad looks. If I go again, I never leave. I die in small white room in small white bed. It better to die here, on top of mountain. If I die here, I die in peace. If I die in hospital, I die like so many people who go there and never leave. I no want to die like them. They not die good deaths."

"The mountains will kill you, Suchin. They are killing you. You can't go on."

"I already dying! Mountains no kill me! If I get to top of pass, my dream for this life come true. All my other dreams already gone. No husband. No children. Why I want to die in hospital when I can die here?"

"It might be easier, less painful."

"I no afraid of pain, Owen."

"But maybe you should be," I countered, frustration rising within me.

"Why? So I can be like you? Afraid and alone? Maybe you no have physical pain, but you have pain in your mind, your soul. I have pain in my body, but my mind, my soul is free."

"If we keep going ... if we keep climbing, you're not going to be free for much longer. You're going to ... you'll die up here."

"Owen, you must understand. For long, long time I not be free. I leave my home, my family. I live on the street. I touch two men I never want to touch. Then I work so hard, but for so little money."

"I know, but—"

"I have no choices for so long. None. But now I have choice. My choice is to climb to top of pass, to finish our journey. If we make it over pass, you can take me to hospital. But my choice is to climb to such a high place in the world. I want to … no, I need to see it. Because if I see it, then I have done something for me. For first time since I am little girl I will do something for me."

I sighed, trying to be strong for her sake, my eyes glistening. What would I do in her place? Would I walk forward or turn around? Would I want my friend to take me to a hospital or to climb with me? "I don't want you to go," I finally said. "There's still too much to see together."

"I always see everything with you. Even when I gone."

"Don't … please don't go."

She traced her forefinger along my eyelashes, wiping away the wetness. "Never forget that if I pull plant from soil, part of plant stay in ground. Then new plant grow from where old one die. This go on and on for all time. And though I will be pulled from you, I still will be there, deep in your heart, like root in soil. As time pass, another will grow to fill my place. But I always be there, always in your heart."

*

Not long after we'd left the village of Pisang I noticed a change in our surroundings. The land was much drier here. Save for impressive numbers of pines, little vegetation existed. It was as if, having reached 10,000 feet, the world had suddenly turned brown.

We were now in an open expanse of land, so unlike the narrow valleys common below. The trail was wide enough to accommodate a car and stretched as far as I could see, disappearing into the base of one of the giants to the west. Suchin and I walked side by side. We'd agreed not to speak of her illness for the rest of the day. She'd even made me promise not to think about it.

A mile back she'd invented a game in which one of us would make up the first line of a story. The other would then ad-lib a second line without pausing. We'd continue to go back and forth until somebody drew a blank—thereby losing the contest. Suchin was exceptionally creative, and as we played, I found myself smiling at her ingenuity. However outlandish my sentences were, she always seemed to outdo me. If I said green men lived inside toilets, she replied that they used pipes to travel from one end of the world to the other, riding miniature dolphins along the way.

The game was good for killing time, and the miles passed quickly. For a while, we actually descended, dropping 1,000 feet in less than an hour. Suchin fared as well as I could have hoped. Though she needed more breaks than usual, she walked with the same speed and determination.

Coming to a crest in the trail, we were startled to see a herd of yaks grazing in a clearing to our left. The creatures resembled cows, except that they had long, shaggy fur and oversized horns.

An enormous bell dangled from the neck of each animal. As the yaks moved, the bells rang, creating a discordant yet strangely soothing chorus.

Though a herdsman must have been near, I didn't see anyone. The yaks stared indifferently as we passed. I knew these creatures only inhabited the highlands and was reminded again of the heights we approached. I watched the yaks eat. We'd been using their milk for our tea, and I wondered how their bodies transformed grass into something calves could drink.

We came to a stone bridge. A stream gurgled beneath it, flowing as it had for thousands of years. I pulled off my pack and sat upon the bridge's edge, dangling my feet over its side. Suchin dropped next to me. She sighed in exhaustion. After pulling a box of cookies from my fanny pack, I handed several to her. Earlier in the day I'd bought the treats from a teenage boy, paying three times what they were worth. Enterprising Nepalese often sold candy and cookies along the trail—goods they'd carried up from stores in the lowlands.

As usual, the cookies were months old—stale and broken into many pieces. Yet they pleased every taste bud on my tongue. Sweets didn't exist in the Nepalese diet, and at least for the moment, the cookies satisfied my craving for sugar. Licking my chapped lips, I lay back and closed my eyes. The sun's heat felt glorious, like a warm blanket lowered carefully upon me. Completely relaxed for the first time all day, I listened to the whispers of the stream. Though it spoke a language that my ancestors understood far better than I, the sound was soothing and I felt connected to the ground beneath me. I began to fall asleep.

I drifted in and out of consciousness. I dreamt of my high school days, remembered they were but fading memories. Sarah then smiled at me from somewhere very distant. I asked her where she was, but before she could respond, an insect landed on my face and I awakened. As Sarah departed, I panicked, realizing she was gone. My fingers sought my ring. The warm gold made me feel as if our bond was somewhat unbroken.

I sat up but closed my eyes again. The sun continued to warm me. "Will it always hurt, Suchin?" I asked softly, my words blending with the stream's.

"Losing Sarah?"

"Losing Sarah … and … and losing you."

"Yes. I think it hurt always … until you die and pass the hurt to someone who loves you. Then it is something for them to carry." She took a slow, deep breath. "But maybe … maybe we hurt because we human. Maybe the hurt shows us that we really lived. You never hurt if you never love. You never hurt if you never live."

"Maybe. But it's hard to accept the hurt. Hard to understand why such things have to happen."

"I know."

Opening my eyes, I tried to imagine Sarah somewhere safe and warm. "I don't want to forget her," I said. "Or you."

"You will always remember our best parts, always remember why you cared for us." Suchin edged toward me and began to sing quietly in Thai. Her voice was soothing, even more so than the stream. Though I didn't understand her words, they echoed within me. I let go of my ring and put my arm about her. I watched a bee as it drifted among flowers.

"What's your song about?"

"This song honors ancestors. Though we no hear them, they sing with us."

I hummed as she sang. I tried to think of Sarah as not wet and cold, but as smiling, lighting a candle between us. When Suchin stopped singing, I held the image in my mind.

"Thank you, Suchin."

"Remember my song when you sad. It better than ring."

"I will."

She nodded. Above us clouds drifted lazily, so delicate that they could have been remnants from the kiss of a painter's brush. Suchin took a sip of water and then pointed to the trail. Not far away a pair of local women made their way toward us. Both used walking sticks and moved slowly. One was middle-aged, the other in her late teens. When they reached us, they dropped their sticks on the bridge and sat down next to Suchin.

"Namaste," my friend said, bowing slightly.

The two women looked startled, as if they hadn't expected us to speak a word of their language. But they recovered and bowed in return. Forcing thoughts of Sarah away, I grabbed the box of cookies, holding it out before them. At first the women did nothing, but then the girl carefully took several pieces, handing two large ones to her companion. Suchin took some as well, then placed more on my lap.

The four of us—an unlikely mix of two Nepalese, a Thai, and an American—munched in unison. When we finished, I bowed to the women and stood. Suchin reached over to help me with my pack, but the older woman rose and vigorously shook her head. Babbling in Nepalese, she pointed to my pack. My head still churned from my conversation with Suchin and I had no idea what the woman was talking about. When my confusion became apparent, she grabbed her companion's skirt. The girl tried to push the woman's hands aside, but the elder merely grunted, pulling up the fabric. The girl's legs were suddenly exposed. Peering closer, I saw that she had a jagged cut across the back of her right calf. It was several inches long and fairly deep.

During the past week, three separate groups of Nepalese had approached us seeking medical aid. After all, the locals knew that Westerners inevitably carried medicine. And they were right, as the nearest doctor might be a four-day walk away.

Although I had plenty of large bandages in my pack, I knew what this girl really needed was a dozen stitches. Not only was the wound deep, but it looked several days old and was clearly infected. The flesh around it was red and swollen, the wound full of yellow pus.

Muttering to myself, I opened my pack and began to dig. I soon found some bandages and antibiotic cream. "Suchin, could you please hold her leg still? This is going to hurt. It's going to hurt a lot."

My companion patted the girl on the back and gently cradled her foot. Opening a bottle of mineral water, I poured its entire contents upon the wound. I then took an antiseptic swab and cleaned the area as gently as possible. The girl's face contorted. She twisted in pain, moaning miserably. Suchin gamely held her leg in place, whispering soothing words.

I squeezed a good half of the antibiotic ointment into the gash. After carefully placing a large bandage over it, I wrapped a strip of gauze about her leg. I wound it tightly. The bandage would have to be secure for the injury to have any chance of healing. I then taped the gauze in place. When finished, I stepped back to judge my work. Though the wrap looked adequate, I feared it was too late to do much good.

The girl was relieved, however, and smiled gratefully. I had numerous antibiotic ointment pouches and gave her five along with more bandages. Gesticulating, I managed to explain that she needed to wash the wound the next day before using the ointment and bandages. She seemed to understand.

Suchin and I prepared to leave, but once again, the older woman stopped us. This time she pulled up her skirt, pointing to a knee that had swollen to the size of a grapefruit. Neither Suchin nor I had any idea what was wrong with her knee, but when she bent it, we could tell she was in intense pain. Reaching forward, I touched the puffy flesh surrounding her kneecap. My fingers probing, I asked, "Hurt?"

"Eeeeeeh—" she moaned, grimacing.

I didn't know how to help this woman, aside from giving her

some aspirin. However, my guidebook stated repeatedly that trekkers shouldn't give locals painkillers of any sort. The author believed that by doing so, Westerners provided them with false hope. For the relief provided by aspirin was temporary, and when the pain returned the afflicted person would only feel more miserable. They'd wish for more of the magical medicine but would have none.

I turned to Suchin. "Should I give her some aspirin? My book says I'm not supposed to."

Suchin hesitated. "If you give her aspirin maybe she make it up mountain. Maybe she go home, go to husband. If you no give, she no make it."

I handed each of the Nepalese two aspirin tablets and several vitamins. They thanked me profusely, as if we'd saved their lives, instead of helped them for a few minutes. When they smiled, I saw the beauty in each of their faces.

"I hope they'll be all right," I said softly.

"Yes, me too. But they very strong people. I think they be okay."

After bowing, we turned, leaving the two on the bridge. For a long time, we heard them calling out their thanks. Then Suchin's song echoed within my mind, though we were silent and all that stirred was the wind.

*

The plump man eyed our trekking permits and us alternately, his head bobbing like a yo-yo from paper to person. He scrutinized Suchin with particular disdain, as if her mere presence offended him. Though I didn't like his attitude, I bit my tongue. He was a policeman, after all, the biggest fish in this very small pond.

After several uncomfortable minutes, he handed us our passports and trekking permits. A pen dropped from his hand to a table, falling into the shadow of his gut. Grunting, he pointed at two lines. When I didn't move, he muttered something angrily, pointing again at the lines.

I smiled and said thank you, knowing it'd bother him if I appeared indifferent to his hostility. After scribbling my name down, I passed the pen to Suchin. It took her a little longer to sign. As the policeman rambled on about something, I studied the checkpoint. Of the three we'd been required to stop at, this post was by far the most dilapidated. Set in the hollows of a deep cave, it contained little more than the table, a chair, and a map of Nepal. A rusty shotgun leaned against the far wall.

Throughout the Annapurna trek, police checkpoints were in various villages. These were used to keep track of trekkers in case one got lost. From what I'd heard, they had saved scores of lives over the years. Unfortunately, that fact was of little solace to me now. I just wanted to leave. I didn't trust this man and knew from my experience with dealing with such characters that he was looking for a technicality that would allow him to fine us.

"Why you together?" he asked suddenly. "You married?"

"No," I responded evenly. "We're friends."

"Where she from in Thailand?"

"Bangkok."

The man belched, his eyes not straying from Suchin. Suddenly he winked at me. "How much she cost?"

"I'm sorry?"

"How many dollars you pay?"

My eyes burned into his. "I'm not going to answer that question."

"You answer whatever question I want," he replied, rotten teeth exposed as he spoke. "Prostitute illegal here in Nepal. Forbidden. You break law."

"Not that it's any of your damn business, but she works in a restaurant washing dishes. We met in a pool hall. And she's my friend." I took Suchin's hand and started to turn around.

"Wait," he said. "I have more questions—"

"I'll tell you what. Ask your questions. But we'll be in Kathmandu in not too long, and I'll be happy to report you to the police chief. You think he'd like to hear that you're bothering trekkers?"

The man's face twitched as he pondered my words. When he disdainfully waved us on, I picked up my pack, letting it knock into his desk as I headed for the door. Though I expected him to yell at me, all I heard was the thumping of our feet falling on the hardened trail.

"Thanks, Owen."

"Well, I'm sorry about him."

"That man make me so angry."

"Don't worry about—"

"He remind me of other men. Of cruel men."

"I wish we'd never met him."

Suchin pulled her hair from her face, wringing it tight into a ponytail with a rubber band. She walked faster down the trail, as if eager to escape. "Policemen give me problems for many years. I no like them."

"I'm sure—"

"Did I tell you story of my Burmese friends?"

"No."

She finished securing her hair and her eyes found mine for the first time since we'd left the cave. "Not long ago," she said, "I meet two Burmese girls. They are twins, only nineteen. They sneak into Thailand because they starving in Burma. They come to Bangkok to make money on streets, like so many girls. They sell themselves to men. After one year, Thai police catch them, take them, and other girls from Burma, back to border. You know what Burmese soldiers then do to my friends?"

"No."

"They give them AIDS test, like all women who is forced back. Women with no AIDS go to jail. Women with AIDS, they take out into field and shoot."

I stopped, shaking my head. "That can't be—"

"True? Why not? Because it too terrible? It true, Owen."

"But why?"

"Burmese government no want women infecting other people. So sometimes they kill them and bury bodies."

"And what happened to your friends?"

"They kill one. Other stay in jail for year. She come back to Bangkok and now begs on street."

"Can we help—"

"Before my friend go to jail, she raped by Burmese soldiers. They hurt her, cut her face bad so that she always live in shame, never get customer again." Shuddering as she started to cry, Suchin looked away. "She once so beautiful, just like a painting. Now she only want to die."

A pain seized me. An instant loss of faith. The horror of it all was too much to comprehend. I saw a muzzle flash in my mind, a torn girl tumble into a grave. As Suchin sat down and wept, I leaned upon my walking stick. Seeing her sob and shake made me want to do something, to change something. But even the mountains appeared ugly, and I felt the familiar, claustrophobic grip of water and waves.

I felt as if the world and I were drowning together.

*

A mile farther along the trail, heading into the village of Manang, silence lingered in a way it that never could in a city. Manang appeared as a ghost town, punctuated by no noise of any kind. No horns. No sirens. No cars and trucks, shouts and laughs.

Dust rose swirling from our boots. Pines churned in the breeze. We were slightly higher than Manang and had an unobstructed view. From what I could see, there appeared to be a few hundred brown, flat-roofed houses separated by narrow alleys. Red and white prayer flags lined the town and were the only vibrant things within it. Just a few miles to the south, the summits of Annapurna III and Gangapurna dominated the horizon.

The valley here was filled with bizarre outcroppings of yellow rock. These rose like hundreds of giant hands. The fingers of most were joined, while a few were solitary, sky showing between clefts of frozen knuckles. The outcroppings must have been formed by thousands of years of erosion. I suspected that one day, long after humanity vanished, the wind and rain would reduce them to nothing.

As we neared the town, I saw a half-dozen scrawny dogs, some chickens, and a few yaks, but no people. The brown buildings were eerily silent. As we approached, flapping prayer flags could be heard, but otherwise all was quiet.

"Where is everyone?" Suchin asked, and then coughed suddenly, cupping her hand over her mouth. When she pulled it away, a thin streak of blood spread across her palm.

I handed her some toilet paper. "I don't know. Maybe they're out in the fields. Maybe—" I paused as a lizard ran across the stone street, darting into the cracked wall of a nearby home. "This place feels like a ghost town."

As we walked, the street grew narrower. The town was laid out haphazardly, with homes jutting into the street and crooked alleys going this way and that. We must have been in its center, for I saw a post office, a stable, and two small hotels. A goat walked toward us, the bell about its neck ringing mournfully. Knowing that wild goats populated these mountains, I was surprised that the creature's owner hadn't tied it up, as it seemed that the goat could easily flee Manang and join its brethren.

Only after descending a legion of stone steps did we hear the high-pitched cry of a woman. A multitude of voices exploded a heartbeat later, sending a tremor up my spine. Clapping and singing rose amid the screams. The clamor wasn't far away—though its source remained unseen amid the congested buildings. We soon came to another staircase, which fell steeply, its stairs zigzagging. After six hours of trekking, neither of us wanted to go much farther. While we descended, I looked for more hotels. Seeing none, we continued to walk toward the noise, which was much louder now.

The road dipped under a stone archway between two homes. We passed through an entrance of some sort and came upon a sprawling courtyard. Surrounded by one-story homes to the south and empty space in all other directions, the courtyard brimmed with hundreds of cheering Nepalese. The locals were all dressed in brightly colored clothes. Most gathered in the courtyard. They formed a great semicircle and appeared to watch something to the north. Occasionally they'd cry out simultaneously, clapping or booing as one.

Taking Suchin's hand, I walked slowly through the chaos. The Nepalese were surprisingly indifferent to our presence. Most merely smiled, though a few bowed slightly. Almost all the villagers held great mugs that they drank from feverishly.

Many of the locals appeared intoxicated. They fell against each other, screaming like madmen. One suddenly thrust a seasoned cup in my hands, motioning for me to drink. When I shook my head, he gesticulated wildly. My reluctance seemed comical to him. He burst out laughing, slapping me on the back.

When I smelled how strong the drink was, I became less worried about the water. Surely the concoction contained enough alcohol to kill any bacteria or parasites. Thanking him, I threw my head back, gulping the liquid. The drink was stronger, by far, than anything I'd ever tasted, and I could feel it warm my innards as it descended. Cringing, I finished the cup and handed it back to him. He held it upside down and howled triumphantly when only a few drops raced to the ground.

After thanking him again, Suchin and I moved on. In a matter of seconds, I could feel the alcohol at work. My mind grew foggy and relaxed. As we made our way through the crowd, other villagers offered us drinks. These we refused politely. A group of children moved from where they'd been standing at the front of the crowd. Eyeing an opportunity, I rushed forward, pulling Suchin with me. By the time the opening had closed, we'd positioned ourselves on the inside periphery of the semicircle. Finally we could see what all the commotion was about.

Ten feet or so ahead of us, in front of the semicircle, stood a group of about twenty men and women. Each held a curved bow with their left hand and was in the process of pulling back on the drawstring with their right. A few hundred feet ahead sat piles of hay with circles painted on them. Well beyond the targets were worn buildings.

When the bowstrings were taut, the crowd quieted. As the archers aimed, those watching ceased their drinking and celebrating. All was still. Then a man dressed in bright clothing and standing next to the archers whistled. The archers released their bowstrings, and the twangs of their weapons reverberated. Arrows leapt forth with surprising speed.

Most of the projectiles were off target, bouncing along the ground well before the piles or sailing far above them. Only three bolts struck home, burrowing to their feathers into the thick hay. The audience cheered for the two women and one man who'd succeeded. The losers were soundly booed.

I quickly realized that most participants were drunk—so bombed, in fact, that they staggered about while searching for another arrow. One man fell flat on his face, provoking a roar of laughter from the crowd. After struggling to rise, he managed to notch an arrow into place. The spectators behind him stepped away.

Suchin and I moved back as well, worried that a derelict arrow might come streaking in our direction. A mug of what I'd concluded was some type of whiskey found its way into my hand. I thanked the toothless woman and quaffed the drink.

"Be careful, Owen," Suchin said. "You get drunk."

Vowing not to drink any more, I turned in time to see the archers pull back on their bowstrings. The crowd grew quiet as aim was taken. The elaborately dressed man stepped forward, raising his hand. He whistled as his hand fell. The arrows blurred, streaking like black rays of sunlight. Several came frighteningly close to a group of bystanders, sending them diving for cover. One lost a feather in flight and suddenly veered to the left, smashing into the roof of a nearby home. Of all the arrows, only one struck a target. The majority fell far short, skipping along the ground.

One of the archers—a squat, sturdy woman—held her arm aloft. She'd hit the target before and was clearly the crowd's favorite. They cheered her relentlessly as she bowed. The other contestants, perhaps hoping to improve their aim, took turns drinking from a plastic bucket.

I was about to get out my camera and take a picture when I noticed how tired Suchin looked. She swayed back and forth, leaning upon strangers. Grabbing her hand, I led her away from the chaos, my other arm around her back and holding her protectively. People pressed up against us, trying to fill the gap we'd left.

After a few claustrophobic minutes, we left the crowd behind. As we passed under the archway we'd seen earlier a young boy ran forward to pull my sleeve. "Hotel? Hotel?"

Wiping sweat from my brow, I asked, "Do you know a good hotel?"

"My mother's hotel, called Karma Hotel."

"Great. Let's get there as fast as we can. My friend needs to rest."

"Okay, mister."

Out of the corner of my eye, I saw Suchin start to fall. Lunging forward, I caught her, wrapping my arms around her shoulders. As I lifted her off the ground I cursed myself for forgetting her. I told the boy to get moving, and he turned and ran. My heart pounding, I followed him quickly, praying she'd only fainted.

*

The Karma Hotel hadn't aged well. From the outside, it looked like nothing more than a wall of misshapen rocks. The inside was akin to a cell block. Rooms branched off every dozen paces from its main corridor. The place was eerily quiet—no humming of electricity, no sound of any sort.

Our room's walls had long ago been plastered with the pages of American magazines. These covered every inch of available space, hundreds upon hundreds of them. The pages were of basketball players, foreign lands, investment strategies, models, advertisements, and everything in between. Many overlapped, creating a wild collage of text and images.

Each page hailed from 1993. Why this was so I could only guess. Perhaps a trekker had once left magazines here that the owner had put to good use. Whatever the case, the pages shone as if they'd come off the press yesterday. Someone had obviously taken great pains to seal them.

My eyes drifted about the walls, studying this snapshot of history. As I glanced from one photo to the next, I wiped Suchin's brow with a wet rag. We rested on the room's only bed.

The Nepalese version of a black hole, the bed bore a wide but hopelessly sagging mattress that sucked us toward its center.

"So sorry I faint," she whispered. "I no want to make you worry."

"No," I said, shaking my head. "It was my fault. Completely mine. We should have gone straight to the hotel and rested."

"But festival was beautiful. If we no go there I no see it." She coughed, her face tightening in pain. "Thank you for showing it to me."

A tiny spot of blood appeared at the corner of her mouth. I carefully wiped it away with the rag, hating to see her bleed. "Suchin, if you don't eat something tonight we're turning around."

"But I not—"

"I don't care if you're hungry or not," I interrupted. My voice growing sharp, I added, "You're going to eat something or the trip's over."

She held back a cough, nodding grimly. "Okay, Owen, for now you number one boss. Maybe you get me soup."

"Good." Gently placing the rag on her forehead, I said, "I'll be back in a few minutes."

I rolled out of bed, left the room, and made my way down the hallway. I soon stopped and peered in one of the many open rooms. Like ours, it was wallpapered with American magazines. Several flies buzzed against the only window. Aside from their tortured gyrations, the room was still.

I shrugged, moving on. The boy heard me approaching and

darted from a nearby room. "Want drink? Want food?"

"I'd like two bowls of soup, please," I said slowly, helping him to understand.

"Soup?"

"Dal baht, please. And some hot tea."

The boy smiled. "My mother already make. I bring to you quickly. Please wait here."

Leaning back against the wall, I closed my eyes. I tried to relax, listening to the wind. As if alive and seeking refuge, it fought to enter the decrepit hotel, wailing while it struggled through cracks in the walls and roof. The sound was primeval, not something you heard in America. It was the same noise that my ancestors' ancestors heard thousands of years ago while they huddled in caves, fearing the night.

I found it amazing that this building could stand up to the elements. Winter after winter it persevered—a disregarded testament to human ingenuity. The Karma Hotel. I liked the name and hoped the place would survive for many more years.

Inspired, I walked into a nearby room and scanned the dozens of magazine pages. Something needed to catch my attention. I quickly spied the image I sought, which turned out to be an old couple holding hands, walking on an empty beach. Though the photo was just part of an advertisement, I liked its depth, the love it symbolized. Pulling my camera from my fanny pack, I took a picture of the ad.

Some day, I promised myself, I'd come back here and look at the ad again. If the hotel was gone, so be it. But if this place, this image survived, I'd rent the room and light a candle in Suchin's memory.

The thought made me want to weep, but I clenched my fists and walked out into the hallway. The boy stood waiting with a tray in his hands, which bore twin bowls and cups, each steaming deliciously. I gave him a tip and thanked him absently—my mind still trapped in the room.

The wooden planks felt strangely reassuring as they slid beneath my bare feet. My composure somewhat regained, I opened our door. Suchin still rested on the bed, her head propped up by several pillows. When she saw me she smiled. "Hello, Owen." Her voice was weak, alarmingly so.

"Time for dinner," I said, setting the tray beside her. After kissing her forehead, I dipped a wooden spoon into the dal baht. I blew upon the liquid before reaching over to feed her. She opened her mouth, lips sucking the soup from the spoon.

"It good," she said. "Much better than before."

"Wonderful. Let's see how much you can eat."

And so I fed her, spoonful after spoonful. Though she ate slowly, she seemed to enjoy the food. The room filled with her slurps. I was afraid if I asked a question or commented on something that she'd lose her interest in eating. So I focused on the soup, shepherding each drop into her mouth.

A good ten minutes later, I scraped the last bit of rice from the bowl. Though I could tell she was full, I tipped the spoonful of dal baht onto her tongue. I patted her shoulder, then wiped all traces of soup from her lips.

"Thank you, Owen," she mumbled, closing her eyes.

"Good night, my friend. I'll get in with you in a few minutes."

"Please hurry. I want to feel you."

"I know," I said, pulling the sleeping bag up to her neck, then kissing her cheek. "And I want to feel you."

She smiled but said nothing. I watched her fall asleep, wishing that, this close to death, she was decades older. I wanted her face to be lined with deep wrinkles—the wrinkles of someone who'd spent a lifetime laughing in the sun. Her face would have looked like that someday. It should have. She shouldn't be so weak and near the end with such a smooth and perfect face. And her hair shouldn't be black and thick and vibrant as it was now, but the color of winter.

I rose from the bed. Kneeling before the table, I ate my cold dal baht and drank my cold tea. I suddenly felt that she was leaving me, and so I left my meal unfinished and climbed into bed beside her. I whispered her name. I then took the photo of her family from where it sat on a bedside table. I placed it under her hand and placed my hand atop hers.

Sleep did not overtake me for quite some time.

CHAPTER 15

The Stand

Sometime during the night, Suchin had grown feverish against me, shivering as if lying in ice water. Though I'd piled blankets atop her sleeping bag and snuggled close to give her warmth, she shook uncontrollably. I'd whispered words of encouragement in her ear, but she hadn't seemed to hear. Her replies, escaping between quiet moans of suffering, were incomprehensible.

For most of the night I had held her. She must have wanted my touch, for her grip was tight. Wildly, she'd stared into the darkness, writhing in pain, biting her lip until it bled. At five in the morning, I'd given her some aspirin and a cup of warm water. This combination eased her pain, and she'd fallen asleep. I had as well, laden with weariness that almost surpassed comprehension.

Now awake, I was surprised to see how high the sun was perched in the sky. Yawning, I turned to Suchin. Though I expected her to be asleep, she was staring at me. A faint smile crept across her face.

"Good morning, Owen," she whispered.

I gave her a soft hug. To my utter joy I realized she was no longer shivering. Holding her, I asked how she felt.

"Tired, but not so cold as before."

"I wanted to find you a doctor … to do something to help you. But I couldn't think of anything."

"You wonderful." Her words—soft and calming—were like chimes ringing in the distance.

"Your body was too cold."

"Yes. I think maybe I die. But then I say that I no on top of mountain pass. It too soon for me to die. So I fight."

"Way too soon," I said hurriedly.

She shook her head. "Not far away, Owen. But not yet. We need three day to get to top. Three day I must be strong. Then you can take me to hospital."

"Three days is too much, Suchin. You're too weak to do anything, let alone climb a mountain range."

Suchin pointed to her head. Voice growing resolute, she said, "Mind more strong than body. If mind can do, body will follow."

"But these three days will be the most difficult of all. They'll kill you."

"My past kill me, Owen, not mountains. They remind me

how special life is. On streets of Bangkok, I forgot how special life could be. These mountains remind me. You remind me."

Nodding, I brushed a strand of hair from her eyes. For the first time, I truly understood Suchin's wish, her dream to climb among giants. I understood her wish because it was a hope that I now also sheltered. Though I hadn't been a spiritual person since Sarah's death, I felt a strange sort of calling.

If God, Buddha, or some kind of power reigned above, I felt that upon reaching Thorung La Pass, a part of my search would be over. I'd have filled some of the hole that my life had become—because if heaven or Nirvana existed, I'd be able to sense it from the top of the world. And if such a place awaited me, surely I'd sense Sarah as well. She'd be there. And maybe after sensing her there, life would somehow again have meaning for me.

Yet no matter how beautiful or spiritual the pass was, I didn't want to arrive there alone. Suchin needed to be at my side. Without her, without the one who'd become my guide, I'd see only rock and snow.

She needed to reach Thorung La as well, needed to sit atop the world. If she didn't, she'd have died the night before. Instead of allowing herself to fade away, she'd fought, suffering for hours to give herself a chance at realizing her dream.

And for her pain, I promised myself—the pain of the night before and the pain of her past—I'd get her to the top.

*

As soon as we left Manang, the trail rose. Jumping over a stream, we headed northwest, our feet falling on loose slabs of rock. The land beneath us was very dry, dust rising like heat. Clusters of scrub juniper and alpine grasses bordered the path. The large pines we'd left far, far below.

Climbing was difficult. My joints felt arthritic, my body tired. Each step seemed to burn what little energy I possessed, drain my fortitude like an unbearable task being assigned to me. My pack—always so tolerable at lower elevations—felt as if it could have anchored an ocean liner. It dragged me toward the ground, pulled me downward when I wanted to stand tall. Walking itself was a challenge, and I leaned heavily on my stick, my hands by now callused from holding it. Though I'd tied my boots as tight as possible, pebbles accumulated within them and rubbed painfully against my blisters.

Suchin fared worse, though she wouldn't admit it. Despite being dressed heavily, she shivered. Her cough came and went, often so intense it forced her to stop. I tried a few times to support her from the side but found it impossible to do so. The trail was too narrow and rocky. And I didn't have the strength to bear any of her weight.

I wished we were still in bed and had the day off to relax. We were supposed to, after all. Trekkers always rested for a day at Manang. My guidebook claimed that a thirty-six hour stop there was necessary to acclimatize. Already we were at more than 12,000 feet, and in the next three days we'd climb about 5,000 feet higher. Though I'd tried to explain to Suchin the importance of acclimatizing, she wasn't willing to waste a day. After a half hour of debate, she'd started up the trail alone, leaving me to pay our bill and catch up to her.

I now followed her closely, ready to catch her should she fall. I found it amazing how her sticklike legs propelled her up the side of the mountain, how she could deny the previous night's suffering.

The trail climbed endlessly. We were making terrible time and I wondered if we'd ever get to the village of Letdar. Consulting my map, I saw that we should have risen into a valley twenty minutes earlier. However, as best as I could guess, the valley was still a good half-mile ahead.

Sticking the map into my fanny pack, I tapped Suchin on the shoulder. "How are you doing?"

"Tired," she muttered, gulping for air. "Very tired."

"We should rest again."

"No, no, I be okay. Rest when we reach valley. Not before."

I nodded, watching a pair of griffons soar. The birds reminded me of other forms of wildlife, and I surveyed the landscape for the rare snow leopards and blue sheep I'd heard about. But I saw only rock—and high above, vast fields of ice and snow.

The griffons soon were specks in the sky, circling specks that rode currents of air, searching for food far below. I envied the ugly birds. How easy it would be to soar over Thorung La, to drift with Suchin forever. Focusing on my jealousy of the birds, I was able to draw more strength from within. We approached some kind of summit, and taking Suchin's hand, I walked faster. The trail here had been hewn through rock—the crisscrossed gouges of picks easily recognizable. Many of the lines ran parallel, reminding me of fingernail scratches.

As we neared the summit, the trail grew moist and slippery— odd considering that a few hundred feet below, it was as dry as a desert. Ferns and flowering plants rose from spots the sun rarely hit. The man-made crevice in the rock abruptly ended and the trail flattened. The valley lay before us. Rimmed by imposing Himalayas, the valley was surprisingly short, perhaps only a mile in length.

An abundance of snow and ice loomed above us. Several waterfalls in the distance cascaded from incredible heights. The air was crisp—much cooler than it had been below. I pulled a long-sleeved shirt from a side pouch of my pack. Taking off my shoulder straps and letting the pack ride on its wide hip strap, I quickly put the shirt on.

"Are you warm enough, Suchin? You could throw on my jacket if you wanted to."

"Maybe that good idea."

I fished the jacket out of my pack and handed it to her. She zipped it up over her other clothes. Now she was nearly as wide as she was tall.

"You look like a teddy bear," I said.

"Maybe so. But you … you look dirtier than a pig I once knew," she retorted, feigning disgust.

It was good to see her old self reappear, if only for a minute.

I playfully swung my walking stick at her, increasing my speed. "Let's go for another twenty minutes, and then we'll take a break."

Soon I heard the rush of water. I didn't remember reading anything in my guidebook about a river here and was surprised when I saw one. It poured from below one of the several waterfalls around us, a good two dozen paces across.

The sun was unobstructed, melting the snow above us and thereby creating the river, which raged with unquestionable fury. As Suchin and I neared it, I searched for a bridge or crossing of any kind but saw nothing. We'd have to ford it. Though the river didn't look particularly deep, its waters moved quickly. Crossing would be problematic. Stopping at its edge, I let my pack fall to the ground.

"Do you think we can make it across?"

She didn't respond immediately. "It look too strong."

I shook my head. "We could cross it here, or go downstream and hope to find a bridge or shallower water. But if we do that we'll lose a lot of time. And there's no guarantee we'll find anything."

"We go here."

I sat down to untie my boots. The two torn fingers on my right hand ached as I pulled on my shoestrings. Thinking the cold, fresh water might do them some good, I removed my bandages. Though blood still seeped from the wounds, they appeared to be healing. I didn't see signs of infection.

Grimacing, I tied both sets of boots to the top of my pack,

then pulled off my jeans and strapped them to the pack. Suchin did likewise. Clad in our underwear, I took her right hand in my left. I was about to move forward when a thought suddenly occurred to me. "How well can you swim?"

She shook her head, obviously afraid. "Not so good in big river."

I swore to myself, wishing we'd get a few breaks. "Then whatever happens, don't let go of my hand. If you have to, grab hold of me or a strap on my pack."

"If it too deep, come back."

"Damn right I will." Stepping forward, I stuck my foot in the water, which might as well have been solid ice. I'd never felt anything so cold. Not even close.

"It too cold!" Suchin exclaimed, leaping back to the shore. "I cannot be so cold again."

"Okay, okay," I said, judging the depth of the water. "I'll carry you across." Before she could protest, I bent down. Placing my arms beneath her back and knees, I hoisted her off the ground. She couldn't have weighed more than ninety pounds, and I lifted her without much trouble.

"Be careful, Owen. I no want you to hurt yourself."

"Just hold my walking stick, and keep your fingers crossed."

I stepped into the water, shivering with its embrace. Slowly, I moved out, feeling the rocky bottom carefully with my feet. After a few steps I was up to my knees. The current was strong, pressing against me, trying to force me downstream.

I was about a quarter of the way across when the water

approached my hips. Despite having serious doubts about whether I could make it, I continued forward. Unfortunately, the deeper the water, the harder it was to keep from being washed downstream. I could now feel the river's might. As if alive and intent on throwing me back to the lowlands, it hammered at my body.

Suchin was no longer light in my arms, and I had to struggle to keep her above the water. She was terrified and hugged me tightly. "I no swim in this!" she yelled in my ear.

I didn't answer. Each step was a battle of will between the river and me. Thinking of Suchin's courage as I struggled, I tried to draw strength from it. I did for a few heartbeats, but when I slipped on a rock and went plunging into the icy water, my first instinct was to give up. I was so tired. It would have been so much easier to let the river carry us away.

But I didn't. I came up from under the darkness, yanking Suchin with me. She screamed as we were sucked downstream, the mountains and sky spinning about us like a giant Ferris wheel. I inhaled a lungful of water, coughing it up as I struggled to find footing. Suchin pulled hard on my hair, shrieking.

The pain gave me strength, focusing my frantic movements. My feet stopped skidding across the rocks and became embedded within them. Crying out, I threw Suchin over my shoulder, once again stepping forward. I now moved with reckless abandon, unafraid of falling again. Dimly I was aware of Suchin coughing, of her thrashing atop me. Cursing the water, I moved through it angrily. Soon it was at my thighs, then knees, then ankles. When my feet touched dry ground, I let go of Suchin. She wouldn't release her grip on me, however—her eyes still clamped shut.

"We made it," I whispered, my voice shaking from fear, my body shaking from the cold. "Suchin, we made it across."

She opened her eyes slowly, absorbing our surroundings like one who has awoken from a deep sleep in a strange place. It took her a few seconds to realize I was speaking the truth. "I thought we would die," she stammered.

Gently pushing her from me, I pulled off my pack, which was heavy with water. After dropping it to the ground, I picked up a rock and hurtled it into the water. "You call yourself a river?" I shouted as a strange combination of delirium, euphoria, and rage coursed through me. Another rock went sailing. "Is that the best you've got? Nothing more?"

Watching me rave, Suchin laughed despite her shivers. When I handed her a rock, she thanked me and tossed it into the river. "Why you so weak?"

I hollered, told the river of our victory. All the stress of the past few days was surfacing, being released. It felt so good to laugh that I forgot our troubles, forgot how far we had to go. I screamed at the river again, tossing a large rock at its center.

"You crazy man," Suchin said, giggling as she started to pull off her wet clothes. "When we get to Kathmandu, I take you to hospital. I think you need many, many help."

"Maybe," I replied, dropping the rock in my hand and unzipping my pack. Fortunately, it was much less wet than I had feared—just a few of its side pockets were full of water. Besides, as a precaution against rain, most of our clothes were wrapped in plastic bags. Still smiling, I opened one of the bags and pulled out shirts, pants, and socks. I handed Suchin everything she needed, pleased I'd had the foresight to waterproof everything.

Only when she was completely dressed did I change. We then wrung out our wet garments. Suchin started to cough again. Inspired, I looked up and down the river. A few hundred yards below us, I saw what I sought. "Wait here a few minutes," I said, running south.

Our bout with the stream gave me renewed energy. The cold water had left my skin tingling and had cleared my mind. I ran with surprising quickness, racing the fast-moving water. For the first time in days, my boots didn't feel like size-eleven rocks. Moving without my pack was wonderful and liberating—only now did I realize the magnitude of the physical and mental toll that its weight took upon me.

A pile of driftwood materialized amid some boulders. I tore through the pieces. The branches closest to the stream were wet, but atop the pile, limbs were dry. Grabbing as many as I could, I hurried back to Suchin. She sat with her arms wrapped about her shoulders, swaying back and forth.

I dropped the wood, stooping to arrange it like a teepee. I then grabbed a roll of toilet paper from my pack. Ripping off about twenty feet, I shoved it in the center of the wood. Suchin already had my lighter out and reached forward to light the paper.

Within a few minutes we had a beautiful fire going. I set our wet clothes on the stones beside it, placing them as near as I dared. Steam soon rose from the garments.

"Don't burn yourself," I said.

Suchin took a step back from the flames. "I no have fire before."

"Never?"

"Not my own fire."

"You like it?"

"Very much." She was about to add something else when a fit of coughing consumed her.

I grabbed a T-shirt from my pack and dried her hair. "I don't want you to get cold again."

"Me too."

I dabbed at her hair as fast as I could. When finished, I wrapped my arms around her. We were only a couple of feet away from the fire, and its heat was considerable. But the branches were of little substance and burnt quickly. Soon nothing would remain but embers.

"We've got ten minutes, Suchin. Then we should leave."

Disappointment eclipsed her face. "How far to go?"

"I don't know for sure," I said, glancing at my watch. "But I'd guess Letdar is still a good four hours ahead."

When she didn't reply I bent down, warming my hands before the flames. My joyous mood of such a short time ago was suddenly gone as I pondered the walk ahead. Would it be the walk that broke her?

*

Three miles later, we were in the midst of another endless series of stone steps. Because I had nothing better to do, I counted them. "321, 322, 323," I whispered, rarely taking my eyes from the ground.

To our right was a seemingly bottomless drop. To our left, a rock face veered almost straight into the sky. Though the steps were wide and several feet apart, a mishap could easily send one of us falling to our death.

The valley here was tight, confined within itself. The nearby mountains were so steep that I couldn't see the peaks of the much higher Annapurnas in the background. Walking with so much earth above us was eerie, giving me a new perspective on what an ant must see as it navigated about a pile of boulders.

"372, 373, 374—"

"Owen, you miss parents?"

I glanced up, my tired mind immediately losing count. "Ahh, sometimes."

She kept walking before me. "When?"

"Well, they'd love the stars here. I wish they could see them."

"You be happy if they here now?"

"Oh, I'd like them to see these skies, but I'm glad it's just the two of us."

She brightened. "Good."

I grinned, pleased she felt the same way. A gust of wind whipped down the valley, cool and strong. Worried, I looked to the sky, expecting to see dark clouds. But all I saw was blue.

"Thank God," I whispered.

"What you say?"

"I was talking to myself."

"Maybe we getting too high. Maybe if we go higher your brain no work."

"It hasn't worked for a long time."

"That true."

We laughed. When we quieted, I asked, "What about you? Do you miss your parents?"

"I miss drinking tea with mother. I miss helping father in farm." She coughed briefly, her body convulsing. "One time, when I was young child, brother get very sick. Father and I walk all night to next village. When I get tired father carry me on shoulders. He never get angry, never tell me to go back.

"In morning we find good doctor and he come back with us. Father carry me again. We sing old song, never stop to rest. After we bring doctor to home, he fix brother, give him medicine to make pain go away. My father very poor man but he give doctor chicken. But doctor good man, give chicken back. So next day father go with him to work in doctor's farm. So mother and I work in our farm. Make it perfect for father, make it beautiful. When he come back after three days he very, very happy."

"Was your brother all right?"

"Medicine help him. After that he more strong."

I smiled at her. "That's a wonderful story."

"Yes. It make me happy."

I didn't respond, letting her dwell in the past. We'd finally reached the top of the steps but were still in the valley. The trail was wider here. The land was so desolate that, if I'd seen it in a photo, I might have guessed that I was looking at the surface of Mars. We must have been approaching the timberline, for there was almost no foliage.

"Mother and I always talk about my babies," Suchin said suddenly. "She very excited to be grandmother."

"You'd have been the best, Suchin, the best mother anyone could ask for."

"Why you think so?"

"Because there's a lot of love inside you. And you'd share it."

"Thank you."

An airplane appeared in the thin slice of sky sheltering the valley. Its white contrail lengthened, reminding me of a zipper being pulled down, separating blue fabric. "Suchin?" I muttered tentatively.

"Yes?"

"This is none of my business, but shouldn't you let your parents know what's really going on?"

She looked away. "I think of this many times. Many, many. I want so much to call them, to see them. But they too good to know what happen to me. They blame themselves if they find out what happen. It destroy them."

"They've probably already had those thoughts."

"Maybe."

"Well, maybe they'd feel better if they heard from you."

"I want … this," she replied, sadness in the pause between her words. "I miss them like you miss Sarah. Same same. But I afraid to disappoint them."

"I think you owe them the truth."

"Maybe they no love me when they hear truth."

"That's a chance you have to take. But if they created you, such an amazing person, then there's no way that they won't continue to love you."

"You think?" she asked, sniffing.

"They'll always be proud of you, Suchin. And they'll always love you."

"Even with my past?"

"Your past doesn't matter. You helped them. You helped your brother. That's what matters."

Her abrupt hug caught me off guard. "Thank you." She sniffed again, rubbing her eyes. "Maybe I made mistake. Maybe I should write them long time ago and tell them truth."

"Don't worry about that. You did what you thought was best. Anyway, it's not too late."

"But how I reach them?"

"Write a letter. I think you have to tell the truth in it, the truth about what happened to you. If you don't tell the truth they'll wonder why you never came back. And I think that'll hurt them more than knowing what happened to you in Bangkok."

"You really think?"

I shrugged, then wiped my damp brow. "I'm not sure. But

if I were a parent, I'd want to know. I'd want to know so that I could somehow try to make peace with it—just like you've tried to get me to make peace with what happened to Sarah. If I never knew, I don't think I could make peace with anything."

She glanced at me, looking curiously into my eyes for a few heartbeats. "Okay. I do this soon. I tell them truth, at least most of it. Maybe they know by now anyway."

"Good. And tell them about your trip here, tell them that you're happy. Tell them that you're not afraid ... of the future."

"Thank you, Owen. That good advice."

Our conversation, as painful as it was, seemed to give her strength. She walked steadier and didn't look down at the trail but out at our surroundings. Wanting to keep her in this state, I said, "Like you, Sarah would have been a great mother. We talked about it a few times."

"And you? Do you want to be father?"

"Well, I'm sure it's not easy, but I can't imagine anything better."

"Your children be wise and strong."

"Why do you say that?"

"Because you same same. You give that gift to child."

I swatted at a fly. "Well, maybe ... maybe I could show them some of that. But they'd have to find it on their own."

"That true."

"I've actually wanted kids for a long time. Maybe it's because I always wished I had a brother or sister. Sometimes it was hard, being alone. I had to grow up pretty fast."

"I wish we friends as children. Then I keep you young."

Hopping, I pulled a rock from where it rested against my ankle. "That's for sure," I said, tossing the rock aside. "It's crazy that I feel so much closer to you than to anyone back home. I mean, we come from opposite sides of the world, but we're so similar." I paused, wanting to expose my feelings, but uncertain if I should. "If things had been different with us, if we'd met earlier and … and under different circumstances, I wonder if we'd have fallen in love."

She turned and started at me intently. "Could you care for me? So much?"

"I care for you more each day." I took her hand, folding it within my own. "If we'd met—"

My words ceased as two men stepped from behind a nearby boulder. I thought I recognized them and said hello. To my surprise, the men didn't return the greeting but came straight at us. Each carried an armful of wood. When they were a few feet away they dropped the wood. I started to bend down to help them retrieve the logs, stopping when I realized each held a long knife. "What's going—"

The larger man yelled, raising his knife. Abruptly I found it hard to breathe. My heart threatening to suddenly burst from my chest, I managed to pull Suchin behind me. The bandit motioned for us to take off our clothes and boots. When I shook my head he snarled, his knuckles whitening about the hilt of his blade.

"I'll give you my money," I heard myself say, my voice

quivering with fright as I reached into my fanny pack and groped for bills. "Take it and go. But we can't give you our clothes. She'll die if you take hers."

The men moved closer, eyeing Suchin. I didn't know if they understood English. Again the bigger one motioned for us to strip. I imagined Suchin naked, shivering uncontrollably. "Please, please, please don't do this," I stammered. "You can have my money. I'll give you all of it. I'll give you my camera, my bag … everything I have except for our clothes." I pulled out my money and set it on the ground.

The bandits spoke in Nepalese. The smaller of the two angrily pointed at the money, and then at my pack and boots. Suchin had her arms around me and I pushed her back, wanting to be unencumbered. My heart still thumping like the hooves of a racehorse, I stood my ground.

"Maybe we give them clothes," she whispered.

"No!" I hissed. "I'll be goddamned if—"

The bandits called my bluff. The smaller one lunged at me, the tip of his knife darting toward my chest. Fortunately, my walking stick was longer than his arm and I brought it down hard toward his head. I don't think he expected to be attacked, for he barely tried to avoid the blow. My walking stick cracked him atop the skull, and he crumpled.

The other bandit mumbled something and came at me. His face contorted as he feinted with his knife and, as I twisted away from his blade, his booted foot slammed into my groin. Pain was instantaneous—consuming all of me but my arms and legs.

My first instinct was to double over, but I managed to knock him back with the end of my stick. Had I been slower, he'd have surely killed me.

Too scared to take the initiative, I awaited his next attack. Eying me, he switched the grip on his knife so that he held it with its point downward. Screaming, he lunged ahead, his knife flashing toward my chest. Stepping forward, I brought my walking stick up viciously. I'd played baseball for many years and knew how to wield a piece of wood. My walking stick caught him under the chin, snapping his head back. Though my assailant was lifted upward by my blow, his knife still fell at me. Desperate, I ducked down, twisting to try and get my pack between the metal and me. God must have finally decided to give us a break, for my pack bore the full force of the blow, the blade shearing through its thick material.

The man groaned, still somewhat upright. Before he could do anything else, I dropped my walking stick and smashed my fist into his nose. I felt it shatter. The bandit toppled, his head striking hard against the ground.

I fell to my knees. In a kind of suspended animation, I watched Suchin pick up both knives and throw them into a nearby ravine. She stuffed my money into her pants. Then she ran over and yanked on my arm.

"We must go!"

I nodded dumbly and struggled to my feet. Looking at the sky, I mumbled, "Why?"

"Let's go, Owen! They be awake soon!"

"But why?"

"No time. We must go!"

We turned and ran, stumbling against each other. Listening to Suchin cough, I had a sudden urge to hurt our attackers more. But I couldn't have done it, no matter how much they deserved it.

Knees trembling, I ran on. Suchin led me, as strong and bold as the granite around us.

*

The room was damp and cold. It boasted no windows and was as black as a cloudy night. Lying in bed, it didn't matter if I had my eyes open or shut. Either way, I could see nothing.

The bed was miniscule, and even though it would have been confining for one person, we were both on it, snuggling beneath our sleeping bags, sharing our warmth. We'd unzipped our bags to create blankets. Suchin's chills had returned, and I'd decided that I could keep her warmer by lying beside her. I'd done all I could to get her warm, dressing her in my long underwear and a sweater. She even wore a wool hat that I'd bought from a villager.

I was cold as well. The air was so crisp that when I flicked on my flashlight, I saw tiny white clouds escaping our mouths with every breath. We were almost at 14,000 feet, and sleeping in these conditions was like camping atop one of the Colorado Rockies.

The room was drafty, as insulated as an outhouse. I could

feel the wind coming under the door, chilling any part of me uncovered. Suchin was completely under the sleeping bags. Following her lead, I pulled them over my head.

"It much better in here," she whispered.

In the darkness I didn't know if she was facing me. Reaching out, I felt her lips, gently traced them with my fingers. "Are you cold?"

Her chattering teeth told me the answer. "I very cold. No can get warm."

"I'm sorry."

Part of the reason we were so cold was that our sleeping bags were damp. I hadn't protected them as well as I'd thought, and the river had left its mark. At dinner I'd placed both bags near the fireplace. I'd put them too close, however, and the fabric had started to melt. By the time I yanked them away, each bore a fist-sized hole.

As I cursed myself for my foolishness, Suchin kissed my forehead. "You very brave today. I no see this side of you before."

"I'm not proud of anything."

"I no like fight, but you had no choice."

"Probably not."

"Anyway, you hero today. You like knight in shiny armor."

I smiled. "Shining armor."

"No, it shiny armor."

I couldn't resist giving her a squeeze. "You're right," I said, my fingers finding and stroking her cheek in the darkness. "It's strange. I feel like today was … like it was some kind of test. I mean, first the river, then the bandits. And you getting sicker. Did it feel that way to you?"

"This whole trip, Owen, feel like a test to me."

"Yeah, it's a test for both of us. If we get to the top of the pass I think we'll each learn something. Something really important."

"What you learn?"

"I'm not sure. But I know that I've lost track of who I am. Sarah made me feel complete, just like you do. But I want to feel complete when I'm alone."

"How will mountain answer?"

I imagined myself atop Thorung La Pass and pondered how I would feel. "I think ... I hope that if we get to the top the wars inside my head will end."

"Such wars sometimes good. They make us better people. But yours last too long."

"Wars. Regrets. More wars. I'm tired of them all. It's time to live again ... like we're living now."

"Now you understand why I no want to stop. Maybe stopping easier. Maybe stopping better for some people. But not for me. Not for you."

Impulsively, I moved toward her and kissed her forehead softly. "We'll get there together."

She wrapped her arms around my neck. "Owen, can I ask you something?"

"Sure."

"Why you no want to make love to me? Everyone else always want to. You think I ugly?"

"God, no, Suchin. You're beautiful, inside and out. But we can't make love."

"I can make you feel good. If you wear condom it safe."

The room became a cocoon of silence. I longed to see her face, her expression. But the blackness was impenetrable. "You already make me feel good. I don't need anything else. Sex isn't going to change my feelings for you."

"But my boyfriends want it, say I make them feel good. Why you no ask?"

"Because it's something we don't need to share."

She sighed. I tried to edge toward her, but she pulled away. Finally she blurted, "I wish I virgin. I wish we could make love for first time. Then you want me, not like now when you think I dirty."

"That's not what I think."

She didn't reply. I felt a sudden wetness on my hand and knew she was crying. Holding her body close to mine, I ran my fingers through her hair, time and time again.

"I feel you, Suchin. I feel all of you."

"So?"

"You're as clean and beautiful and amazing as any mountain around us."

Once again she didn't answer.

And all I could do was pull her tighter against me.

CHAPTER 16

FRIENDS AND FORGIVENESS

Though she hadn't slept at all, Suchin climbed out of bed at dawn. In the dim light, I watched her dress, layer after layer. She never glanced at me as she got ready, her back always in my direction. My companion's hurt was tangible. I was about to try and redeem myself when she hurriedly opened the door and stumbled outside. It didn't take her long to throw up, moaning between heaves. Though I wanted nothing more than to run out and comfort her, I stayed still, knowing she'd lose face if I witnessed her misery.

Cursing the gods for making her suffer, I closed my eyes, hoping the heaves would end. Seconds seemed like hours. When she finally opened the door and came inside I rolled over, pretending to waken.

"Where did you go?" I asked, yawning.

She paused for a moment, collecting herself. "I go out to see sunrise. It very beautiful."

"Is the sun up?"

"Yes, it now above mountains. I think it be wonderful day. I can see blue sky. No clouds."

When she turned away, I sat up. "Suchin, about last night, please … please don't be upset. I do want to touch you. Of course I do. But I think that making love would be too hard on you now. It's not why we're here."

She bit her lip. "You boss. I do what you say."

Sighing, I got out of bed, dressing quickly. Suchin brushed her teeth as she organized our few possessions. I taped up my blisters and put clean bandages on my fingers. In the growing light, I drank some water and ate a candy bar.

"Do you want any breakfast? Or tea?"

"I want to walk. Let's go."

She started to head out the door, but I reached forward, pulling her to me. "I don't want to argue. We've got too little time."

Though she didn't respond, she didn't push me away. We held each other tightly. I could feel her heart pounding, her breath on my shoulder. A rooster belched forth its cry somewhere in the distance.

"Last night you hurt me," she said quietly.

"I know."

"Please do no more."

I kissed her softly, savoring the fullness of her lips. "I won't hurt you again."

*

Walking in silence, I gazed at the world above. Outlining the horizon were at least a dozen Himalayas. The upper half of each was covered in snow, the white peaks in stark contrast to the azure sky. These mountains were sharp, razorlike in appearance. Though each was uniquely shaped, they were the same height, rising in unison like an assembly of sisters.

I kept my eyes on the mountains as I couldn't bear to watch Suchin. Every step was a journey for her—one filled with pain, one that depleted her strength. How she went on I'd never know. But she did, forcing one foot ahead of the other, swaying unsteadily.

She'd thrown up bile twice during the hour we'd been walking. She'd fallen, dusted herself off, and gotten up numerous times. Though I tried to help, the extent of what I could do was limited—frustrating me to no end. The climb was a struggle for me as well. Forever ascending, rising past 14,000 feet with little sleep and not one good meal in a week had taken a collective toll upon me. My back, feet, and knees throbbed. I longed to drop my pack and walk unencumbered.

I couldn't imagine what the climb was like for her. It must have been hellish, an endless series of tests of her will. Amazingly, though I occasionally glimpsed her agony, for the most part her face bore a strange look of contentment, as if she'd made her peace and didn't begrudge her suffering.

A short while earlier, the group of Germans had caught up with us. This development was hardly surprising since they'd hired several Nepalese to carry their packs. Following the Sherpas, they'd quickly left us in their wake, wishing us well in English.

On several occasions I'd been tempted to hire a Sherpa but had resisted the urge. It didn't seem right, paying someone five dollars a day to lug my gear up the side of a mountain. More important, I didn't want to be helped, didn't want my suffering to be any less acute. To walk without pain while Suchin struggled would have broken me.

Pulling out my battered guidebook, I studied today's route. A long but very gradual climb lay ahead. Though it was a good seven-hour walk, it looked like we'd only rise about six hundred feet. Such a small gain in altitude was welcome news, as I could already feel the effects of the elevation and worried about the next day's brutal ascent.

Far ahead on the trail—which now was nothing more than a groove atop these naked mountains—I noticed other climbers. At first they weren't much more than tiny black dots, and discerning whether they were walking up or down was impossible. But then, almost imperceptibly, they grew defined, descending like snails on a boulder.

A half hour later, we were upon them. One was a huge man with a thick beard. His companion was a woman clad from head to foot in yellow rain gear. She wore silver sunglasses. Her blond hair cascaded upon her shoulders, bouncing with each step. Both trekkers looked like athletes, though they moved very deliberately.

"Hello, mate," said the man, his thick accent marking him as Australian.

I nodded, stopping as they approached. "Good morning."

"Ah, nothing too good about it."

"Sorry to hear that. Where are you guys coming from?"

"The bloody pass," said the woman, shaking her head. "I reckon it was damn near the end of us."

"Come again?"

"Ah, Simon and I got these dreadful headaches."

The big guy nodded. "Bloody altitude, mate. We got about halfway up Thorung La and me head feels like it's about to explode. Our guide insisted we turn around."

Suchin sat down on a rock beside us. I winked at her. "So where's your guide now?"

"Probably getting pissed on the other side of the pass with the rest of our group."

"Pissed?"

"Drunk, mate. Drunk."

"Well, I'm sorry you had to turn around," I said, immediately liking the two.

"Can't be helped," interjected the woman. "Anyway, as soon as we started descending, the headaches let up a bit. I reckon they'll be gone by tomorrow."

"I'm glad we're not up there anymore," said the man. "We

walked damn near three hours and hadn't even reached the bloody halfway point."

Glancing at Suchin, the woman asked, "Is your friend all right? She looks a bit ill."

I waited for Suchin to respond. When she didn't, I said, "She got some food poisoning a few villages back. Can't seem to get over it."

The woman grimaced. "Well, she'd better rest before the pass. It's a devil of a rock."

"Yeah, you're probably right."

"Anyway, good luck to you both. Maybe we'll meet in Kathmandu."

"I'll buy the first round," I volunteered.

Laughing, the man added, "And we the second, third, fourth, and fifth."

"Sounds good." When they started to turn, I added, "By the way, yesterday a couple of bandits ambushed us. If it hadn't been for some really good luck, we'd have been in big trouble. So be careful, especially since you're alone."

"Any advice?" asked the woman, taking off her sunglasses to stare at me.

"Well, they didn't seem to like my walking stick a whole lot. Get yourselves a couple of big ones and keep your fingers crossed."

"Thanks, mate," said the big guy. "You get yourselves up that damn pass. And when you're up there, take a good look 'round so you can tell us what the top of the world is like."

"We will," I said, and then bid them farewell. After helping Suchin up, I kissed her lightly on the forehead. "We're going to do it," I whispered. "And when we get to the top I'll tell you a secret."

Her eyes sparkled for the first time all day. "Please tell now."

"No, it'll be better up there, better on top of the world."

*

Two hours later, we moved methodically up the trail. Suchin's pace was so slow that I had to remind myself not to go too fast. She'd started coughing again, and the rag she often held to her lips was stained by blood.

What upset me most was that she could never get warm. No matter how many layers she wore, or how fast we moved, or what medicine I gave her, she always shivered. It seemed that if she could just warm up, her suffering would ease considerably. But she couldn't, and I squeezed my walking stick in frustration.

"Are you glad we came?" I asked, knowing the answer but desperately needing to hear it.

Suchin saw my pain and took my arm in hers. "If I die today I happy. You give me hope."

"Hope? How can you feel hope when you're hurting so much?"

"Because you make my life better. Because my dream come true. So maybe my dreams for my brother and for Ratu come true. That give me many hope."

I pulled her closer. "I wish I had your strength."

"You do. If you not have, you not here with me now."

"No," I said, shaking my head. "Don't give me too much credit. I was drunk when I asked you, desperate for a companion. There was no strength in what I did."

"You wrong, Owen. You bring me here. Everyone else walk by; not care about me. Maybe before, when I good-looking, they stop, want to talk. But now they never do. They want to stay far from me. Even my friends leave. They afraid I give them disease."

"Friends don't—" I stopped, waiting as she violently coughed. "Friends don't leave you when times get hard. That's when they should be by your side."

"It not always their fault."

"Why not?"

My question didn't seem to register with her. "Once I have best friend," she said.

"When?"

"Oh, five or six years ago, before I get sick. One day I see girl almost hit by bus. She very scared. I buy her tea, we talk for long time. After that we become friends." Suchin trembled as coughs came and went. She tried to subdue a moan, but I heard her pain. "She high school student," she continued gamely. "I not want her to know about me, so I buy high school uniform, always wear it when I see her. Soon we like sisters. We go to movie, dancing, talk about boys. After while she introduce me to her older brother. He later tell my friend that he think I beautiful, want to ask me on date."

"Did he?"

Her eyes darted mischievously. "Yes, he ask many, many times. Finally I go with him. He wonderful gentleman. He take me to many beautiful places in Bangkok, places I never see before. We go to gardens, to art museums, to floating restaurants."

"And what happened?"

She smiled. "I discover that he gay. He try to like girls, but he like boys."

"And your friend?"

"I still have my friend, but now she lives in Singapore. She working as maid."

"I've heard it's pretty there."

Suchin stumbled, falling feebly to her knees.

I dropped beside her. "Let's rest. We've still got a long, long walk ahead. You'll need all your strength."

We sat on my pack, staring to the west. A massive, rock-strewn meadow stretched toward infinity. Behind it lay a group of nameless mountains. These giants were barren of all but snow. Clouds drifted by their summits, as white and pure as the peaks themselves.

"I understand why people from all over the world come here," I said softly. "It's magical, like stepping back into time."

"Or stepping into time," she said, wheezing for air. "Mountains be same in thousands of years."

I hadn't thought of it that way, but it was easy to see her point. Perhaps my great-great grandchildren would someday stare at these peaks. Though they might do so from space or through a computer monitor, I found it hard to believe that the land would be any different.

I remembered my mother telling me once that some mountains on the moon were taller than any on Earth. Though that seemed impossible right now, I absently wondered if Armstrong had glimpsed one as he eyed the lunar landscape.

"Owen, after trip, what you do?"

Suchin's question yanked me back to reality. "Well, I've been thinking lately about doing something … doing something good."

"What?"

"Going back to Bangkok and helping Ratu. He needs to be in school."

She smiled. "I so happy to hear that. It magical thing to say."

"No, it's not magical, it's—"

"It beautiful, Owen. Maybe these mountains make you think of beautiful thing."

"Maybe. Maybe that's why people are drawn here. So that they see things differently."

"For sure. Please go back. Please go back and help him."

"I will. I promise."

"Thank you. Thank you one million times."

I grinned, unlacing a boot. When I turned it over a slew of pebbles fell. Dust rose from the little stones and was borne away by the breeze. "And what about you?" I asked. "If you could be anything, or do anything, what would it be?"

"Anything?" A pair of coughs came and went, wracking her. "Even impossible dream?"

"Yes."

"I be doctor. Help people with AIDS. I be kind to them when they need friend."

I envisioned her with the sick. "You'd be the best. The absolute best."

She smiled and closed her eyes. I leaned back and did the same, relaxing as the sun drove into me. The strength of its rays made it seem as if someone had painted my eyelids orange. Motes drifted within this vortex, alone and clustered. I groaned, my body somehow comfortable upon the rocks and rubble.

A sudden, distant roar caused my heart to skip. I sat up, immediately drawn to a sweeping mountain across the valley. Against the backdrop of blue sky the mountain seemed to fall upon itself, as if bowing deeply to the world. Immense plumes of snow were cast in every direction as the avalanche gathered speed, cascading down the mountain. Even from where we sat, at least two miles away, I could feel the ground tremble. I watched in awe as the snow reached the lower third of the mountain, obliterating vast stretches of pines in an instant.

Suchin found my hand. I didn't take my eyes off the spectacle, knowing I'd never see it again. For a good half minute the avalanche dominated me. I listened to its fury, studied its path of destruction. Then the avalanche slowly quieted. The ground grew still. As the snow cleared I saw that the mountain looked different, as if it had metamorphosed. Many of its trees were gone. The peak seemed thinner, the snow more evenly distributed.

I realized then that Suchin and I were possibly the only people on the planet to have seen the event. I felt blessed, intensely aware of our good fortune. Taking out my camera, I focused on the mountain through my telephoto lens. But no matter how many different angles I tried, how close I zoomed in, I knew no picture would ever do the sight justice.

I took a shot anyway, a simple image framed by the other peaks. Spinning, I captured Suchin as she yawned, and again as she blew me a kiss. As I stowed the camera she started reluctantly up the trail. Her feet dragged, and she slumped forward like an old woman. By the time I reached her, she was already feeling faint.

But still, despite her exhaustion and pain, she asked me about avalanches and how they came to be.

*

The village of Thorung Phedi, which meant "foot of the hill" in Nepalese, was really nothing more than a few shacks and a sprawling, ramshackle hotel. Thorung Phedi stood well above the timberline at 14,700 feet, encompassed by windswept mountains and little else.

Night hadn't fallen within the valley quite yet, and the sun hung stubbornly over a distant mountain. Suchin and I were a few hundred paces away from our hotel room, near the edge of a colossal chasm that fell to the valley's floor. Too exhausted to stand, Suchin lay on my sleeping bag, watching me as I used a narrow plank to bat rocks into the abyss below.

The plank felt good in my grasp. Tossing a rock into the air with my left hand, I spun, smacking the rock high and far. I watched it disappear from sight, waiting for it to hit the ground but never hearing it do so.

"You good," she said weakly.

I tried my best to smile, wishing she could play. When I swung hard at the next rock, I missed completely, almost losing my balance. Frustrated, I picked up a larger stone, crushing it. As I hit the rocks, my anger grew. It pained me to see her lying there, struggling to breathe. No matter how brave she was, no matter how much she meant to me, death would soon claim her.

I knew without question that the climb to Thorung Phedi had nearly killed her. The last mile had been nightmarish—a two-hour stretch where I'd practically had to drag her. She'd fainted at the end, not coming to her senses for a good half hour.

Since our arrival, she'd rested, trying to put on a brave face. She'd even made a joke—telling me that she'd finally decided that I was smarter than most pigs. In a way, her boundless good nature made the experience even harder for me.

Dusk was falling quickly, as it always did in the Himalayas. After smacking one final rock into the abyss, I turned, making my way toward Suchin. I was about to ask how she was feeling when I realized she was asleep. Reaching under her sleeping bag, I lifted her off the ground. She mumbled but didn't waken. Cradling her, I walked to our hotel, my eyes rarely straying from her face. She seemed at peace.

I passed a group of Nepalese farmers, quietly saying hello. Several sharpened tools on a grinding stone. One wished me good luck in English. Each stared at us, his face echoing his curiosity.

The hotel was silent. I stooped to unlock our door, supporting most of her weight with my left arm. The door swung inward on leather hinges, banging against the wall. Suchin's eyes fluttered open.

"Where we go?" she whispered.

"To bed, my sleeping friend. I want you to dream."

"But I no tired."

"I don't believe that," I said, placing her on the bed.

She shuddered, pulled me close. "I afraid if I go to sleep I never wake up. I never get to top."

"Tomorrow we'll get to the top. We're going to rise before dawn and walk all day. You'll need a good night's sleep."

Moaning softly in pain, she nodded. "I try. But first talk to me. I want to hear your voice."

"Okay," I said, stroking her hair. Realizing how tangled it was, I got up off the bed and walked in the growing darkness to my pack. After pulling out a comb, I sat down beside her. Gently, I lifted her head up and placed it on my lap. With great tenderness, I combed her hair. The wind had made a mess of things, and her long locks were impossibly twisted. I untangled them slowly, careful not to pull too hard. I stroked her brow periodically.

"That feel good," she whispered. "Mother do same to me long, long time ago."

"Did she sing, or tell you any stories?"

"When I tired she sing. But most time we talk."

"What about?" I asked, prying out a small twig.

"Many … th…"

"I'm sorry?"

"Many thing," she replied, her words barely audible. "We talk about Buddha. About how someday I be woman … have family of my own. She tell me many secret. How to make husband happy. How to save food if no rain."

"She sounds like a wonderful woman."

"She is. I very … so lucky to have her." Suchin motioned weakly to my pack. "Last night … when you asleep, I write parents letter. I put in backpack. Please give to them. Their names and my village name on letter."

"I'm glad you wrote it."

"Me too. It tell most everything … good and bad. But it feel only good to write."

"I'll bring it to them."

"And another thing, Owen. If you give my parents money … just little money, they could take Ratu. He could be their son … my brother's brother. Then everyone happy."

My hand froze for an instant, then resumed its task. "That's a wonderful idea," I replied, my mind overwhelmed by a dichotomy of emotions. I was consumed with grief yet touched by the beauty of her thought. My eyes watered.

"Please tell parents I miss and love them."

"I will. And I'll tell them how much … I'll tell them about everything you taught me, about how proud they should be."

"Thank you, Owen. Ratu know their village … he take you there."

After wiping away my tears, I unfurled our sleeping bags, spreading them over her. When I started to undress, she reached out to me. I noticed that her eyes also glistened. "Owen?"

"Yes?"

"I scared … scared to die."

I tried to speak, to tell her something that would give her solace, but I didn't know what to say. How could I tell her not to be scared when death scared me? When I'd seen it up close and still cringed from what I saw? Feeling inept, I hugged her tightly until warmth spread between us. Finally I whispered, "Suchin, just remember what you believe. Remember that it isn't an end, but a beginning."

"I do believe. But I afraid to leave … so much behind. Colors, tastes, smells. They so beautiful."

I didn't try to stop my tears, and they fell from me like raindrops. "You'll take … those things with you. All of them."

"I hope so. I hope … I also take you."

"You will. I promise. You'll take colors, memories, me."

"What else, Owen?"

I sniffed, biting my lip as she had bitten hers so many times.

"Touch, voices, laughter, friends. And visions ... visions of the stars, of the sea." I reached into my pack and withdrew her family's photo, tucking it beneath her hands. "You'll take your loved ones. They'll never, ever leave you. Neither will I."

"Promise?"

"I do."

"Th ... thank you ... Owen."

Hearing the profound weariness within her voice, I bent down to kiss her lips. "Good night, Suchin."

"Good night ... number two boss."

She closed her eyes. I picked up the comb and continued to groom her hair, brushing each strand until it was free. As I worked, I occasionally bent down to kiss her forehead. Finally, I put the comb down and crawled into bed beside her. When she mumbled my name and edged closer to me, my tears came harder and faster, cool against my face.

CHAPTER 17

ASCENTS

Suchin's gasp startled me. I heard her try to suck in air, as if she'd just inhaled a lungful of water. While my mind cleared, she gasped again, her body unconsciously fighting for oxygen.

Panicking, I bolted upright in bed. She convulsed, her body arching like a bridge. Not knowing what to do, I pulled her up. She moaned as her head swayed, falling back limply. I caught and cradled her head with my left hand, yelling at her to awaken. Her eyes opened a fraction and she gasped again. Foam bubbled at the corners of her mouth.

"Suchin!" I shouted frantically.

Seconds passed. Ticked by in slow motion. One. Two. Three. Four. Then she coughed, her body shaking violently in my arms. She mumbled something in Thai, which I asked her to repeat. She must have recognized my voice, switching to English, saying something about my face.

"What?" I asked.

"So beautiful—"

"Wake up, Suchin! You have to—" I stopped shouting when her eyes abruptly opened. She looked bewildered, as if she'd not expected to awaken. Then she groaned, her body slumping against mine.

"It's okay, baby," I said, hugging her tightly. "You're okay."

She coughed again and again. When she finally quieted, she put her head on my shoulder. "I ... not ... ready."

"I know," I whispered, tears running anew. "I'm not either."

"I no ... not want to die here."

"You won't."

"Let's go," she wheezed, sounding like an old woman on a ventilator.

"Now?"

"Please, Owen."

I propped her against the pillows. Throwing on my clothes, I stuffed our possessions into my pack. I talked to her while I worked, worried that she'd black out. When finished, I helped her dress, knotting her boots in the darkness.

"Can you do it?" I asked, dropping some bills on the bed.

"Yes."

"Then let's get going."

*

Walking in the darkness, with mountains and stars and the moon looming above, I felt remarkably small. The light my flashlight cast reached out a Frisbee's toss into the night, revealing ancient faces of rock that rose quickly until they disappeared. When I shone my light on such faces the trail beneath us vanished and we blindly stepped ahead. When my light was on the trail the faces disappeared, untold tons of rock draped instantly by the cloak of night.

I held the flashlight with my left hand and Suchin's arm with my right. Fortunately, the trail was distinct and, as long as I kept my light on it, easy to follow. Though it rose quite steeply, the trail was barren but for countless shards of rust-colored stones.

My watch showed that it was just after midnight. I should have been tired, having slept only a couple of hours. My mind was clear, however, and my body responsive. At least for now, the aches and pains that had been my companions for the past week had subsided.

The Himalayas slept above us, rising into the blackness like dimensionless, infinite shadows. I didn't know how tall these mountains were, only that we were at about 15,000 feet, almost 3,000 feet short of the pass. At the rate we were going it'd take at least five hours to reach the summit.

Aside from our feet striking the path, the only sound was of Suchin's tortured breathing. She could never get enough air. Never satiate her lungs or her need to cough. Though I felt fairly strong, I had to make a conscious effort to breathe deeply. Were we at sea level I'd have quickly hyperventilated.

But here the technique served me well.

Suchin stumbled. Fortunately, I caught her elbow and pulled her up before she struck the ground. "Can you go on?"

She nodded, trying to smile. "It difficult ... to talk," she said weakly. "I no have energy."

"Then don't speak. We'll talk later."

Lifting my flashlight, I followed the trail upwards with its beam. The path zigzagged above us like a slithering snake. At its sides, neither bush nor flower nor weed lived. Only rocks endured this lunar landscape. At the edge of the trail they lay atop each other, cracked and splintered. I'd never seen so many rocks. They might as well have been grains of sand on a beach.

We soon walked along the spine of a desolate ridge. Leaning on my walking stick, I pushed myself up a particularly steep section of trail. The village of Thorung Phedi had already disappeared from sight. I couldn't even see its lights.

"God, we're rising fast," I whispered, hoping the trail would level off. Five hours of this kind of climbing would surely break us. We'd have to pace ourselves and rest often.

I lost track of how many times the trail switched directions. The ridge was exceedingly steep and would have been nearly impossible to ascend straight up. The switchbacks, while making the route longer, also made it bearable. I'd have liked to have seen them from the air. From a few hundred feet up they'd resemble cracks in a vast expanse of marble.

A sudden noise caused me to turn. Directing my flashlight's beam uphill, I searched the darkness for the clamor. A hundred yards above, a mountain goat bounded down the slope. The goat moved with surprising speed and agility. Rocks cascaded before it, picking up momentum, creating miniature avalanches.

But the goat's quickness was not what stole my breath. What did was its color. The animal was completely white, its woolly hair falling to the ground. It must have come from the highlands, for it wore no bell. The goat ran frantically down the slope, often falling and rising again in nearly one motion. In just a few seconds it was below us, quickly dropping from sight.

Above the goat, I heard a snarl. I followed the noise upward with my beam, my heart dropping when I saw the snow leopard. A majestic creature—white with small black spots—it ran in great leaps. The cat's mouth was open, displaying a set of teeth that matched the color of its fur.

The snow leopard moved with a sort of fluidity that I'd never dreamt possible. It ran straight down, muscles contracting, legs propelling it like wings. I couldn't maintain my flashlight on the cat and caught only glimpses of its brilliance. Even so, I knew that no human could ever match its grace. The snow leopard never tripped or stumbled. Its body was a steel spring, catapulting it ahead, propelling it closer to its prey in magnificent strides.

Both animals quickly vanished, leaving only tumbling rocks in their wake. Still transfixed, I watched the stones roll, wondering if the goat would escape. Far below, I heard the cat snarl. Peering into the night, I searched hard for it but saw nothing. The world had once again gone dim.

*

Forty-five minutes later my mind was on the cat. Nepalese believed that snow leopards were good omens, signs that the world was strong. I found myself hoping that the locals were right, and that the snow leopard's spirit would give us strength.

Suchin and I hadn't talked since our encounter with the animals. I'd tried to initiate conversation a few times but soon realized she lacked the strength to speak. Her silence troubled me, made my gut ache with fear. As I followed her, I kept my flashlight's beam on the ground beneath her feet. For the most part, the trail was free of debris other than the small rocks. However, it continued to rise at a sickening angle. We'd been climbing for almost two hours and had probably gained a thousand feet.

The air was much thinner here. I felt like I'd had several beers, and was slightly off balance from the lack of oxygen. Luckily, my knees and back weren't hurting too badly. By constantly adjusting my pack's shoulder and belt straps, I shifted its weight upon various parts of my body.

I wished I could have done something to ease Suchin's pain. Climbing was a titanic struggle for her. She'd already fallen three times—a trio of crashes that left her moaning. Each time she'd fallen, I put her head on my lap and we rested. Stroking her brow, I'd told her everything I'd read about these mountains. I'd spoken of the snow leopard as well, explaining how the Nepalese believed them to portend magical, wonderful events. As I'd talked quietly, Suchin had nodded on occasion.

Sometimes she'd muttered a simple question. But for the most part, she had rested with her eyes shut. Trying my best to ignore her raspy intake of air, I'd talked until she was able to stand.

The fact that she could go on was nothing short of miraculous. It would have been infinitely easier for her to just lie down, go to sleep, and never awaken. Most anyone else would have been in bed, waiting for death to claim them. And yet Suchin tackled it head-on, pressing forward with what seemed to be an unbreakable resolve.

The trail unraveled like an endless ball of yarn thrown down the side of the mountain. Suchin followed it slowly, never raising her eyes or voice. I was about to ask where she found the strength when she tripped on a rock and fell hard to her knees. Groaning, she toppled forward, sprawling out on her stomach.

I swore and dropped my pack. Turning her over, I placed her head on my lap. An angry bump already had risen on her forehead. Her eyes wandered, unwilling to focus.

"Suchin? Can you hear me? Suchin?" Something escaped from her lips but I couldn't comprehend what was said. Bubbles appeared at the corners of her mouth, which I wiped away with my sleeve. "What can I do?" I asked, helplessness overwhelming me. "Please tell me."

Air wheezed in and out of her lungs. "It … hurt … to breathe," she stammered.

Not knowing what to do, I stroked her forehead. "I'm sorry. I'm so, so sorry. It shouldn't be this way. We shouldn't have come. I shouldn't have taken you."

"I no more ... walk. No more—"

"Let's just stay here," I interrupted. "It's a beautiful place."

"So close. My dream ... so close."

Wiping more bubbles from her mouth, I watched her cry. Tears rolled down her cheeks like rain on glass. Soon she was sobbing, her frail body shuddering with each moan. In her sobs I heard the many sorrows of her life—the pains that I knew of, as well as the secret agonies that she had kept hidden from me. These miseries she had repressed so deeply that they were only surfacing now, as her spirit shattered.

Seeing her this way made me not only despondent, but also angry, so full of rage that my body trembled. I cursed in despair. I pounded my fist into the ground, knowing that her journey couldn't end this way. Not when we'd come so far. Not when she had suffered so long. I had to get her to get her to the top, to show her the sunrise from nearly 18,000 feet. Then she could rest, could fall asleep forever.

I hit the ground again as inspiration struck. "We're not done yet, Suchin. We haven't reached the top."

"We ... I done," she sobbed.

I didn't respond. After unzipping the sides of my pack, I lifted it up, dumping its contents on the ground. I emptied the pack of everything. When finished, I stuffed my sleeping bag into its bottom. In one of the side pouches I stuck my wallet, camera, water, first aid kit, CD player, guidebook, our passports, Suchin's letter, and her picture frame.

My pack's top had no zipper and cinched shut like a garbage

bag. However, two zippers ran down each side of the pack. This feature allowed the user to gain access to the bottom or middle of the pack without disrupting the above contents. Moving the two top zippers up and the two bottom zippers down, I created a pair of huge openings. I then uncinched the pack's top as far as possible. Anger turning to hope, I pulled the pack toward Suchin's feet, guiding her boots through the top.

"You've gotta move down into this," I said.

She managed to raise her legs off the ground. I lifted the pack, pulling it over her, watching as her feet, knees, and hips passed through the opening. I kept pulling until the pack reached her shoulders.

"You'll be able to dangle your arms just fine," I said. "And your legs will fit nicely in these holes."

After pulling her legs out each side of the pack, I positioned my sleeping bag beneath her. It would serve as a pillow. I then pulled my pack's top zippers down and its bottom ones up, effectively sealing the bag around her legs. Knowing the zippers would separate, I tied them together with dental floss.

"You go … crazy," Suchin said weakly. "I no understand."

She looked like a mummy, entombed inside my pack. "I haven't gone crazy yet," I replied. Grabbing the pack's shoulder straps, I pulled it, and her, off the ground. Groaning with effort, I put the straps over my shoulders, then tightened the belt about my hips.

The front of Suchin's body pressed against my back. Her legs fell from the openings, her bent knees pushing against the sides of my ribs. Suchin's head was actually higher than mine, and her arms draped around my neck. The contraption was really no different than the backpacks that parents used to carry toddlers. Mine was just bigger.

Though the pack was much heavier than before, the weight was bearable. Bending awkwardly, I picked up my walking stick. "We're going to make it," I announced, taking a step forward.

"Sure sure you crazy. We … we never make it."

"We'll make it. You don't weigh much. And I'll carry you to the top."

She coughed. "You number … one, Owen."

I didn't like how weak her voice sounded. "Keep talking. I don't want you to fall asleep."

"You talk. I too tired."

"But you'll listen?"

"Sure."

Knowing she'd like the story, I described how my mother had prematurely given birth to me in the desert. As I leaned heavily on my walking stick, I explained how my parents had been at a remote observatory studying binary systems. My father and their colleagues had delivered me, cutting the umbilical cord with a pocketknife and wrapping me in a sweater.

When I finished the tale, Suchin poked my shoulder. "What … what binary system?"

"A solar system with two stars at its center. It'd be like having two suns."

"Strange."

I didn't respond, still getting used to her weight. Realizing that I couldn't carry all of it on my shoulders, I tightened the belt about my hips. This caused my knees to ache, pain radiating up and down my legs. My breath quivering with effort, I trudged ahead, trying to make good time, wondering if I could make it to the top.

"I see Orion," she said, her voice barely audible.

I searched the sky, quickly finding the giant. He was low in the horizon to the west, hovering magically over the vague silhouette of a jagged mountain. "He's looking in our direction."

"Maybe … maybe he see us."

"I think he's watching over us, making sure we get to the top."

"I like … the midnight suns. Thank you for teaching me them."

"Midnight suns," I replied softly. "That's a wonderful way to describe them."

She moved her head closer to mine. I felt the warmth of her breath on my neck. "Owen, after I … when I gone, please remember me … remember me when you see Orion. Remember … our trip together."

"I will," I said, leaning my head back slightly, so that it touched her brow. "But you know, I'd rather … I would rather see you in the stars."

"I no understand."

"It's simple, Suchin. I'll search the sky until I see your face. And when I do, I'll memorize it like I have the other constellations. You'll be the most beautiful one of them all."

Suchin's arms tightened about my neck. When I twisted to look at her, I could tell that she was searching for herself in the heavens.

*

As the night progressed, we grew silent. Aware that my obsession to get Suchin atop the pass might have fogged my judgment, I struggled on, growing more exhausted with each step. The trail continued its brutal ascent.

An hour earlier, we'd left the maddening switchbacks for good. Now we seemed to go straight up Thorung La. In the darkness I found it impossible to get a feel for my surroundings and had no idea what the mountains or the pass looked like. I did know that I was exhausted, so weary that I was dizzy with fatigue. Suchin felt like a marble statue in my pack. Except she wheezed between my vast intakes of air. She might have been asleep, might have been dying, for she didn't respond to my questions. As always, I tried to make her suffering motivate me. And to some degree it did.

But the mountains mocked my effort. I felt like an amoeba climbing a skyscraper. No end was in sight, no summit awaiting my embrace. I knew only pain, knew it in every joint of my body. My knees were like pinpricks of fire. My back felt shattered, each step sending a jolt of agony up my spine. The blisters on my ankles had popped with the extra weight of Suchin, and my dirty and bloody socks felt like pieces of sandpaper rubbing against my wounds.

Fortunately, the pain was exploitable. I used it to propel me onward. The more I hurt, the more determined I became. Pain was short-term. It could be controlled. What troubled me was my head. The altitude must have been affecting me, for I felt drunk, so bombed I could hardly think straight. Staggering, I kept the flashlight on the trail, never glancing at what lay about me. I was coherent enough to realize that staying focused on the path was essential, placing one foot before the other. If I veered from the trail I'd get lost and we would never reach the top.

I had read about the false summits of Thorung La, which were legendary for making trekkers turn around in frustration. As I came upon the first of these false summits, I heard voices. I didn't know if I was talking or if someone else spoke from somewhere distant. But I was aware of a conversation taking place. It might have been in my head. It might have fallen from the heavens.

Through the blackness I climbed, cursing the false summits, damning them for all of time. Though great distances separated the rises, I felt as if they were always upon me, crashing into my body as if endless waves. The summits seemed to go on forever. I climbed them for hours. I climbed them like a robot. Like a child. Like an old man. Never did I stop, cease in my plight. As I neared the crest of each rise my spirits would briefly soar, only to come crashing down when my flashlight revealed the next brutal ascent.

The cold, oxygen-deprived air assaulted my lungs. It chilled me like seawater, the chatter of my teeth incessant. I grew frightened, wanting to turn and run to a warm bed far below. This world was too harsh. It wasn't meant for living things— certainly unintended for a pair such as us. Never had I so yearned to see green. I craved it like an addict craves heroin. Like someone scorned craves love. I'd have given damn near anything for five minutes in a field of grass.

As I struggled, forced my body beyond its limits, delirium gripped me. The ground moved. The world spun about in frenzied arcs. To keep from fainting, I bit my injured fingers until they bled. This new pain kept me going long after I'd have otherwise collapsed.

Squinting, I continued on. All I knew was the trail. The trail was the only thing in my life that mattered. I followed it up and up, through clouds and fields of snow. As I followed it, voices rang in my head, rang like chimes in a foreign land. I recognized a few words but wondered what the rest meant. Perhaps I was listening to another language from another time. Perhaps Suchin spoke to me in Thai.

My own thoughts were nearly incomprehensible. I didn't know who I was or what I was doing, only that I had to get to the top of this godforsaken rock. Despite finding it impossible to get enough air, I struggled on, continuing to climb until I suddenly pitched forward and fell hard on my chest. I moaned, so full of agony I couldn't move. Barely aware of what was transpiring, I unstrapped my pack. To my surprise I saw that someone was in it. She looked asleep.

My head as heavy and dense as an anvil, I doubled over and threw up. The bile scalded my throat. I gagged as the world spun faster about me. Falling on my back, I closed my eyes, hiding from the whirling stars. Thinking of their frantic dance, I threw up again, moaning like a sick child.

The bile's taste was overwhelming. Reaching into my pack, I pulled out my water bottle. I had a hard time getting it open, but once its cap was on the ground, I gorged on the liquid. When satiated, I managed to screw the cap back on and drop the bottle next to a pool of someone's vomit. Then I closed my eyes, not caring if I ever woke up.

I drifted between conscious and unconscious thought. Visions visited me. The first was of Sarah. I saw myself making love to her on a deserted beach. She was smiling, her fingers tracing the contours of my face as the sun bathed our naked bodies.

Sarah transformed into Suchin. Staring into her dark eyes, I watched as she leaned forward to kiss me. Her lips were soft, full of life and vigor. A pink orchid graced her hair, swimming in the darkness. I smelled it and then kissed her again, loving everything about her.

But she soon left. I saw them both walk away, vanish slowly. Just before they disappeared, Sarah turned around and motioned for me to follow. I nodded, knowing what had to be done, focusing my strength to do it. I started to reach for the ring about my neck but let my hand drop.

I don't know how long I lay there. Time had no meaning. But gradually, as gradually as a frost-covered tree shedding its amber leaves, my mind began to clear. Pain crept back into my body. I was no longer numb. Opening my eyes, I scanned the darkness and recognized Suchin in my bag. Rolling to her, I felt her pulse and rejoiced when it was strong.

The beat of her heart gave me resolve. I rose to my knees, pulling the first-aid kit from my bag. My bloody fingers opened a bottle of painkillers, and I swallowed four of the white capsules. Taking a huge gulp of water, I washed the medicine down. I then splashed water on my face and let it run down my shirt.

My watch said it was 5:14 a.m. We'd been climbing since midnight and I knew we were close. There couldn't be many more of the false summits. Glancing around, I realized we were in the midst of a vast expanse of snow. The trail was a dark line that bisected the snow, rising until I could see it no more. Though the night was as dark as ever, I sensed that dawn was near.

Fumbling in my pack's pocket, I pulled out the waterproof bag containing my portable CD player. Inside the bag were also several CDs. U2, Moby, Eric Clapton, Otis Redding, and others I set aside. Though I rarely listened to classical music, and had only brought Beethoven's Fifth Piano Concerto because my mother had given it to me, it seemed an opportune time for the music. After inserting the CD, I hooked the player to my belt. The old-fashioned headphones went around my skull.

I quickly ate two candy bars, savoring the chocolate's taste. The painkillers were working, for my body ached less. My mind continued to clear. I looked down the trail and tried to remember the latter part of the ascent. Though my flashlight's beam revealed only two of the false summits, I knew many more were down there, waiting to attack climbers until none were left to vanquish. Praying that no more of the devils hid above, I glanced up, following the trail's sickening ascent.

I shuffled to my pack. Suchin was still out cold, though her breath was strong against my hand. Moving carefully, so as not to awaken her, I lifted the pack off the ground, fitting it about my shoulders. Though it felt frightfully heavy, I stood straight, promising myself I'd not think about the discomfort.

After grabbing my walking stick, I stepped forward. I hit the play button on my battered music maker, waiting for Beethoven's magic to fill my ears. And it did, slowly at first, the stirrings of the second movement building quietly. In the darkness each instrument's cry was particularly acute. The violins wept. The notes of a piano were melodious raindrops.

The music grew, blending like lovers in the night. Its chords filled my ears and its meaning filled my heart. And as I walked, I grew stronger, more determined than ever to make it to the top. Though my body ached, I didn't mind the pain. It made me feel alive, made me feel as if this journey had been good to take.

I'd heard somewhere that artists claimed to discover their best pieces rather than create them, and in some sense the fifth concerto was as old as these mountains, or at least as old as any human account of them. It was almost as if Beethoven had glimpsed the truth of these worlds of rock, the longing and wisdom echoing inside them.

Turning up the volume, I hurried forward, attacking a steep slope. Rocks churned beneath my feet. I stumbled but regained my balance and moved on even faster. Something told me that I was close to the summit, close to the time when Suchin's suffering would end.

When I rose to the top of the ridge and realized it was only another false summit, I took a slow breath and prepared myself for the next climb. Legs pumping, I marched up the trail, following my flashlight's dying beam. My legs were shaking violently, but I paid them little heed. Instead I listened to the music, letting it drown me with emotion.

I imagined a symphony orchestra as its members sweated under the glare of stage lights, fought to hit notes perfectly, rose and fell as one. The music continued to empower me. I saw a ballerina, dancing on her toes, back arched like the snow leopard's. The dancer flew through the air, whirling and spinning as if a goddess. The music soared with her, empowering me. I wanted to run, to take Suchin in my arms and sail to heaven. I'd place her in the hands of whatever force loomed above.

I shouted out when I saw it—a dim line of light outlining the rise ahead. The light was the color of the sea. It portended the dawn, screamed to me that the endless night was over. As I rose, the light grew in strength. Rays of sunlight gleamed like fire in the sky.

Beethoven's brilliance soared in my ears. The music exploded to a crescendo, culminating in wondrous, sweeping torrents of sound. Listening to it while light filled the land was simply overwhelming. I was in awe of beauty, of miracles, of sunlight embracing me as I crested the summit. Tears streamed down my face when I reached the top. Crying out, I dropped to my knees, shuddering.

Heaven had fallen to this patch of Earth. The sky to the east glowed, streaks of amber and crimson chasing the darkness away. Encircling us were the mountains of my dreams. They resembled the teeth of a giant canine, impossibly tall and sharp. Snow blew from their peaks, diffusing into the voids that separated them.

I wept, watching the sun embrace the world. I didn't know if my tears stemmed from grief or rapture. All I understood was that I was moved beyond comprehension—truly alive for the first time since Sarah's death, perhaps since well before it. Pulling off my pack, I lowered Suchin to the ground. The music raging within me, I kissed her gently. And when her eyes fluttered open, I smiled, leaned down to hold her.

I saw her lips quiver and turned off the music. "We're here, Suchin." She tried to say something, but no sound came forth. Placing a finger to her lips, I said, "Just wait. Wait until you see it."

Reaching to the bottom of the pack, I untied the zippers. After opening the pack, I pulled it from her. She tried to push it away but could barely move her arms. Knowing she was impatient, I threw the pack aside. I then dragged the sleeping bag out and spread it upon the ground. Lifting Suchin, I sat her down on the middle of the bag. She started to fall sideways, but I caught and steadied her.

"Look," I said, pointing to the east. "It's better than we imagined."

The Himalayas glowed faintly, rows of stained glass in this timeless cathedral. I watched a tear streak down Suchin's face, felt its wetness against my cheek when I leaned forward to hug her.

"It … perfect … better than perfect," she whispered.

I nodded, knowing words couldn't capture how I felt about this place. "Thank you, Suchin. Thank you for bringing me here."

She tried to shake her head. "You … you carry me."

"No," I said, my voice cracking. "You made this happen. You've carried me for two weeks." I stroked her chin with my thumb. "Not long ago, I wanted to give up. Not on these mountains, but on life. You changed that. You changed everything."

Another tear christened her cheek. "You make … me happy," she said, her words faint.

I took her hand in mine. I kissed it. I pressed it against my tear-dampened cheek. "Remember the secret I told you about?"

"Yes."

"Well, the secret is that I love you."

The pain disappeared from her face. "You do?"

I nodded, hugging her. "I think … somehow I always have."

She smiled. "Kiss me."

I parted her lips with my own, caressing them. I tried to ignore how cold she felt, instead smelling her skin, running my hand through her hair. When she gently pushed me away and stared into my eyes, my tears were many.

"Don't cry … Owen. This not sad time. I very happy."

"Tell me why."

She struggled mightily to draw air. "This place … you love me … I love you."

"I don't want … to lose you."

"You no can lose something, Owen … that is … that is a part of you." Her voice trailed off, began anew in a whisper. "My pain gone. I see only light."

I pulled her close, my voice cracking as I spoke. "Take my love with you."

"Yes."

"Promise?"

"It with me."

I pulled her closer, kissed her again. "What do you see?"

"Miracles."

"What kind?"

"Mother smiling … brother laughing … you holding my hand. Life miracles."

"It must be wonderful."

"It is."

We watched the sun slowly rise over the mountains to

the east. Its climb was sheer beauty, a climb of reincarnation. Golden clouds drifted by the glowing orb, reminding me of the prayer flags we'd seen so far below.

Take her gently, I prayed. *Bring her into your world with the greatest of care. She deserves peace, the sanctuary found here. Please, please, let her flourish, soar as she was meant to. Please love her. She's one of your best.*

"Owen?"

"Yes?"

"Always be happy."

Nodding, I watched the sun continue to climb. Amid my tears, it occurred to me then that such moments made life precious, made the many hardships worth the pain. Yet such moments were things that a child sees and cries out joyously over, but a man or woman sees and walks quietly past. I didn't want to walk past such moments anymore, didn't want to drift through life rather than be a part of it.

And so I concentrated on the sunrise, then focused on her face. I memorized every detail of her skin—her almost invisible freckles, the faint laugh lines around her mouth. I looked past her beauty, beyond the shadows of her life. I saw her as a child, a woman, a treasure I was fortunate enough to embrace.

And I believed her when she whispered that she'd soon be a part of these mountains; that she could feel herself merging with the world around us. I knew she was right, knew that in time I'd merge with all around me, as would my children, and my children's children. That was the beauty of the soul.

"Thank you ... my love," she whispered, blowing me a kiss. "Someday ... someplace ... we meet again."

"I'll find you ... my ... my midnight sun."

Suchin smiled, as if pleasantly surprised. Then she went limp in my arms, died staring into my eyes. Calling out her name, I gazed at the heavens, wanting to see her spirit take flight. But I saw only the sky. Nothing save blue emptiness.

Shudders consumed me, for I wasn't ready for her to be gone. As my tears tumbled, the wind suddenly stirred, pushing her hair across her face.

"Suchin?"

There was a brief pause, the silence of dawn. But then the breeze came again, caressing me as I knew she would, touching me the way her hands and her words once did. I was overwhelmed by a sense of peace, the taste of her soul as it passed through my own. A part of it stayed there. A part rose to the sky and the world beyond.

Knowing she was home, I carefully closed her eyes.

CHAPTER 18

Rebirth

The pile on Thorung La served me well. Comprised of colorful flags, walking sticks, stones, and about anything else one could imagine, the pile was about ten feet wide and five feet tall. I wasn't really sure what it meant, other than it was a place where trekkers left a sign of their passing.

I raided the pile for its timber, taking armload after armload of old planks and walking sticks to a distant knoll. I stacked the sun-bleached wood carefully, filling in the cracks with hundreds of crumpled pages from my guidebook. I then set Suchin's body atop this new, chest-high pile of old timber.

As I worked, stuffing the last few pages into the hollows beneath her, I noticed a shepherd approaching. He had a dozen yaks with him and swatted at their flanks with a long stick. The man waved to me. I nodded, straightening out Suchin's jacket.

The shepherd moved nearer. As his yaks passed, he walked in my direction. Though he'd seen many decades, he moved with the strength of a young man. When he reached me, he paused to look at Suchin, mumbling a quick prayer. His fingers touched her brow as he blessed her.

I thanked him, pulling out my lighter. The man nodded and hurried after his yaks. I waited for him to disappear. When he was gone, I leaned over to kiss her one last time. I held her one last time. I then withdrew my wedding ring and placed it in Suchin's hand, gently folding her fingers around it. I realized that she was right. Sarah had always been with me. And always would be. The ring was never what truly bound us.

I lit the paper, blew on it softly. The flames died and I tried again. This time the fire spread, slowly at first, then hungrily, blackening the pages. I stepped back and watched the flames grow higher. When the fire raged, consuming her and the wood, I said good-bye and turned away.

The trail felt reassuring beneath my feet. Though I wished Suchin could share it with me, I knew she was watching; knew our love was like an ocean that touched two continents. I was no longer afraid to swim in the depths of this ocean, to feel the pain and joy of its currents. Sarah didn't dwell there anymore. Long ago, she'd found the same peace as Suchin, the same peace I'd someday discover.

It was a beautiful day in the Himalayas—clear and pure and

timeless. As I started the long descent on the other side of the pass, I blew a kiss to the sky. And though my body and soul wept, I knew that in time, my sorrow would waver.

In time, I would love again.

The End

ALSO BY JOHN SHORS

Beneath a Marble Sky
Beside a Burning Sea
Dragon House
The Wishing Trees
Cross Currents
Temple of a Thousand Faces
Unbound
The Demon Seekers: Book One
The Demon Seekers: Book Two
The Demon Seekers: Book Three

ABOUT JOHN

John Shors is the internationally best-selling author of eleven novels, which have been translated into nearly thirty languages. In addition to *My Midnight Sun*, he's written *Beneath a Marble Sky*, *Beside a Burning Sea*, *Dragon House*, *The Wishing Trees*, *Cross Currents*, *Temple of a Thousand Faces*, *Unbound*, and *The Demon Seekers* trilogy. He has won multiple awards for his novels.

Boulder, Colorado, is home to John and his family. In his free time, he enjoys traveling the world, reading, and fishing. He also leads literary tours to the settings of his novels.

For more information on John, please visit **johnshors.com** or follow him on Facebook or Instagram.

Photo: John on the Annapurna Circuit in Nepal.

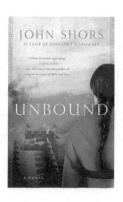

UNBOUND

BY JOHN SHORS

John Shors reimagined one of the world's greatest love stories—
the romance that inspired the Taj Mahal—in his critically
acclaimed, international bestseller *Beneath a Marble Sky*.
Now, with *Unbound*, Shors recreates an ancient and celebrated
Chinese legend about a pair of young lovers separated by war
and the Great Wall.

The year is 1548, and the Chinese Empire faces an imminent
Mongol invasion. All that prevents the violent end of a
dynasty is the Great Wall. Yet even this famed fortification has
weaknesses, and against his will, a talented Chinese craftsman
is taken from his home and wife, so that he may labor alongside
the wall's defenders.

Fan has been missing for a year when his wife, Meng, decides to do the impossible—to leave everyone and everything she knows in a daunting effort to find him. At a time when many women fear even stepping outside their homes, Meng disguises herself as a man and begins a perilous journey of deliverance.

As two armies gather at the Great Wall, the fates of Fan and Meng collide with a Mongol horseman seeking redemption, a Chinese concubine fighting injustice, and a ruthless general determined to destroy them all.

"*Unbound* is utterly captivating—an epic, historical page-turner with a beating heart. I loved it." —Jamie Ford, *New York Times* best-selling author of

HOTEL ON THE CORNER OF BITTER AND SWEET